There was no possible way the *Enterprise* could stop the Deltans from firing, no way to prevent a war from breaking out between worlds. This mission had certainly changed his thinking about the Deltan people.

"Vale, any options occur to you?"

The security chief thought for a moment, eyes straining at her station. "Without additional firepower, we're right now sitting in the potential crossfire. Too many ships, spread out in a classic pattern, and everyone's hot to shoot first. We're out of luck, sir."

Riker nodded in agreement and continued to pace the bridge. Walking eased some of the strain, but not enough of it. The standoff was growing tenser and the addition of more Deltan vessels spoiled any hope of a diplomatic solution. Starfleet had not responded to his last communiqué and the Diplomatic Corps was equally nonresponsive. He did not have the authority to contact the Deltan homeworld directly and he wasn't even sure if he should bother. Oliv was determined to gain possession of this dead rock, for whatever good it would do the Deltan people.

He wasn't sure what to do next: make popcorn to watch the inevitable fight or pray for Q to turn up.

Milan shook his head
in amazement.

STAR TREK
THE NEXT GENERATION®
GATEWAYS

BOOK THREE OF SEVEN

DOORS INTO CHAOS

Robert Greenberger

Based upon STAR TREK®
THE NEXT GENERATION
created by Gene Roddenberry

POCKET BOOKS
New York   London   Toronto   Sydney   Singapore

For information regarding special discounts for bulk purchases, please contact Simon & Schuster Special Sales at 1-800-456-6798 or business@simonandschuster.com

This book is a work of fiction. Names, characters, places and incidents are products of the author's imagination or are used fictitiously. Any resemblance to actual events or locales or persons, living or dead, is entirely coincidental.

An *Original* Publication of POCKET BOOKS

POCKET BOOKS, a division of Simon & Schuster, Inc.
1230 Avenue of the Americas, New York, NY 10020

STAR TREK is a Registered Trademark of Paramount Pictures.

A VIACOM COMPANY

This book is published by Pocket Books, a division of Simon & Schuster, Inc., under exclusive license from Paramount Pictures.

ISBN: 0-7434-1856-5

First Pocket Books printing September 2001

10 9 8 7 6 5 4 3 2 1

POCKET and colophon are registered trademarks of Simon & Schuster, Inc.

Printed in the U.S.A.

*For Deb, who indulges me, encourages me
and makes life complete*

HISTORIAN'S NOTE

This novel takes place shortly after the events depicted in "Pathfinder," a mid-sixth-season episode of *Star Trek: Voyager.* This would place it at approximately Stardate 53500 in the Starfleet dating system, in the year 2376 on the Earth calendar.

Chapter One

THE FIRST THING they noticed was the stench. A rotting-food kind of smell drifted from the open window at the rear of the museum. Its visitors were long gone, its doors locked. The building itself wasn't terribly large, just two stories tall but a block wide. In fact, it was a rather ordinary building, without much in decoration, which made Jhen sneer. They showed more respect for their past back home, he decided.

Four figures moved quietly toward the window, ignoring the odor. Street lighting was minimal toward the rear and this helped hide their tall and thin silhouettes. After all, few Andorians were seen on Tellar, each race preferring to keep to themselves.

It occurred to Jhen that he never quite knew what the original problem was between these two people. He knew they had found one another long before there was a United Federation of Planets, but why two aggressive races did not form an alliance and conquer nearby worlds such as Alpha Centauri and Vulcan made no sense to him. It didn't matter, because the Andorians had their pride and if the Tellarites wouldn't be their allies they were to be considered potential adversaries.

When the dormant doorway lit up and Tolin saw it led to Tellar, it was she who suggested they step through and retrieve the revered artifact, the colAndor Scrolls. Jhen knew the history: how the Scrolls were brought to Tellar as part of a cultural exhibition. How they were used to show Tellar another way to organize their government. And how Ger, High Councillor to the First Seat of Tellar, spirited them away and threw the Andorian delegation off the planet. The Scrolls had been lost to the Andorians and skirmishes almost led to a war. Changes in both governments led to a truce some years later, but the Scrolls remained on Tellar.

Tolin tugged at Jhen's loose sleeve. He turned and saw her gesture toward the window. Below it was a stack of containers, sturdy enough to support them. How very careless of these arrogant creatures, Jhen thought. With a wave of his hand, Jhen directed his small party forward, inching toward their goal. No sound came from the building, so if it was guarded, it was from an artificial, not living, source. This made it simpler, as Tolin thumbed a palm-sized cylinder. Its purple light flared and she nodded in satisfaction. Now the automated surveillance would be fooled and they could move freely. She placed the cylinder just inside the window, fastening it to the interior wall.

Okud was the first one through the window, open

more than enough to allow their slender forms through. The drop to the polished marble floor was less than a meter and was done with only the slightest of noises. Tolin followed, then Mako, and finally Jhen. All four stood within the room, breathing through their mouths to ignore as much of the stench as possible, which was stronger inside the building. Lighting was dim and Jhen could spot the various sensors, none of which changed from their amber status. The room they had entered was cluttered with stone carvings and paintings on metal. He knew even less of Tellarite culture than his companions, so he couldn't begin to guess what he was looking at. What he did know was that the workmanship was crude, like the Tellarites themselves.

Mako looked closely at one statue, that of a boy at play. He smiled at it, earning him a disapproving glance from Tolin. As far as Jhen was concerned, there was nothing to like about the heathen race, and Tolin seemed to agree. Reaching into a hidden pocket within her leather tunic, she extracted a folded piece of paper, opened it, and studied the map. Satisfied, she replaced it and pointed one light-blue-skinned finger to her right.

The quartet ignored the rest of the items surrounding them, heading straight for their objective. Passing through two more rooms, they finally saw a large chamber with a glass-covered pedestal. Within it was their objective: the Scrolls. Jhen silently counted to five, smiling that they were all together. Tolin grinned at him. Mako walked ahead of her to peer at the placard underneath the glass, trying to read the description. He growled in frustration; his knowledge of the Tellarite language was almost nonexistent, so he couldn't understand the words.

Remaining silent, Jhen pointed at Okud, who opened up a brown satchel that had been strapped to his back. The first object was palm-sized, oblong and dark. He removed it, thumbing a control set deep within the item. Its low hum indicated the localized disruptor was scrambling a spectrum of frequencies normally associated with security shielding. Withdrawing thin, elegant tools next, he made quick work of the sealant around the glass's base. A glance at the disruptor showed no warning lights, so Tolin and Jhen gently lifted the glass upward. Mako reverently touched the Scrolls, then placed each of them in the satchel. He nodded toward Jhen, signaling he was done. Okud absently disengaged the disruptor while Tolin reached once more into her bag when they were interrupted.

As expected from the outset, an undetected sensor was triggered and a keening sound came from the pedestal. The Tellarites weren't entirely stupid, they knew, but they figured they would get this far before being detected. They had speed working in their favor.

None of them hurried, but walked with long strides toward their window exit. Jhen saw that a metal plate was sliding down to cover it—a standard security tactic. Tolin unholstered a hand-sized phaser, and fired. The amber beam turned the metal plate into molten slag, halting its movement. With a little more speed, they exited and began strolling away. Jhen had successfully found the back-alley route that would return them to the door, and home.

When a security detail arrived five minutes later, they went from room to room checking for damage. As they approached the chamber that once contained the

Andorian Scrolls, they saw in its place a small figurine. It was of an Andorian female, in cleric's robes, praying.

"Grand Nagus!" The voice was urgent, if high-pitched. It sounded like that of a child entering adolescence, cracking and nervous.

"Yes," said Grand Nagus Rom of the Ferengi Alliance. There were still mornings he woke up convinced this was the longest dream he had ever had. But no, he was really the Grand Nagus. He still remembered the day it happened, with vivid clarity: Zek, gnarled and cackling as usual, telling him it was time he and Ishka—Rom's mother—settled down into retirement. Since Rom shared Zek's vision for long-term changes in Ferengi society to insure its viability in an ever-shifting universe, the outgoing Grand Nagus asked Rom to succeed him. With his Bajoran wife Leeta by his side, Rom considered himself the luckiest man on the face of the planet.

Of course, not everyone agreed with Zek's logic, most notably Rom's older brother Quark.

"Three Orion ships approaching orbit. They've already disabled forty-three percent of our satellite defenses!" His voice grew even more excited, if that was possible.

Rom raised a hand to his left ear, making sure it was not blocked and that he heard the warning properly. Orions! They had no respect for the Rules of Acquisition, just plunder. They had proven incredibly unreliable business partners and even his older brother avoided working with them. But they had never ventured anywhere near Ferenginar before, so what did they want—and how did they get so close without triggering the deep space sensor net?

Jumping to his feet, Rom left his soft, warm bed, letting the tall and sultry Leeta remain slumbering. If she was anything, he mused, slipping into a shiny robe, Leeta was a good sleeper. He began flipping switches on the desk he used for late-night accounting reviews. While he might have been poor with business, Rom was good with matters technical, and this got his curiosity aroused.

"Errr, just stay clam," he muttered into the communications system. "Have we mobilized the Treasury Guard?"

"Yes, Your Grandness."

"Oh, okay," he replied. "Make sure we have forces surrounding our key trading facilities and, um, let's mount an aerial force to keep them from landing."

"Yes, Your Grandness!" Rom wasn't sure who this shrill man was, but he assumed he was from the morning watch, and had never experienced the unexpected before. The current Nagus had certainly seen plenty of that during his time on Deep Space 9, both as the "assistant manager of policy and clientele" for his brother's bar, and later as an engineer during the Dominion War—a war in which Rom had fully expected to become a casualty. In the months since he had returned home to rule, Rom had fallen into a new routine and it gave him comfort. While letting business continue as usual, he began exploring the various ways off-world trading was conducted, drafting reforms that he would phase in. It was like solving any engineering problem, as Chief O'Brien used to tell him: don't try and fix anything until you're sure you know the full extent of the damage. "Shortcuts can lead to short circuits," he used to mutter in his Irish brogue. Rom

missed that voice and idly wondered how the chief was faring back on Earth.

With a shake of his head, he turned his attention to the feeds from the remaining orbital satellites. Telemetry was coming in and he began to notice odd energy readings just a few tens of thousands of kilometers from Ferenginar. The readings were massive, emitting an energy signature he didn't recognize, but clearly a portal of some sort, large enough to allow Orion starships to traverse through it. This was disturbing, if the Orions found some way to alter the scale of trade. Should they manage to just show up and attack worlds or shipping lanes, no one would be safe.

Again, he wondered why would they come to Ferenginar. Zek was no fool, and had made certain their wealth was spread out far and wide, controlled through some of the most sophisticated software imaginable. Rom saw no reason to change what worked.

"Grand Nagus!" shrieked the voice once more.

"Yes?"

"They've established orbit and are engaging the aerial police. But we've detected transporter activity."

This wasn't good. Orions would not beam down just to trade or make a deal. They came to steal and his people would not know what to do. This would be worse than the Great Monetary Collapse. "Where?"

"Your home."

Rom bit his lip in surprise and he yelped. His home! Not that he had a lot of gold-pressed latinum on hand, but he had mementos brought from both Deep Space 9 and the house where Ishka raised him and Quark. "But I don't hear . . ."

His words were cut off by a loud crash, as the front

door was kicked in. Orions, Rom knew, were physically imposing and preferred brute strength to weapons, and if they needed weapons, loud and destructive ones over anything subtle. Hands flew over his ears as the thumping continued, growing closer.

Rom hurried over to his bed and spent a few precious seconds gazing at his wife. How he loved Leeta, he thought. Then, with rising panic, he shook her awake with almost violent force.

"What's the matter, sweetie?" Her voice was still sleep-thick.

"We're being invaded! Quick, to the closet!" Rom tugged at her and Leeta rose from the bed, eyes wide in shock. Her next few words were garbled since she couldn't quite form a coherent sentence, which suited Rom just fine, since he didn't think he could give her a proper response. Tapping two studs in the wall, a hidden panel opened up and Rom practically shoved his wife, still in her diaphanous gown, through the doorway. "You stay there," he advised her. "I'll see what they want."

"Want? They want everything!" she exclaimed as the hatch sealed itself, once more looking like an ordinary closet.

Rom turned and headed back to his desk. He studied the data from space, marveling over the size of the aperture that allowed the invading force. Was it stable like the wormhole he lived near for so long? Could the Prophets of Bajor come for his meager profits? His thoughts were stopped when his bedchamber door was obliterated by a booted foot. Six Orions, each in his own version of fighting gear, walked in, weapons waving in every direction. The leather they wore was dark, well oiled, and reflected the hall lights. The weapons seemed almost as big as the average Ferengi and they hummed with power.

"You!" the first one shouted. He had scars along the right side of his face and, Rom noted, had rather dainty ears. He suppressed a giggle.

The next few minutes had the Orions rampage through the room and the rest of the house, taking what looked valuable, breaking a few things when they were frustrated, and demanding Rom quote open-market prices on just about everything. He had a hard time keeping up with six determined shoppers but through whimpers, he managed. Rom could hear fighting going on, in the rainy streets. Thank the Great Exchequer, he thought, his people were defending their Nagus.

Finally, satisfied they each had enough, they tapped identical blue buttons on their forearms and were transported back to their ship. Rom stood, shaking, amid the litter. Some of his favorite items were gone, others cracked or broken. Still, he was alive and they never found Leeta. As he returned to the bedroom to retrieve his wife, Rom remained fascinated by the engineering that was used to create the passageway.

"Macan deserves its unity! Macan's people deserve peace and prosperity! Macan does not, however, deserve its corrupt government!"

The small throng of people listened intently as the portly figure spoke. He was tall, broad, and had perfectly coiffed hair. His clothes were neatly pressed, the sixteen buttons on the jacket gleaming in the afternoon sun. For the last month, he had met with small groups such as this one, speaking with a lilt in his slightly accented voice, which the people of Sherman's Planet found appealing.

Jiggs Cardd had escaped his homeworld of Macan, fearing for his life. Now, several systems away, he once more was an outspoken critic of his government. Since unification came to his world, it had struggled to band nine continents and three dozen smaller governments into a cohesive whole. To accomplish this meant a merging of ideologies, finances, and a plethora of other details. What Cardd had learned was that along the way, those left to organize this glorious new beginning for the people of Macan were accepting bribes and favors to help shape a government that would favor some countries' peoples over others. There was even word that deals with off-planet interests would weaken their ability to conduct trade or apply for admission to the United Federation of Planets.

The people leaned in, engaged by the tenor of his voice but also by his spirit. Cardd was not the only one to speak out, but by being first, he was seen as the leader of a rebellious faction. On more than one occasion he avoided being arrested by the hastily formed Planetary Defense Initiative—Macan's secret police. His home had been burned to the ground, he had lost his job, and he had been roundly criticized on the information networks.

And still he spoke, making sure his people knew they were being sold out.

When things got so difficult he could no longer speak out in public, he found sympathetic friends who took him away from Macan. Now, speaking out in exile, Cardd tried to keep people focused on the problems before they were too entrenched to be fixed.

"We have over two hundred cultures and languages

on my world, two hundred different ways for describing a sunny day. Should fifteen of those ways be given preference over the rest? I think not. Nor should those unfortunate enough to live in poverty be subjected to testing to qualify for relief. Pooling together these countries means redistributing all the resources to help everyone. These are the overriding principals that allowed Vulcan to become one of the leading races in the galaxy. These are the same reasons that allowed Earth to put countless world wars behind them and seek a better way of life. And that's all I ask for Macan."

As Cardd spoke, no one noticed the three men that entered the town square. They wore dark brown uniforms and visors that covered their eyes, and had energy weapons clipped to their sleeves. With determined steps, the men neared Cardd. Once they spotted him, they fanned out in a well-practiced formation, unclipped the weapons, and took aim. Without a word, they fired in unison and all three bright violet beams struck the speaker. Cardd slumped forward, people screaming in shock.

The men merely turned away and walked back through the town, to the doorway that remained patiently open, waiting for their return.

Delta IV and Carreon were separated by four solar systems, each populated with up to eleven planets. And yet, they each laid claim to one planet in a nearby system. Admittedly, the planet was mineral rich unlike any of the others. In fact, the solar system was devoid of life, so the planets were ripe for the exploitation.

In the past, to avoid a war that would devastate both cultures, they signed treaties to leave the planet alone. But now, a small number of Carreon ships emerged through a gateway, figuring the instant transport to the planet would go undetected by the generally peaceful Deltans.

The Deltans clearly had the same thought.

Now, a total of seven ships hung in space, none close enough to orbit the planet—which had curiously gone unnamed all these years—and unwilling to give an inch.

Aboard the Carreon lead ship, Landik Mel Rosa looked through his viewscreen and tried to guess what his counterparts would do next. His red-gloved hand stroked his stubbly chin as he fine-tuned a sensor reading. Their bridge, located deep within the center of the vessel, was bright and well staffed by veterans. Mel Rosa liked that about his crew; they had all tested their mettle together and formed a battalion that was undefeated.

While he had protected his world from threats such as Orion pirates and exploratory Klingon ships, Mel Rosa had never led his crew into battle against the Deltans. Those days were lost to him, he assumed—that is, until recently.

Just days before, a gateway opened near their twin moons. No one knew it was there, hidden as it was among asteroids that floated in a loose ring around Carreon and its moons. One brave pilot led a scout craft through the gateway to see what lay beyond and within an hour returned with word: it was a direct pathway to the coveted planet. The transition was instantaneous and did no damage to life or equipment.

Quickly, Mel Rosa was asked to lead a small fleet through the gateway, finally laying claim to the planet and establishing a presence before the Deltans had a clue that anything had changed. He remembered laughing with his subordinates as they took the fastest journey of their careers yet went farther from home than ever before.

The laughter quickly turned into something less mirthful when Mel Rosa spotted flashing pinpricks of light near the world. Sensors confirmed four other ships, Deltan in design. He snapped an order to his weapons officer and sure enough, another gateway signature was spotted, a little farther out in the system. It appeared the Deltans had the same sneaky idea.

Now they faced off, neither one answering the other's hails. Mel Rosa could not go back for reinforcements; **they were** already outgunned by one ship. He couldn't reduce the odds without letting the Deltans think they had won. The world was needed to help a shaky economy and the timing was opportune. Once more he rubbed his chin and looked at the readouts. The gateways had identical signatures, so he knew it was not of Deltan origin. They also had not moved into a fighting configuration, and their weapons remained offline.

Mel Rosa turned to his second and asked, "What do you think?"

"I think they're ripe for the picking. Deltans go for all things sensual; they're not fighters. Four against three, I still like our chances."

The captain looked around his bridge, the determined looks on the crew's faces. All of them knew the stakes, knew the need for the world just within their grasp. He took a deep breath, let it out slowly, and began giving orders.

The first volley rattled the Deltan craft. Inside the flagship, Oliv, leader of the expedition, nearly fell from his chair. "Shields, return fire!"

Confirming calls went out from the crew and he watched as crimson streaks crossed his forward viewscreen. As expected, the Carreon were prepared and began moving away, letting the shots graze their shields.

Oliv knew the Carreon were practitioners of battle. Their vessels were better armed and protected. The Deltans had the advantage of numbers, but not the experience of bloodlust he knew was required. Which was why the moment the Carreon starships floated through the surprising second gateway, Oliv sent out a hail to Starfleet for help.

"We should have expected this," Hath said. "After all, why should we be the only ones so blessed with this miraculous transportation device?"

The captain looked at his companion, noting the sweat adding a shine to his bald head. This was a vessel full of miners and explorers, with just a handful of security. Still, Oliv was one of the few to have actually participated in battle. He had recently returned to Delta IV after volunteering with a mercenary band that fought in the Dominion War. It was that experience that led his government to ask him to undertake the current mission.

"Oliv," the communications officer called. She was incredibly attractive, with thick eyebrows and high cheekbones. "We've received word from Starfleet that help is on the way. They say it's the *Enterprise.*"

Oliv's own eyebrows rose in surprise. "Now we just have to survive until they arrive."

Chapter Two

CAPTAIN JEAN-LUC PICARD stood at the window, hands clasped behind his back, looking at the sunny day. As was typical of San Francisco most of the year, there was a breeze, keeping the environs cool, and the wind brushed the lush trees dotting the campus that was Starfleet Command. He gazed at the buildings that were just about completely reconstructed after the Breen attack on Earth a year earlier. There were some stylistic differences from what originally stood there and he nodded in satisfaction that the Federation had prevailed.

Starfleet and the United Federation of Planets had expended much in the way of manpower and matériel during that war. The costs were quite high, probably the highest since the first Romulan War nearly two centuries earlier. Picard and the crew of the *U.S.S. Enter-*

prise fought in the battles, doing their duty, but did not play as decisive a role as one would have thought of the Fleet's flagship. Still, he was proud of how his people had conducted themselves, and appreciated the last few months when the majority of missions were satisfying, short, and didn't require the phasers. But now he found himself back at Command headquarters. The communiqué from Admiral Ross was precise: return with all haste.

No sooner did his ship achieve orbit than a series of orders were issued. Picard and Counselor Deanna Troi were to beam to headquarters while Will Riker was to take temporary command and assist a border dispute between the Carreon, an independent world, and the Deltans, one of the older members of the Federation. While he trusted Riker with his ship, Picard was curious as to what was important enough to keep him and his counselor behind.

A day before, Picard mused, he had noticed a higher than normal incidence of daily briefings dealing with problems throughout the Alpha Quadrant. People going missing, races tangling over problems when peace existed merely a week earlier. It got him curious, but before he could begin investigating, he received his orders back to Earth. He was equally curious and more than a little anxious to tackle a big problem.

The sun was warm against his skin and Picard enjoyed a relaxed moment, although he was also growing tenser as he awaited the admiral and the briefing to follow. Troi was elsewhere, receiving a briefing of her own. He imagined they were connected but one could never tell with Starfleet Command.

"Calm before the storm, eh, Captain?"

Picard turned and saw Admiral Ross rounding a corner, his hand already out to greet the captain. Ross was slightly younger than Picard, but commanding the Fleet during the Dominion War took a lot out of him. Even as he tried to smile, Ross couldn't shake the hangdog look on his face. His dark hair was flecked with gray and his eyes seemed tired. He looked fit, however, filling out his uniform nicely if a few kilos over the norm. Picard grasped the beefy hand and was approving of the firmness in the grip.

"It's a pleasure to see you again, Admiral," Picard replied.

"You tended to avoid our conferences fairly regularly," Ross chided him. "Now I'm blessed with your presence twice in as many months. The pleasure is truly mine, even if we do only tend to see each other during crises."

They stared out the window in companionable silence for a few brief moments and Picard suspected times like this came all too rarely for the admiral. Cadets and officers strolled leisurely by, ignoring the construction going on around them. Picard could see a substantial space for a new garden, a memorial, he was informed, for those who gave their lives during the war.

"All those lives given for our ideals," Picard said.

Ross just nodded in agreement. "Not just ideals, but for the freedom to enjoy our choice of destiny. Worth fighting for again and again.

"Captain, we're due to begin the conference in a minute, we should go in and get ready. Once it's over, we'll speak privately."

"Yes, sir." Picard was curious. How many others were summoned to Earth? There didn't seem to be a preponderance of activity at Spacedock or in orbit. He hadn't a chance to visit the Quantum Lounge so he couldn't even pick up any gossip. Just as he could sense when his ship was the merest bit out of trim, he usually could tell when something was afoot at Command, but not this time.

"Our final speaker will be with us shortly, but we should go in to begin."

Ross led the way to a set of double doors and walked through. The captain recalled this area as a simulator room, a chance for Command to run contingency plans before implementation. Certainly an odd choice for a meeting but once again, the mysteries of command preceded him.

The space was lined with holo-emitters in the usual crisscross pattern, all deactivated. A small console was on the far side of the room with a lieutenant, small in form, dark-skinned and utterly silent, standing by. And it was empty. Picard frowned in mild confusion.

"Singh, is the captain in the building yet?"

"Yes, sir, he's just beamed down and should be here in three minutes."

Ross walked toward the center of the room and gestured for Picard to stand by his side, about two feet away. The admiral nodded at the other man and small lights winked on in the space above and around them. In a matter of seconds, several dozen humanoid forms began taking shape and the captain began recognizing fellow officers. Quickly, he scanned the faces, looking for patterns, and it became apparent that these were captains of patrol and fighting vessels from all points across Federation space, as well as starbase commanders from strategic regions. The new holotechnology had clearly been improved, hence the lack of starships in orbit—they weren't needed.

Picard noted, with some satisfaction, Mackenzie Calhoun among those gathered. The Xenexian officer had been thought recently dead, but managed to turn up quite alive just as Picard was dedicating the new *U.S.S. Excalibur,* after the original was destroyed, presumably with Calhoun still aboard. Calhoun spotted Picard beside Ross and gave him a relaxed smile. Also among the officers was Calhoun's new wife, Elizabeth Shelby, now captain of the *Trident* after briefly commanding the *Exeter.* In fact, Picard had the pleasure of conducting the marriage ceremony right after dedicating the new starship. While he had his problems with Shelby's style, Picard kept the opinion to himself since Calhoun obviously saw something about her to love.

Off to his right, a little farther behind the newly commissioned commander of the *Exeter,* whom he did not know, was Colonel Kira Nerys, from Deep Space 9. He had worked with Kira recently and found her to be hard-edged, nothing at all like the previous commander Ben Sisko, but definitely a worthy successor. She was also the only non-Starfleet person participating, but given DS9's importance, her presence made a certain sense. Standing beside her, looking intently curious, was Commander Elias Vaughn. The assignment of the enigmatic older officer to DS9 as Kira's first officer seemed to agree with him—he looked more relaxed than he had when he'd been temporarily assigned to the *Enterprise* on their mission to the Badlands weeks earlier.

"Good afternoon," Ross began in a deep voice. Many returned the greeting, some nodded; Solok of the *T'Kumbra* offered the Vulcan salute. "It's nice to know our relay systems are fine-tuned enough to allow holo-conferences like this to occur. It certainly beats trying to find parking orbits for all of you." He smiled but he instantly knew the joke fell flat.

"I'm placing you all on yellow alert until further notice." He paused a moment to let that sink in before continuing. "As for why we're doing this, we have a new problem. A few days ago, the Federation Council was approached by a group of beings who identified themselves as the Iconians." He paused again, letting the name seep into the minds of those assembled and waiting for the general reaction.

Sure enough, many widened their eyes, some nodded, others quickly asked "off-camera" officers to check the name.

"Captain Picard, would you please detail what we know of the Iconians?"

"Of course, Admiral." He straightened his uniform and looked out among the sea of holo-images. Moving slowly in circle, he began. "The Iconians were known to exist in this quadrant of space some two hundred millennia ago. Their culture and technology were unparalleled in that time period but records about them are scant. About a decade ago, Captain Donald Varley of the *U.S.S. Yamato* determined the location of their homeworld in the Romulan Neutral Zone, but was lost along with his ship when a destructive Iconian computer program inserted itself into the *Yamato*'s mainframe. Even after all this time, the technology on the Iconian homeworld remained functional—including the gateways.

"These gateways provide instantaneous transport between two points that could be meters or light-years apart. Two functional gateways have been found over the last few years: one on the homeworld, which I myself destroyed rather than allow gateway technology to fall into Romulan hands; and one, discovered by the Dominion, in the Gamma Quadrant, which was destroyed by a joint Starfleet/Jem'Hadar team from the *U.S.S. Defiant.*"

"Thank you, Captain," Ross said with a nod. "The Iconians who have come forward now have offered us the gateway technology for a price. The Council is considering the offer, but it's a bit more complicated than that. First, they are offering the technology to the highest bidder. Similar offers have been made to governments throughout the quadrant. Clearly, this could have a devastating impact should any antagonistic or ambitious government obtain the technology exclusively.

"Second, and most immediate: the Iconians have chosen to demonstrate how useful the gateways can be by activating the entire network. Gateways have opened up all over the quadrant, and beyond. The Iconians have seen fit to withhold how to control them and they have chosen not to provide us with any form of useful map."

As Ross paused, several captains passed on comments as the missing puzzle piece was provided to them. Picard was pleased that so many of his peers also noticed the higher number of incidents and now they knew why. However, Picard frowned, recognizing just how dangerous such a move was and how it struck him as wrong for a race as revered as the Iconians were.

Now he knew why Ross looked stressed and tired.

"As the gateways came online," Ross continued, silencing the group, "we immediately began studying their output, trying to get a handle on how they work. We became rather alarmed at some of the readings, and so turned the study over to the Starfleet Corps of Engineers. We now have a preliminary report."

As he stopped speaking, Picard became aware of a figure approaching him. The captain was so caught up in Ross's revelation, and its implications, he never heard the doors open.

"Captain Scott, thank you for joining us."

Montgomery Scott nodded at Ross, and then beamed at Picard. The crew of the *Enterprise* had rescued Scott from a transporter loop seven years earlier. Shortly thereafter, the original *Enterprise* engineer was loaned a shuttlecraft to find his place in the new universe. Picard heard Scott had spent some time actually working on Risa before accepting Starfleet's offer to act as liaison between the S.C.E. and the admiralty. Their paths had crossed just a month or two previously and Picard couldn't help but smile at the living legend.

"It's nae a problem," Scott began, his Scotch brogue a little heavier than before. "Those gateways, to be blunt, are behavin' in ways we never imagined. It seems that when they exhaust their power, they tap into any other power supply that's available. Like pussy willows here on Earth, that seek water and break into pipes to find it. These gateways are so beyond our ken tha' figuring out how they tick and stoppin' them will be almost impossible."

Ross looked alarmed, even though he must have had some inkling of this prior to the briefing. "Do you mean, they could tap an entire planet's resources and drain them dry?"

Scott took a deep breath. "Aye. Worse, for those worlds using predominantly geothermal or hydraulic power. Their ecosystem could be compromised. We don' have all the figures in yet, but one o' my ships is measuring solar consumption. My fear is some stars might be destabilized by additional power demands. It's a very nasty bit o' business."

"All the more reason for us to mobilize the Fleet. Duty packets are going out now with specific sector assignments. We'll need to maintain the peace. Some of our scientific vessels will be working with the S.C.E. to determine just how severe the problems might become. Captain Solok. . . ."

The Vulcan captain raised an eyebrow.

"I will want you and your crew to begin monitoring all incident reports from gateway activity. If the Iconians won't give us a map, I want us to make one."

"Understood. I should point out that it will not be complete and therefore not entirely accurate."

"Noted," Ross said. "I'll take whatever we can get since it's better than the nothing we have right now." He turned to Kira and Vaughn. "Colonel, Commander, our scientists have done some preliminary mapping based on the gateway power signatures and we've discovered something very interesting out your way. We're estimating no gateway activity within ten light-years in any direction of Bajor."

Vaughn's eyes closed to slits. *"The wormhole."*

"We think so, yes."

Kira added, *"It could be the Prophets protecting this region."* Picard instinctively wanted to dismiss the idea, trying to keep possible deities out of the complicated mix, but he had to admit, be they Prophets or alien life-forms, they wielded considerable power.

"That's certainly a possibility," admitted Ross. "Vaughn, given your experience with the gateways, I want you out there, finding out why there aren't any gateways near Bajor. Is it something natural? Is it the doing of the aliens—that is to say, the Prophets?" he amended with a respectful glance at Kira. "What properties are being displayed, and can they be harnessed beyond your sector?"

Nodding, Vaughn said, *"You're hoping we can turn it into a practical countermeasure."*

"Exactly."

Picard was more interested in what Ross had said about Vaughn's experience. As far as he knew, he, Worf, and Data had been the first to discover a functioning gateway, and he'd always been a little jealous that Worf had encountered a second. "I was unaware, Admiral, of any encounters with gateways beyond those by the *Enterprise* and the *Defiant.*"

With a look at her first officer, Kira said, *"Neither was I."*

"It was a few years ago," Vaughn said neutrally.

Ross gave Picard a reassuring look. "The relevant portions of Commander Vaughn's mission will be declassified in light of the present emergency."

Picard nodded. "Good."

As Ross and Kira discussed another assignment of DS9's relating to the Europa Nova colony, which needed to be evacuated, Picard stared at Vaughn. There was layer upon layer of story shrouding the man. How much of it could be true? he mused. Given DS9's own checkered history and its enigmatic wormhole aliens, Vaughn was probably even better suited to the place than Picard had imagined.

Before he could let his mind wander further, he heard Calhoun's name.

"Captain, you and the *Excalibur* will go deep in

Thallonian space. There's a concentration of gateway signatures that bears investigation."

"We don't habitually go shallow in Thallonian space, Admiral. 'Deep' is our status quo. Can you give us a bit more of a hint than that?"

Picard inwardly winced at Calhoun's comment. Even after all this time, the warrior showed through the veneer of Starfleet training.

"We'll forward the coordinates to your science officer," Ross said curtly.

"Thank you. What do the gateway signatures say, by the way? 'With all our love, the Iconians'?"

"Captain," said Ross, his voice sounding less pleased by the moment, "I'm obviously referring to energy signatures, not autographs, and this is no laughing matter."

"You're only saying that, Admiral, because your joke didn't get a laugh."

Picard glanced over at Ross and saw his hands forming fists, knuckles whitening.

"Admiral," Shelby cut in, *"if I may . . ."*

"Please do, Captain," Ross said. At least Shelby knew proper protocol, Picard thought. She might help defuse the moment.

"I have a new crewman on my ship. She came to me through the Temporal Displacement Office, and she described the means through which she got here as a sort of 'gateway.' I don't think she used the term in the 'official' capacity you're using here, but it may well be the same technology."

"Transporting through time *and* space?" He looked grim. "These things may be even more powerful than we had previously imagined. Was she on the Iconian homeworld or in the Gamma Quadrant?"

"I don't believe it was either, sir. She'd filed a report with the TDO; obviously it wasn't passed along to you."

"Damned paperwork trail," Picard said. "Thanks to modern technology, the left hand can be oblivious of the right hand's activities with greater efficiency than ever."

This drew more chuckles. *"Careful, Picard,"* Calhoun said. *"He hates it when other people get more laughs than he does."*

"Captain!" Ross snapped.

"Yes, sir?" said at least two dozen of those present.

Ross winced, then spoke to Shelby even as he gave Calhoun a withering glance. "In light of the current situation, Captain Shelby, speak with this crewwoman and see what further details you can learn. Send a report directly to me, if you'd be so kind."

He handed out a few other specific assignments, especially to vessels near the Klingon and Romulan borders. Then he concluded with: "These will be some trying days ahead of us all. I want to keep in constant contact and I'll be reachable any time you need me. Good luck."

The holo-images winked out almost entirely at once, leaving Ross, Picard, Scott, and the technician standing in the barren room. It was a quiet moment, filled with both energy and tension.

"Ye know," Scott said, "we may have found it first."

"Found what?" Ross asked.

"A gateway. Tha' talk of temporal displacement had me thinking back to my *Enterprise*'s encounters. And well, one thought led to another and I recall my *Enterprise* being a thousand light-years from its origin point in just a blink."

Ross looked at him askance. "Gateways aren't that big."

"Who's to say," Scott said in turn, rocking on his heels, looking a little satisfied. "How else do ye explain that?"

"I don't," Ross said curtly. Clearly he disliked the direction of the conversation and fell silent.

Picard allowed that silence to last barely half a second and then finally raised his own concern. "Admiral, I still do not see why I was brought to Earth . . . and my ship sent on without me."

Ross gestured for them to head for the door. Scott ambled over to the technician, knowing the two needed to be alone. The two officers left the room and began walking down the gleaming corridors of Starfleet Headquarters. It dawned on Picard how empty they seemed, with office doors closed and overhead communications muted. Now he felt the vibration of work being done, as if everything went into motion as the holoconference was being conducted.

"Jean-Luc, you and Varley shared a deep interest in the Iconians. In fact, you may now be Starfleet's foremost authority on them."

Picard nodded but added, "In the Fleet maybe, but Professor Chi Namthot at Memory Alpha has continued to analyze what we found on Iconia."

"Be that as it may, you have the qualifications to help us." Ross continued walking, barely noticing those around him. His voice grew grave. "To be candid with you, we in Starfleet do not think these are really Iconians."

Picard paused, turning to look at Ross's expression. He saw only seriousness and maybe exhaustion as the eyebrows hunched further down. Despite all the findings on Iconia, not a single image of an Iconian had been identified, so they remained a visual enigma.

"I've read your logs, I've even seen excerpts of Namthot's work. None of us believe a race as sophisticated as the Iconians would merely want to sell this technology. The Council, however, cannot dismiss the possibility after all this time and are negotiating in good faith. We have to be fully prepared for whatever the outcome. If we gain the technology, another race such as the Breen might see that as a prelude to war. If we do not gain the technology, other races might use it to dominate this quadrant or more. The Orions are engaged in aggressive negotiations with the Iconians on Farius Prime right now, and I don't have to tell you what a disaster it would be if those pirates got their hands on the technology. Should these prove to be other than real Iconians we need to know who they really are. Right now, diplomacy is going on so we cannot do invasive medical scans. From surface scans, we do not recognize the physiology so they are at least alien to this section of space. Their starships are also of unfamiliar design using some ion-based propulsion unique to themselves."

"How do they act?"

"Formal, following all of our diplomatic protocols. They came already knowing Federation Standard so we can't guess at their native tongue. I attended two working sessions at the President's request and came away feeling uneasy. I guess winning a war gets me a little credibility because once he heard that, I was authorized to begin mobilizing the Fleet, just in case."

Picard looked at him, steeling himself for the hard question. "Are you afraid of another war?"

Ross shook his head slowly. "We can't afford one, Jean-Luc. The Fleet is seriously stretched thin after losing so many ships to the Borg and Dominion. Shipbuilding takes time, training crews takes time, and if that technology ends up with the Romulans, or the Orions, or even the Jem'Hadar, we might become very, very vulnerable."

"I see," Picard replied slowly. Already, he was creating and rejecting scenarios that showed how the Federation would stack up against an aggressor gifted with a gateway network. The picture was grim, adding further importance to the mission, whatever his role was to be.

"We're surprised by how easily the Iconians are operating on Earth since our gravity differs from Iconia. Also factor in over two hundred millennia of genetic growth and they seem too comfortable. My gut says we have two problems: them *and* the gateways. I've sent everyone else out, including your boy Riker, to handle the gateways. I need you to handle the Iconians."

Picard was surprised, since it sounded like he'd be apart from his ship and crew for longer than he would have liked. By now, their wandering had led to a briefing room, on the opposite side of the building. Ross had led them here, through the silent, empty corridors, and escorted him inside. Seated at the grand, U-shaped table was Troi, a data padd by her hand. Her eyes grew wide, signaling to Picard that she still wasn't certain why she was here. The captain smiled and nodded slightly.

"Counselor Troi, it's nice to see you again." Ross greeted her with a quick handshake, while at the same time gesturing for her to remain seated. The admiral slipped behind the podium at the open section of the U and tapped on a console. The screen behind him came to life and a map of the Alpha Quadrant appeared.

"I suspect we do not have a lot of time," Ross began.

"Therefore, since we're spread thin, I'm asking for your help in assembling a quadrant-wide delegation. I have two vessels ready for you, and one for myself. Ambassador Lojal has been freed up by the Diplomatic Corps to pay a few visits on our behalf. We're going on a journey, asking for representatives of the key races in our quadrant to come speak as one with the Iconians. If nothing else, I want us to present a united front, asking them to close the gateways until negotiations are over. I'm hoping that will buy the negotiating team some time, and give the Fleet a chance to regroup in a more battle-ready way. Captain Picard, I will ask you to head up that delegation."

The captain looked sharply from the map to Ross. "Me? Sir, if you're helping to assemble this group, it should be the ranking officer who . . ."

"Picard, you have a reputation almost unequaled in the Fleet. When the Borg attacked Earth, you took command and managed to knock out the cube."

"Disobeying direct orders to stay away," Picard added quietly.

Ross's eyes twinkled for a brief moment. "All's forgiven. You have dealt with the key races: Klingons, Romulans, Gorn . . . and have earned their respect one way or another. And, you know the Iconian culture better than I ever will. My gut instincts got us this far but I need you, your experience, and your own instincts to take us further."

"And me, sir, what is my role?" Troi asked.

"Counselor, you carry the standard of the *Enterprise,* just as respected as Picard himself. Your empathic skills will be necessary to help us sort out who our real allies are and to back up Picard's sense of the Iconians. You make an excellent team."

Troi smiled. "Thank you for the vote of confidence."

"It's earned, Counselor. "

"But why not more from the Federation's diplomats?"

Ross looked grim. "The gateways have caused so much trouble that the entire Diplomatic Corps has been sent out to help mediate problems or escort lost people home. There's no one left to send. You'll join the *Mercury* and approach the Gorn first. I have your flight plan already worked out."

Troi nodded. Then Ross turned to Picard. "Our ambassador on Qo'noS has already arranged a meeting for you with Chancellor Martok. That'll be your first stop aboard the *Marco Polo*."

"Sir, I'd much rather do this aboard the *Enterprise*," Picard protested.

"I need that ship out there on active duty. You don't need it to make these visits. I'll be out too, starting with the Romulans. Our alliance remains intact, but this will no doubt add strain so I need to give it the personal touch. Then it's off to the wild-card regions—Melkots, Metrons."

"Any thought about Organian intervention?"

"No, Counselor. They haven't appeared in so long, it's our opinion that they forced a peace between the Federation and Klingons to steer us where we are today. Whatever their concerns are, they are clearly not directed our way."

"I see. That does make sense."

Ross smiled tightly. "Of all the powerful beings out there, I'm more than thankful that only one of them seems interested in dealing with us. Imagine if we were bothered by the Q, and the Organians, even the Excalbians, and . . ."

"We understand," Picard said, cutting off Ross. It pained him to see how the admiral was handling the new pressure. As far has could tell, Ross saw this as a larger problem than the Dominion. And he couldn't argue.

"Gateways are marvelous tools, but in the hands of those who would exploit it, the problems clearly outweigh the benefits." He stood, tugging his uniform into place. "We had best get to our ships and begin lining up our allies. If Mr. Scott is right, and I'm willing to bet he is, we have entire planets to worry about."

Ross agreed and handed them padds from the lectern. The captain and the counselor accepted them and strode from the room in one direction while Ross went the opposite way. Once they were some distance, Picard slowed his gait and turned to his counselor.

"What do you think?"

"Ross is a good man. He's very concerned over how many variables have to be kept in check and he's very worried that Starfleet is not yet up to a challenge of this magnitude. He needs to head this off now. That's why four of us are making the contacts."

Picard slightly nodded in agreement. "He's right that the *Enterprise* is best off helping those in need but still . . ."

Now Troi smiled. "I know, it's not the same: not the same ship or same crew. It's just to gather the people together, you'll be fine."

"Am I that obvious, Counselor?"

"Just to those of us you've led."

Changing the subject, Picard added, "Did you know Mr. Scott may have beaten me to the gateways?"

"Do tell," she implored. She liked Scotty and had

grown to appreciate the exploits of that *Enterprise* and its crew, so any new story was welcome.

"I can't. I need to look up the facts since Ross interrupted. Still, imagine a gateway big enough for a starship . . . how that could change space travel."

Troi smiled and said, "If you had gateways, you wouldn't need such huge ships. Seems almost wasteful to use that much power to open such a large hole in space."

"And I thought you were the dreamer in my crew."

"Oh, I am, sir," she said. "I just don't dream about holes in space."

"Landik Mel Rosa, I must insist you stand down."

"Would that I could, Commander Riker, but you see, I have weapons trained on me and were I to lower my shields, well, I certainly would be tempted to fire if I could."

Stroking his smooth chin, Riker shifted uncomfortably in the command seat. On the forward viewscreen was a tactical display showing the planet standing between the Deltan and Carreon vessels. Sensors showed both sides were running hot, although neither had fired since the *Enterprise* dropped out of warp, entering the solar system. Were a firefight to break out, the *Enterprise* could not protect any other ship. Since he was still unclear on the dispute itself, Riker could not take sides although, strictly speaking, since the Deltans were members of the Federation they deserved his protection. Still, if they were the aggressors, they might have it coming.

"Stand by," Riker declared and signaled for the com channel to close. He stood, crossing the short distance to where Data sat at ops. Putting one foot on the side of the console, he leaned forward, resting an arm on the raised knee. "Opinion, Mr. Data."

The gold-skinned android turned his head slightly and frowned. "Sensors have detected identical readings in this system that I match with that of the Iconian gateways."

Riker looked at him in surprise. "I thought we destroyed the one on their homeworld."

"We did. It seems there are others, as suspected, throughout this section of space. As a result, both races could have come here through the two gateways and found themselves in conflict over the planet."

"Does either have a legitimate claim?" Riker's mind raced through his memories of the gateway encounter, recalling being on the bridge throughout most of the action. Picard knew the Iconian legends; Riker only had a passing knowledge. Clearly, the first officer needed to brush up on them if those gateways were the cause of the conflict.

"Negative. Computer records indicate both sides have clashed over this planet in the past. It has remained unclaimed and undeveloped."

Riker nodded.

"Commander, three more vessels approaching this system," called out Lieutenant Christine Vale. Currently security chief, she took over the tactical station once the *Enterprise* left Earth orbit and had provided briefings on Deltan and Carreon ship configurations and armaments. She even found time to drill the photon torpedo teams in case the flagship got caught in the crossfire and they needed to stop both sides simultaneously. Despite her diminutive size, Vale commanded respect and got it from Picard on down.

"Whose side are they are on?" Riker asked.

"Deltan vessels, hot and ready for fire."

"Advantage, Deltans," Riker muttered, watching the ten vessels on the screen.

In a clear voice, he spoke out. "Captain Oliv, this is Commander Riker of the *Enterprise*. I must ask that your support ships stand down and remain at the edge of the system. If they come closer, the Carreon will see this action as hostile."

A moment later, an audio-only response was heard. *"I'm sorry, Commander, but too long have we waited for a chance to tame this world and my government would have it be today."*

Riker grimaced, sensing the battle to come. "That's for the Federation diplomats to decide. Let's get a negotiator out here to meet with you and the Carreon and we can get this settled without a fight."

"I'd rather not wait, thank you," the Deltan replied, the voice soft, milky. Then he cut the connection.

"I always thought they were lovers, not fighters," Riker said.

"Actually, Commander," Data said, "the Deltans are known for their passions. While renowned throughout the Federation for their physical prowess in the art of lovemaking, they are also passionate in all their tasks including fighting. Some fourteen different boxing, fencing, and armament titles are held by Deltans and have been for the last decade."

"Swell." Riker furiously tried to think through the options available to him. After all, the last thing he wanted was to bear witness to a slaughter, especially over an uninhabited world.

Chapter Three

"PICARD'S COMING?"

"Is it true, is it really Picard?"

"Four of us heard it's Picard, you make five, so it's got to be true."

"I dunno, an hour ago, we thought Admiral Jellico was being assigned."

"And he never left Earth."

"Which is a good thing."

"Mia and Kal heard it, so that's two. I heard it . . ."

"Yes, but you heard it from them so you don't count."

"But you heard it from Sacker, so you're three."

"Sacker would be four."

"Jessie thinks she's heard it, does that count?"

"Picard or not, I still don't care." And that seemed to settle the debate on the bridge. Everyone had arrived in

36

hurried fashion, throwing their gear in temporary cabins, quickly logging in to check duty rosters, and then grabbing a bite before some captain arrived. Everything had been rush-rush, orders cut, people pulled from other vessels. No one felt properly oriented and it grated on Kal Sur Hol, the newly named science officer.

"Picard can throw his weight around, but what's the big deal? I was scheduled to depart with the *Gettysburg* and now I miss out."

"It's Jean-Luc Picard! Don't you realize what we're dealing with?" The woman asking was Mia Chan, the conn officer. She belonged on this vessel and seemed to welcome the sudden change in routine. Her equanimity grated against Hol.

"Yeah, yeah, commander of the allmighty *Enterprise,* discovered this, settled that, Arbiter of Succession for the Klingons, once a Borg . . . what's he doing on this miniature starship?"

Chan toggled a switch, swiveled around, and stood up. Hol noticed she was young, probably on her first posting and grateful for any deep-space assignment. She had auburn hair, cut short, a smooth unlined face that told Hol she had not had much experience at much of anything, and dark eyes that took in everything. There was that freshly minted Academy glow about her; he was glad his had worn down over the years through experience starting with even smaller craft in remote portions of the sector. He had returned to Earth, a land-based assignment in the wake of the Breen attack on Starfleet. Finally, he was given a fresh assignment and then this came up: short duty but vital to the Federation.

"He's taking us places," she said. "Serving with him, impressing someone like that, can do us all wonders."

Enthusiasm dripped from her every word. Had he ever sounded so sincere?

"This milk run will not be a chance to impress him at all, Chan," he said with disdain. "We're running him from point to point, just being good footmen. You think we'll discover some new stellar phenomenon along familiar routes? Find another Q? Always heard how the *Enterprise* stumbled across this spatial glitch or that space-breathing life-form. You ask me, he's just trying to outdo April and Pike. Now, they were explorers."

The younger woman tugged at her right ear, an annoying habit, and was staring at the Tiburonian with dismay. "Picard helped stave off wars and his crews always got the best postings. Wouldn't it be great to serve on the *Sovereign*-class ships like *Enterprise?*"

Hol sighed. "The *Gettysburg* would have been big enough, thank you. Better take a station, though. Davison went to meet him and I bet he comes right here."

"So it is Picard, then?" she asked, seeking that final confirmation.

"It better be, wouldn't want him disappointing you," he said archly.

The main transporter facility at Starfleet Headquarters was in constant action when Picard arrived. He could see officers, young and old, being beamed to their ships, belongings sometimes coming along, other times left behind in haste. In his right hand was a data padd filled with the roster of the *Marco Polo,* and he had had scant time to even look through the names, let alone service records. He had never felt more rushed, less prepared for an assignment. Still, he recognized the need for speed and was doing what he could to keep things moving along.

Yet, he felt like he was only a step ahead of a tidal wave.

He went to the duty officer and announced his destination and was given priority clearance so he could skip waiting on line. Everyone seemed to know who he was and there were nods of acknowledgment. Picard returned them, wishing to know if any of them were to be among his crew. As the person on the pad dematerialized, he heard his name, and turned to face the speaker.

"Ah, Counselor, ready for your journey?"

Troi rushed up to him, still adjusting her jacket collar. She seemed as rushed as he was and he gave her a sympathetic smile.

"Just about. Captain Brisbayne is anxious to depart. Are you ready for a new command?"

"It's just temporary, Counselor. We'll be back with Will and the others soon enough." He eyed the platform and saw it was empty and waiting for him.

"This is a new crew and they only know you by reputation," she pointed out. Picard took a step toward the platform and paused. He looked at her as if there was a deeper meaning to her words. His silence prompted her to continue.

"It's a young crew, and that means they don't have the experience yet. All they have are lessons and simulations. You'll be something larger than life to many of them and you need to keep that in mind."

"Am I some sort of ogre?"

She laughed and touched his shoulder with reassurance. How lucky Will was, he considered. "Not at all, but there will be nervousness trying to live up to your reputation. Don't let it distance you from them."

"Thank you," he said quietly. In all the rush, he never considered his impact on the crew. He saw them mainly as a means to an end; she gave them substance. With a final smile, he walked to the platform, carrying his baggage himself, and placed it on the pad beside his own. His final image was of Troi, giving him one of her patented broad grins.

Just three hours after the conference, Picard and his belongings were aboard the *Marco Polo,* which had just finished a maintenance check before being crewed and launched.

She was a *Sabre*-class vessel, a light cruiser built for speed and maneuverability. The first such vessels, Picard knew, were launched just prior to the Borg attack on Earth two years previous. Most of them were attached to the S.C.E. these days—in fact, Picard had lent his chief engineer to one, the *U.S.S. da Vinci,* for about a week, and he had almost had to pry Commander La Forge away. It was a snub-nosed vessel, with nacelles close to the hull and painted a dark gray.

The captain noted that its complement was only forty, spread over four decks, and that at 310,000 metric tonnes it was smaller even than the *Stargazer,* which he had commanded prior to *Enterprise.* From the padd Ross gave him, Picard learned that the crew was thrown together from Starfleet resources: original crew complement still on Earth during shore leave, other personnel pulled from ships in orbit, and even one or two volunteers when word got out that something was happening.

Picard grew concerned that a crew that had never worked together, under a captain unfamiliar with the ship and its capabilities, would never perform well in combat. For a rush diplomatic mission, such as this, there was a slight hope this would be fine. In fact, he mused, this might be good for their training. Picard was among the captains that noted their concerns with Starfleet Academy that recruits were being pushed along too fast, not enough were logging sufficient star hours before graduation and ship postings—particularly both during and after the war when the greatest concern was refilling the ranks. There was a genuine concern that such ill-prepared crew might be a danger to their ships and themselves.

As the transporter beam coalesced, a middle-aged woman with long brown hair piled high on her head greeted Picard. She wore her gray duty jacket open, her red shirt showing a fit figure. "Commander Jessie Davison" was all she said.

"Captain Jean-Luc Picard," he replied by way of greeting.

"Welcome aboard, sir. I'll have someone bring your bag to the captain's quarters."

Picard nodded, preferring not to disturb the ship's real commander, who was off enjoying a conference on some distant world. Gripping the padd in his right hand, he said, "Let's get up to the bridge and head out."

"Agreed. The crew is anxious to meet you."

Troi's words echoed back in his mind and he marveled at her accuracy. "Are they?"

"You do have a reputation, Captain. And it's not every day they get a chance to serve, however briefly, with such a storied commander." Her voice seemed full of joy and enthusiasm; this was a veteran who still loved every star hour logged.

"I see." He was concerned over the gateway damage, not being on the *Enterprise,* the true nature of these Iconians, Will doing something to his ship, and making these rapid-fire diplomatic contacts. And he wasn't aboard his familiar command. He wasn't sure there was time left to coddle a boatload of youngsters. Still, he had to make the effort.

In the turbolift, Davison explained that all forty members of the makeshift crew had now reported in and they had received priority clearance to leave Space-dock and clear the system. Picard nodded at both Ross's efficiency and Davison's.

"We achieved a new record," she said proudly.

"Haste is not always useful," Picard warned.

"True, but we wagered at being staffed before *Mercury* and beat them once you reported in."

"Really? What was the wager?"

"An advance copy of the latest Risa solar surfing holoprogram." She grinned at Picard.

He took one final glance at the roster, then lowered his arm as the doors opened to the bridge. It had been over a decade since he last took command of a ship that wasn't called *Enterprise.* He liked to think he had learned from the experience, wouldn't be as stiff and distanced as he was back then.

Picard ignored the captain's seat for a moment, strolling around the circle of duty stations that ringed the command center. Starting to his left, he walked by the tactical station and said, "Good to have you aboard, Lieutenant Rodriguez." He continued walking by the science, engineering, and environmental controls aft, then flight control and operations console at the bridge's front, and the science station. Along the way, he greeted each officer by name, making him or her feel welcome.

"Mr. Sacker . . . Ensign Chu-Fong . . . Lieutenant Sikluna . . . Mr. Putski . . ."

Once he took his place in the captain's chair, he let out a deep breath and turned to Davison, who had a grin on her lined face.

"Was I even close?"

"Pretty close on two of them, but I'm sure they appreciated the effort."

Picard stifled a sigh, looked around once more, and then checked the readouts on either side of the command chair. It was time to get to work.

"We're cleared to depart, helm, take us out. Engage."

Chan smoothly eased the smaller vessel out of Spacedock and across the solar system. Picard watched everyone at work, satisfied that they knew what they were doing. It pleased him that he had to revise his estimates at the total youth aboard the ship as evidenced by Davison and Hol.

"We're making a series of brief visits, Ensign Chan. Please review the flight charts and make certain we're taking the most expedient course."

"Aye, sir," she replied at once. He noticed the withering stare Science Officer Hol gave her from the ops console next to her.

"Best speed to Qo'noS," he ordered.

"Leaving the solar system in five minutes, before engaging warp," she said.

"Very good. I'll be in the ready room. Commander, will you join me?"

* * *

Once the captain left the bridge, leaving the conn to Hol, Chan turned right around to address her colleagues. "So, that's Captain Picard, huh?"

Hol looked at her with penetrating eyes, emphasized by his race's lack of hair. "And?"

She shrugged, pulling at her ear. "I thought he'd be, I don't know . . . taller."

"He is what he is," Hol replied. It didn't seem pertinent what size the captain was. On the other hand, he was concerned over the mission. "As I understand it now, we're to bring him to a number of targeted worlds. An interesting collection of non-aligned races."

Chan adjusted the heading and checked the readouts, nodding to herself with satisfaction. "Well, the Klingons aren't exactly non-aligned."

"She's right," chimed in Rosario, the tactical officer. He was a tall, broad-shouldered man, the fitting image of a security chief. His blond hair, cut severely short, reflected the light so it always seemed to shimmer around his skull, which took nothing away from the penetrating blue of his eyes. "Klingons. I am so ready for warp speed."

"We will need warp speed to maintain our schedule," Hol said skeptically. It drew some chuckles from around him.

"Warp speed is very good," said Chan.

"Good, because I would hate to think warp speed meant something other than the velocity."

"Oh, it does," Rosario told the Tiburonian. "We've left orbit, making a direct line for the Klingon Empire, where we will be greeted by the chancellor himself, and our leader is none other than Captain Jean-Luc Picard."

"So, that means we're at warp speed," Hol said hesitantly. Clearly this banter was beyond him. It promised to be a long trip.

"Yes it does," Rosario said with a broad grin.

"Do you think Picard is at warp speed?" Chan asked.

Chan turned to Rosario, hoping for a positive reply. Hol looked at her, noting the intense interest in Rosario's reply. He considered the question thoughtfully. "I don't know if that man ever gets to warp speed. Seems beneath him."

Within the ready room, after dismissing Davison, Picard settled back in the chair and sipped his tea. The chair, he noted, was not as plush as the one he had grown accustomed to on the current *Enterprise*. In fact, *Marco Polo* was built for immediacy.

On the viewscreen built into the desktop, Picard had called up all existing records on the Iconians. Although he had committed much of the information to memory, he sifted through Varley's logs, his own, as well as Data's and Worf's from the visit to Iconia; those taken by Worf and the rest of the *Defiant* crew at Vandros IV, which had been sent directly to Picard from Deep Space 9; and the declassified portions of Commander Vaughn's mission to Alexandra's Planet, which, like Picard's own Iconian experience, also involved the Romulans.

The Iconians were spread far and wide throughout the galaxy, yet only three worlds had been found with direct links to the Iconian heritage. Their gateways were a marvelous example of an advanced technology, but so was their expertise with computers and computer interfaces. He felt saddened by the loss of Varley and his crew but gratified that his loss was not an empty one—it gave the *Enterprise* a chance to comprehend the discovery and, in turn, managed to save the Romulans. More closely, it also meant they managed to save Data when the programming tried to rewrite the android's neural pathways.

The Iconians, with their technology and reach, had always impressed Picard. Of all the long-dead races he studied over the years, they captured his imagination and held it. The time they flourished in the galaxy was long before sentient life even existed on Earth or Vulcan or Qo'noS. What they managed to build and achieve, where they traveled, how they did it . . . all of it showed a sense of achievement mixed with purpose.

Picard agreed with Ross: there was little reason for the Iconians to return after so much time merely to want to sell their technology. True, he did not know all about their culture and he certainly knew nothing of their governing structure. But his instincts screamed at him that this was all wrong.

Putting down the tea, he looked away from the screen, and let his mind wander. He needed to absorb the enormity of the task ahead, make plans in case some of the races said no. And for the ones that would say yes, what if they lied? Without his complete command staff, Picard did not have trusted voices for feedback and would have to make do with the *Marco Polo*'s ad hoc crew. He would force himself to keep an open mind when they ventured an opinion, and he would also make sure they had a chance to offer their thoughts.

He looked forward to seeing his old comrade Worf once more. They last were together when the *Enterprise* brought Worf, newly appointed ambassador to the empire, to his posting. Picard also looked forward to speaking with Martok, a vastly different sort of chancellor than Gowron was. As his mind began focusing on details of Klingon government, he grew anxious. Finally, he admitted he was looking forward to at least this first portion of the mission.

Satisfied for the moment, he returned to the bridge, where obviously the crew had been chattering, forming a working relationship. However, the voices drifted toward silence as he emerged and took his chair.

"Status, Ensign Chan?"

"Proceeding on course to Qo'noS, sir. Nothing unusual between here and the empire border."

"Very good. Mr. Rodriguez . . ."

The tactical officer cleared his throat. "Rosario, sir."

Picard looked over his shoulder, in mild surprise. "My apologies. Mr. Rosario, maintain yellow alert and make sure weapons remain offline until I say otherwise."

"Very good, Captain."

Picard studied the bridge and the collection of unfamiliar faces. "We have a little time before we arrive at Qo'noS but I must say, I am looking forward to this," he added, a tone of pleasure in his voice. "Have any of you been?"

Murmurs in the negative came from around him.

Picard nodded and began telling them of the world, and its people. He made sure to cover some of the customs that would need to be observed and pointed out the Federation ambassador and staff would be present to help smooth the way. The talk went on for several minutes, with none of the crew daring to interrupt even though Chan appeared to have many questions. Davison herself remained quietly respectful by his side.

When finished, he turned command over to her and re-tired to his quarters.

As he left the bridge, Davison looked at the other members of the bridge staff and commented, "That man is at warp speed."

Chan broke into a wide smile. "Yes, he is!"

Captain Brisbayne was not waiting for Troi when she arrived on the *Mercury.* Instead, the first officer, Ranjit Srivastava, an exceedingly thin, dark-skinned man with a face of indeterminate age despite his graying temples, greeted her.

"The captain offers his compliments but is preparing to leave orbit," Srivastava explained in a soft voice.

"It's not a problem," she said. "I can understand the rush."

"We will have to travel at top warp for each leg of the journey to stay on Admiral Ross's schedule. This has the captain concerned."

"Why is that?" she asked. They had left the transporter room and began walking down the corridor, toward the turbolift. The few they passed rushed by as if they were in a race. And perhaps they were.

"We're a smaller ship than you're used to, Commander," the first officer said, using her official rank rather than job title. "We're not built to sustain such speeds for long and it's going to prove a challenge to the engineering staff."

Once inside the lift, Troi was surprised they were heading directly to the bridge. "Is this crew as quickly put together as the *Marco Polo?*"

"Fortunately not," he replied. By then, they had made the quick trip to the top of the vessel and emerged on the bridge. It was certainly smaller than she was used to, but it was of little concern to her. In the center sat the captain, who was issuing orders while reading a data padd and waving off a hovering crewman. He was burly and older, a career officer, she knew. She heard him demand clearance from command to depart while still ordering a final container of medical supplies be beamed aboard.

The first officer quietly took his place to the captain's left with Troi standing beside them. Srivastava made the introductions and Brisbayne merely nodded in her direction as he squinted at something on the padd.

"Excuse me," he said to her. "Brisbayne to engineering. Solly, did you get the extra FTL nanoprocessor units I ordered?"

"We're just storing them now, Captain."

"Fine. Bridge out." He turned to the counselor and gestured for her to take a seat on his right. Still holding her baggage, she shrugged and did as requested.

"We're going to get out of here in record time and then hit warp. Soon as we clear the solar system, we'll convene department heads for a briefing. Will you be ready?"

Troi nodded. "I'm as prepared as any of us are."

"I need you to be better prepared than I am," he said. "We've had our orders changed four times in the last twelve hours, and I'm flying a tired crew that came here for shore leave. We cut short the overhaul the ship needed to take you places, so I hope to God you're ready."

The waves of agitation washed over her and she steeled herself to handle them. She suspected he would remain so until they had made their stops. Her empathic feelings indicated he was dedicated to the mission but worried about both ship and crew. She couldn't tell if his manner was always so blunt but would adjust her reactions accordingly.

"I'm ready, Captain."

"Good."

"Entering orbit," Chan said, as the *Marco Polo* approached the green world of Qo'noS.

"Very good," Davison said, as Picard entered the bridge. "Tactical, contact the consulate and ask for any updates to the schedule. Science, now's a good time to look for gateway activity—just in case."

Picard watched from near the turbolift, satisfied with Davison's handling of the crew. He felt refreshed and ready for the meetings. It had been made clear that although a pleasant stop since the Klingons were an ally, it was also to be a brief one. Starfleet felt a personal approach to Chancellor Martok was best and Picard couldn't disagree. With their codes of conduct, just expecting them to fall beside them could be seen as an insult. Picard also did not fully know the tenor of the Klingon government since Martok took control of the Council. As he understood it, Worf killed Gowron in combat and earned the title himself. Instead of seizing the power, once and for all restoring glory to his family name, he felt unworthy of the position. Instead, Worf decided a race of warriors needed to be led by one who had seen battle, and lived long enough to learn from it. Martok took control of the Klingon people that day, and, after a rather tumultuous transition period, had effected changes that benefited his people. In a society that had seen more than its share of corruption, Martok sounded like the right man for the times. And Picard was immensely proud of Worf's actions, feeling more than a little like a parent.

He took his place in command seat and asked for a direct link to Worf's office at the Federation embassy. Rosario complied but rather than an image of his old friend, Picard was greeted by a human of very mixed ancestry; Worf's aide, Picard recalled.

"Giancarlo Wu at your service," the human said.

"I was seeking Ambassador Worf," Picard said.

"So you were. He is overseeing the preparations for your meeting himself and so is unavailable. How may I help, Captain?"

"I was just calling to make certain all is in readiness and to see if I needed any further . . . preparation for my meeting with the chancellor."

Wu nodded and smiled. *"The ambassador did suggest you bring along a mild analgesic. The chancellor has decided there will be a meal during the meeting."*

Picard gritted his teeth and nodded. "Fresh *gagh* no doubt."

The adjutant smiled and shrugged. *"It's not the chancellor's favorite, but whatever is served will absolutely be the freshest available."*

"Delightful."

Worf had to force himself to stop pacing in the transporter room. Even though he and Picard had seen each other since his appointment as ambassador, he still didn't wear the mantle well in front of his former comrades. A part of him missed the journey through space, the battles to be fought, and the glory to be found in the unknown. Still, he recognized the responsibility that came with the honor of representing the Federation. They were his chosen people and despite that loyalty being tested time and again, he had found a steadfastness that saw him through each adversity.

"Welcome to the First City," he rumbled as Picard stepped off the platform. They looked each other in the eye. Picard seemed fit and healthy, as befitted the captain. Worf respected a great many members of Starfleet, but Picard was one of two he held in the highest esteem. He had watched as Picard took a reputation from his days on the *Stargazer* and forged it into a legend with the *Enterprise*.

"Ambassador Worf, it's good to see you again," Picard said, a warm smile on his face. "How goes it?"

"Well, sir," Worf replied. He didn't see any reason to review the litany of problems, issues, and politics that filled each day. Picard could change none of it, nor could speaking of it do him well with any who overheard.

Worf walked through the door and Picard followed, leaving the cramped transporter room behind. The stone-carved hallways were filled with Klingon officers moving about, few even acknowledging the ambassador in their midst. Unless they had need of the Federation, he was largely left alone, which suited him fine. It was a short distance to the council chamber, where Martok awaited. Armed guards stood on each side of the wide, heavy doors, and looked at both ambassador and captain with suspicion. These were Martok's elite, and after the Dominion War and the invasion of the changelings, Klingons chose to remain in a heightened state of paranoia.

"Have you found a gateway here?" Picard asked casually.

"No, but remnants of one were located on the remains of Praxis," Worf said. "Once the government learned that the entire network had been activated, the High Council ordered an immediate check. When nothing was recorded here, they sent a team to check the moon."

"I assume it was destroyed when the moon exploded eighty years ago?"

"Yes."

The explosion of Praxis, overmined and under-cared-for, was actually the event that started the Klingon Empire on its inevitable path toward peace with the Federation. It wasn't a straight path but with each passing generation it grew a little easier.

"Has the Empire found many active gateways?"

"The chancellor keeps that information to himself but I take that to mean there are more than a few."

Picard digested that information for a moment. "How will your people react?"

"When threatened, they will defend their homes," Worf said. "I cannot say if the lost and bewildered will be made as welcome here as they might in the Federation."

"There are more than enough Federation planets that can just as easily act out of fear or territorialism," Picard noted.

"My people may see the gateways in more than peaceful ways," Worf said. "There will always be those who do not see benefit from allying ourselves with the Federation. Some, like the House of Duras, would try and buy the technology for themselves, dividing the Empire."

"Few have gone to the lengths that House has," Picard said. Privately, Worf was just as glad Lursa and

B'Etor had been dead for years. They had dishonored him and brought shame to his people on more than one occasion.

"A civil conflict was not something I had anticipated," Picard said.

"Martok continues to instill order, but the strain on my people has been great. Gowron ruled unwisely and some Houses have bided their time. He will have to remain strong."

Two guards gripped the handles and opened the doors inward, admitting the ambassador and captain. The room was dimmer than the halls and Worf noted that the full complement of the Council was missing, a protocol insult that few but Picard would even notice. Leaning over a dark wooden table was Martok. Worf appraised the chancellor, noting that he seemed unchanged since taking control of the government. He knew some leaders visibly aged when in power, but Martok seemed fueled by the authority. Not reveling in it, but with newfound purpose which suited his sturdy form. The body was thin, tall, and rangy, battle-hardened. Martok's face showed interest and the one good eye gleamed in the light.

He imagined looking at the chancellor from Picard's perspective. Gowron, the man the captain helped attain the leadership role, was fierce, a true warrior. But he was not a veteran of war, had not led men and ships into battle. Gowron knew how to play the political games that seemed to be preferred to matters of honor on Qo'noS and his eyes bulged in delight. Martok, though, had seen more than his share of battle. He had risen through the ranks and had collected something more valuable than political chits: respect and loyalty. His bearing and tone spoke of each battle, each death achieved in defense of the Klingons' interest. It was a voice that had seen more than enough senseless bloodshed as well, Worf knew, making him the right man at the right time to help steer his people.

It certainly wasn't going to be easy as the political machinations within the council chambers and many of the influential Houses still remained active—too active if anyone bothered to ask Worf. Like Martok, he disapproved of such games, feeling it cheapened the honor of those Houses and their inhabitants.

Martok looked up with his good eye and made a noise that sent the courtiers away from him. The chancellor straightened and strode forward, studying the captain. Martok stopped about six feet from Picard and held his ground. Picard straightened as Worf launched into the formal introductions—not, strictly speaking, necessary, since the parties all knew each other, but one thing Worf had learned in his short time as a diplomat was the importance of protocol, even with Klingons.

"May I present Captain Jean-Luc Picard, son of Maurice," Worf said. "Captain, I bring you before Martok, son of Krigar, leader of the High Council."

The two men nodded at the other as Worf continued.

"Know before all that this meeting between the Klingon Empire and the United Federation of Planets is duly authorized and is overseen by the ambassador." As he spoke, trying to make it sound smooth, he eyed the other councillors around the chamber. They had stood at attention, but there was some whispering back and forth and Worf knew that meant speculation was running between them.

"Captain, welcome," Martok said, when Worf had concluded the formal introduction. "A drink?"

Picard nodded and tankards were brought forth and quickly handed to one and all. Worf saw Picard sniff at his drink and hid a smirk. Picard would gamely drain the tankard, not to be bested by the most basic of Klingon tests. Sure enough, Picard smiled and nodded toward Martok and took a very long pull.

The chancellor smiled and took an equally long drink. "Excellent vintage."

"I know a thing or two about vintages," Picard said. "I don't know this one, though, but it is remarkably . . . smooth."

"From my wife Sirella's family," Martok said.

"Chancellor, this is a fine drink but I do not have time for a lengthy visit. I do not mean to be rude. . . ."

"What does the Federation need of us?" Martok put the drink down, studying Picard with his usual intensity. Worf hoped this would be brief but without rancor.

"The gateways," Picard replied.

"Very efficient mode of transport," Martok said, not changing his expression. Worf stood to the side, between the two leaders, watching with only his eyes.

"But right now, very dangerous," Picard replied. "The Iconians are seeking the highest price for the technological plans but until they are satisfied, the gateways remain active and the chaos is already being felt throughout the quadrant. I was hoping we could form a fleet, made up of several races, and approach the Iconians at their base position."

Martok took another long drink, clearly thinking. Worf knew his friend, and leader of his House, to be a shrewd judge of character. He already knew of Picard's exploits before the ambassador could even begin to speak on his behalf. Worf also knew the Iconians had a representative on Qo'noS a week earlier making the same offer.

"Have the gateways not already caused your empire trouble?"

Martok paused, thinking carefully before answering. "We have had some unwelcome visitors" was all he would say.

"Imagine invading hordes," Picard said.

"We'd train our disruptors on each gateway if need be."

"Admirable," Picard said. "But a waste of men and equipment given their dampening fields. Wouldn't you be better off securing the other side?"

"Each gateway opens to multiple locations, that would spread our resources even thinner," Martok said. With his left hand, he gestured to a guard at the door. He nodded and disappeared into another room.

Picard nodded and held his tongue for a moment, letting Martok consider.

"I would sooner encase each one in a block of duranium than expose my people."

"And the starship-sized ones?"

Worf rarely saw Martok surprised but this was one of those opportunities. Clearly, anything more than humanoid-proportioned had not occurred to him. The ambassador also saw that it told Picard nothing of that nature had been spotted within the Empire. The captain was filing that away with all the other arcane information he needed.

Attendants brought in platters and bowls, setting them at a side table that was already prepared. Steam rose from one bowl, its scent quickly making its way toward the men. Worf recognized it as a spiced soup, one Martok liked.

"The Romulans think us weak after the war," Martok said, looking at no one in particular. "We lost many warriors, many ships. To have the ability to walk from one room on Qo'noS to Rura Penthe in a second would mean much for the Empire."

"Oh, there's little doubt that anyone controlling the gateways would find their culture transformed," Picard said. "It would revolutionize your economy and place within the galactic community. But what if it was not the Klingon Empire or the Federation that gained control?"

"Bah, then we'd be picking Ferengi out of our teeth every day," Martok spat.

"We need to show solidarity, need to show the Iconians that they cannot divide us. I cannot do that alone, Chancellor."

Martok strode over to the side table and looked at the food. He nodded once in approval and gestured toward Worf and Picard. The ambassador hoped Picard took Wu's advice and had come prepared. He knew Riker could handle the raw meats, but Picard always struck him as preferring things . . . cooked.

"Try the soup first, Captain," Martok said. "Something I learned to live on as a young warrior."

Picard filled the bowl, letting the steam fill his senses before taking the first sip. Worf was amused by the way his former captain tried to contain the reaction. If anything, the soup's spices were even more potent than habañero peppers from Earth. Picard breathed in again and then took a sip, smiling all the while. Worf was proud of how well Picard handled himself, but also felt himself grow hungry.

The unease of the moment grated on Worf's nerves. He had tremendous respect for both men and would dislike seeing them at odds. To distract himself, he filled a plate with flat bread and some of the *gagh*.

"Your name has been known to me for some time, Picard," Martok finally said, as he reached for some *gagh* of his own. "The exploits of the great *Enterprise* may be the most studied in the Empire. The first such ship certainly caused enough dishonor to several Houses. But, your own actions redeemed that ship's honor and I respect that."

Martok took a deep drink of the soup. "Like you, I worry about our community and the Klingons' place in it. The Iconians tempt us with technology but there is something I do not trust about them. Do you feel it?"

"I have not met them in person, Chancellor, but Starfleet Command shares your suspicions."

"Of course they do," Martok said loudly. "Starfleet has people who are suspicious of everyone and everything. Why else have an intelligence division?" Martok drained his drink and held it out, arm stiff, for an attendant to collect. "While you have my people's respect, Picard, know that the honor carried by being Arbiter of Succession is over. Gowron is dead and I lead the people. However, K'mpec saw honor in you, as does the ambassador. You therefore have my trust. I will assign two battle cruisers, but they shall act under my direction."

"Do you mean to join us?" Picard asked carefully. If Martok joined him, he would have to defer more often than not, which would weaken the plan.

"Not at all. The captain shall follow my directions but do not worry, Picard, if the Iconians fire at you, my ships will stand at your side."

Picard bowed with formal thanks. Then, to seal the point, took a handful of the *gagh* and stuffed it into his mouth. Worf exhaled, sensing the momentum had shifted in his former captain's favor, and Martok laughed.

As Worf finished his plate, he was stunned by Picard's next comment.

"Chancellor, I wish to bring along an experienced diplomat. I feel I may need the help. Can Qo'noS do without Mr. Worf for a little while?" Worf recognized Picard's excessive formality with Martok; a gesture of respect. After all, permission wasn't required.

Martok stared at Worf, his mind clearly turning over the possibilities, but the strategic importance made the answer clear. He quickly replied, "We won't be negotiating with the Iconians any time soon. Whatever problems the gateways bring us will be internal ones. Being a Federation initiative, Worf can do better with you."

"Thank you, Chancellor."

"Qapla'!"

Worf had to contain his smile, but bowed toward the chancellor. He stole a glance at Picard, who seemed more than satisfied with the way things had gone.

"Chancellor, not to rush matters, but I have more stops to make before we can visit the Iconians and with every moment, I suspect we're risking some unforeseen calamity."

"Go, Picard," Martok said. "The Empire will stand beside the Federation once more. Oh, and do bring Worf back in one piece."

Although the sun was bright and there was nary a cloud in the sky over Armus IX's capital city, Clandakin sensed only doom. She had been elected governor of the planet less than a year ago and had just completed consolidating the bickering factions into a coalition that would allow her people to finally move forward after a decade-long economic crisis.

She returned to her chambers after a Regency session, unfastening the bright yellow and orange-feathered cloak she wore when conducting official business. The cool air felt good after the five-hour meeting that was not stopped once. The business at hand was serious indeed. An hour earlier, her Surgeon reported that at least one-third of the planet had quickly contracted the disease. The Guardian had also announced that the culprits had been found but the Regency didn't know what to do with them.

Pictures had been displayed of the aliens who had unleashed the virulent disease among her people, shown alongside a picture of a hospital ward filled with people vomiting and bleeding. They seemed most benign with their oblong heads, dusty skin, and oversized ears. Their expressions showed a lack of comprehension, as if they had no idea where they were or what was happening around them. None had been armed; in fact, none had anything remotely resembling a weapon or communications device. One carried a satchel full of food and drink while another had a tubular item, similar to a ball. Her best guess was that they were out for a walk, not at all intending to sabotage a planet.

Doctors, nurses, and volunteers, wearing as much covering as possible, were also seen. She was heartened by their heroics but saddened that the death toll was already beginning. Clandakin, all of twenty-seven years old, was watching the worst medical crisis the people of Armus IX had encountered in three centuries.

The last time, such a violent epidemic left one-quarter of the planet's population dead and the world took two generations to get itself back on course.

Would this be the same?

A sweaty hand smoothed out the long crimson dress she had worn under the cloak. Leading the people was such a thrill and a chore at the same time. But now it felt like a crushing yoke around her neck, threatening to snap the spinal column. The Surgeon had said testing determined the people to be responsible but it would take time to isolate what germ was unleashed, how it spread, and how to combat it. Those in custody looked bewildered, neither known enemies of her planet nor fanatics with a cause.

She shut her eyes but pictured them again, noting the look of terror in their own eyes. She winced. They were clearly as scared as the Armusians.

Why shouldn't they be? she mused. To them, it was a chance for a lark, a simple picnic for three families taking a short holiday.

Of course, the fact that they lived ninety-five parsecs away might have been cause for some caution, she realized. Still, wouldn't she have been tempted had a gateway, spinning like some jewel, opened up on the outskirts of their village on Tavela Minor? A chance to see another world, meet an entirely different culture, would certainly be too tempting to resist.

No one had stopped to think how their worlds might have differed. Germs and microbes that meant nothing to them suddenly became the cause of plague on Armus IX. Never had her people been victim to so innocent an act.

Could her Surgeon find a cure before too many more

died? A distress call to the Federation had already gone out and the hope was that one of the medical starships could be dispatched. The call went out a day ago and Starfleet had yet to respond.

She knew why, of course. Armus IX was just one of several worlds cursed by the gateways.

"The planet is heavily industrialized in just one section," the science officer announced.

The commander turned and looked at her. "Population?"

"No life signs. It appears to be entirely designed for automation."

"Is it active?"

"Not from our readings."

The commander nodded and looked once more toward the forward viewscreen. The world looked like so many others, nothing distinguishing it at all. He did not recognize it, or the stars around it. In fact, he couldn't recognize any of the formations. This, more than the planet's emptiness, disturbed him.

"Long-range scan," he said, continuing to prowl the cramped bridge.

"Nothing to indicate any vessels have been this way. All we detect is the gateway."

It spun lazily in space, large enough to allow the entire ship to fly through, its aperture showing three, no four, differing locales. He thought he recognized the one he came through, but it spun just fast enough to elude confirmation. Regardless, the ship's computers would isolate it when it was time to go home.

But first the world needed exploration. It was not like most civilizations to build a factory and leave it alone.

"Approach and orbit, helm," he said quietly.

"Orbit in five minutes," came the reply.

"Good. Place us in geosynchronous position to the factory and let's get a complete reading. Navigation, have you determined where we are?"

There was a long, uncomfortable pause before the navigator spoke. His voice betrayed his youth and his nervousness; the commander would welcome neither. "Commander, from our charts, I believe within Federation space." There was silence around the bridge and the commander nodded just once.

"Where precisely?"

"I believe it to be a star system near the galactic barrier, one called Delta Vega by the Federation."

The commander was surprised and more than a little concerned. Although the galactic barrier was nowhere near his homeworld, ship commanders around drinks of strong ale spoke tales of it. People went mad there, it was said; ships were never heard from again, and monsters were created. Improved shielding meant it could be traversed, but none dared try . . . just in case. Better he survey the world, grab what riches might remain, and return home intact.

"Study this factory world. What did they produce here? Are there weapons?"

The officer turned and saluted, fist to heart.

"If the Federation abandoned it, let's see what the Romulan Star Empire might learn and profit from the planet."

The first Bolian coughed in the thick atmosphere. His companions had dwindled to three from an original group of nine. All felt scared with one going almost catatonic, refusing to say or do anything, just shuffling after the others.

Felk had somehow become the group leader and he didn't like it. It was one thing to lead them in a magnoball contest, completely another to handle this emergency. No one else seemed willing to take point and explore the hot world so rather than stand still, he had them move forward.

Just an hour earlier, they were finishing their weekly game, having bested the Gropla Team from Engineering Division. They usually beat the Groplas since they were always looking for opportunities to try obscure patterns and angles, treating the games more as experiments than competition. Felk didn't care, since it was another notch on their tally sheet and got them ready for the championship bout, coming in another month.

Everyone was relaxed and happy when they stepped out of the courts, going for their groundcars. Instead, they found the swirling device where their vehicles were. The ten men and women, five each from the two teams, gaped at the bright aperture.

"I recognize that, it's Mount Seleya on Vulcan!"

Another stared and saw a rounded, tall building surrounded by lush foliage. She didn't recognize it, which seemed to fascinate her all the more. Felk's partner, Helt, pointed and noted the aperture was rotating and three locations were distinct: Vulcan, the building, and an unidentified ice floe. Sure enough, a member of the engineering team whipped out a recorder and took notes, speaking quietly into the device.

"I wonder if we can enter it?"

"Who'd want to?"

"I like Vulcan, always wanted to visit."

One picked up a small stone and tossed it at the whirling gateway and it got swallowed up without so much as a sound. This seemed to embolden the engineers who wanted to explore, their curiosity getting the better of them.

Two made it through and then the others stumbled when it became obvious the device would spin at the same speed so getting to Vulcan would require timing. One woman tripped while hesitating, and ended up on the ice. This seemed to sober the group, but one, an overweight player from Felk's team, pushed forward, knocking several into the gateway, scattering them.

Felk and Helt could see Opel on the ice, shivering. They silently counted among themselves, gauging the rotation and timing their action. If they could get it right, travel through to Opel, then they should be able to reverse themselves and get her home safely.

Their count was off, however, and the two men were suddenly in the humid air of the unknown world. Four others were standing and shaking themselves off, all looking to Felk for leadership. With a swallow, he began timing the rotation once more, trying to compensate for the error. Helt, on his signal, stepped through, hoping to reach Opel. Instead, he was back on Bolarus IX and running to get help.

There was a growing buzzing sound that bothered Felk and, fearing the worst, he debated between staying by the gateway, waiting for help, or moving toward the building, a sure sign of civilization. None of them recognized the planet they were standing on, noting the gravity seemed lighter than home. The air stank of rotting vegetation and something unknown, which scared them all the more. It was that fear that drove them toward the building, which was round, made from metal, and tapering toward the top. It must have been fifteen or twenty meters high, twice that around, Felk estimated.

It had higher technology based on the devices they saw scattered around the structure's exterior. No doors were obvious, or windows, which concerned Felk, but he figured they needed to walk around the entire perimeter before finding an entrance. Here by the building, they took comfort in the buzzing sound growing more distant.

Balit pulled out his magnoball and tossed it back and forth, from hand to hand, trying to channel his nervous energy. Felk didn't pay it any attention as they continued around the structure, tying to guess where in the galaxy they might be. He wasn't much on travel and didn't immediately recognize the world and noted it was not a place he'd want to see again unless the people inside the building proved to be the friendliest folk this side of Wrigley's Pleasure Planet.

A few minutes more, and the party made its way around to the other side of the structure, fending off growing vines, thick underbrush, and oppressive heat. Balit had taken to tossing the ball to Felk every now and then so it almost seemed like an outing, just a little more adventurous than any of them had hoped for.

They stopped to catch their breath and immediately heard loud buzzing once more. Notan, the silent one, looked up and stared, pointing with his left hand. Rising from the top of the structure were three beings, looking more insect than humanoid. They were black with yellow markings, had antennae and wings. Each also carried some sort of weapon that was strapped to their short arms, drawing power from a device at their chest. The insects buzzed among themselves and then began to descend toward the now-paralyzed quartet.

"You have encroached on Jarada's colony Torona Alpha," one of them buzzed. "Why do you invade us?"

No one said a word, continuing to stare, trying to comprehend the sudden turn of events. The trio eased down a little lower, but clearly keeping their distance from the blue-skinned Bolians. For long moments, neither side moved nor said anything.

Finally, Balit, gripping his magnoball, let out a scream. It was a scream of fear, fear of the unknown, fear of dying, just plain fear.

Then he threw the ball. The three Jaradan sentries scattered, avoiding the hurtling spheroid, and watched it strike one of the devices attached to the building's wall. Despite being on an alien world, the ball's magnetic core did its job, obeying the universe's physical laws, and stuck to the building.

What happened next was unexpected. The ball's magnetic charge caused an overload to the device, which turned out to be a sensor. The overload surged through the structure, tripping relays and causing havoc. As the sounds grew ominous from inside the building, the sentries were shaken back to action. Taking aim, they swiftly let loose volleys of plasma energy, which quickly killed the Bolians. The lead Jaradan began to make a report, but was cut off as the entire structure, now supercharged to overload, began to spark. The Jaradan patrol scattered toward the rain forest before them, narrowly escaping the firestorm. Two hundred of their brethren remained trapped within the burning hive.

* * *

"You watched them hatch?"

Troi smiled at the ensign, brightening to the topic. "Sure did. They are fast growing to become the ruling caste for the Gorn, insuring stability for at least another generation."

The ensign, a young Asian named Linda Liang, grew wide-eyed. She was dividing her attention between the counselor, standing to her left, and the conn console before her. Troi had read the roster reports three times to familiarize herself with the *Mercury* and its crew and had come to know them fairly quickly.

"Eyes front, Ensign, wouldn't want you to hit any planets." That from the captain, Carter Brisbayne. To Troi, the silver-haired by-the-book career officer seemed to take every order with a determined grimness. Troi found herself overcompensating, forcing herself to be relaxed with the crew, even if her posting was extremely temporary.

"Captain?"

The question came from Ranjit Srivastava. He had been with the ship since its launch, surviving the Borg attack on Earth and several skirmishes against the Jem'Hadar. This, Troi felt, gave him enough experience to get past the eagerness much of the crew exhibited.

"Yes, Number One?"

Troi suppressed a smile. Anyone other than Captain Picard calling anyone other than Will Riker Number One just struck her as wrong.

"Entering Gorn space in five minutes."

"Understood. Mr. Livingston, full sensor sweep and then let's hail them."

"Aye, Captain."

Everything according to the command directives, she

noted. Inwardly, she realized their mission objective had an entirely different library to follow. With the Gorn, it could be tense. She and the *Enterprise* crew had recently helped stopped a civil war. The Gorn took some time to heal and proved to help during the Dominion conflict, but to a much lesser degree than the Federation had hoped. Time having passed, Troi hoped the reception would be a warmer one but she knew their point of view would not be in synch with the UFP's.

A loud sound interrupted the idle thought and Troi saw the red lights before her.

"What is it, Ensign Liang?" barked Brisbayne.

"Gorn patrol vessel, closing fast at warp two. Weapons online, shields up."

"Yellow alert. Mr. Livingston, keep weapons offline until I say otherwise. Damn, not what I need right now."

A chorus of affirmative sounds was returned and Troi nodded in satisfaction. She turned to the captain and explained their opponents. "They value strength over diplomacy but let's not bare this ship's teeth. We need to get past them and reach the current leader, Lord Slessshh."

"That's a mouthful," Srivastava commented.

"Well, they have a lot of teeth," Troi added with her characteristic smile. Brisbayne ignored her, studying readouts on his screen.

"Ship closing, refusing to answer our hails," Livingston said. "Fifty thousand kilometers."

"Slow to impulse, helm," the captain said.

"Weapons lock!" the tactical officer cried.

"Shields up, red alert," Brisbayne said.

Damn, Troi thought, as the red lights bathed the

bridge and the klaxon sounded, this was the last thing she wanted.

Before another command could be given, bright light emitted from a speck in space. Too far, she figured, for an accurate shot. She pushed her mind, hoping to get some idea what was going on with the alien ship, but they were too far away—too alien to do her much good.

The light, a projectile actually, streaked in front of the *Mercury,* and detonated, some four thousand kilometers in front of the ship.

"A warning shot," Livingston said.

"Good guess," Brisbayne muttered. "Do not return fire. Try and raise the bastards."

It was tense on the bridge, which Troi could feel without even trying. A good third of the crew were newly assigned and had probably never seen battle. Liang, Livingston, and Srivastava had, which helped. The counselors were playing an instrumental role in spreading out veterans among the Fleet, making sure senior staffs were populated with enough experienced personnel to get the jobs done without problems. Moments passed in silence, waiting to see if the Gorn were now ready to talk.

"No reply."

"Open a channel. This is Captain Carter Brisbayne of the United Federation of Planets. We seek access to your homeworld and a chance to speak with Lord Slessshh."

Before he could say another word, Troi uttered a throat-wrenching phrase that no one on the bridge could understand. Brisbayne stared at her coldly.

Once again there was silence. She leaned forward and saw a readout showing neither ship had moved. A good sign, she hoped. Looking around, she spotted Science Officer Alfonzo bent over her console, learning what she could. Next to the science station was Chief Engineer Donald Agbayani, sitting intently. She had been introduced to them as the Double A team, a reference that made no sense to her until it was explained it was an archaic Earth term used in a sport called baseball. The legendary game was just making its presence felt once again on distant worlds.

"Captain," Livingston said in his slow British tone, "I have Lord Slessshh."

"On screen," he said.

A green-scaled figure filled the viewer, with huge glittering eyes devoid of emotion. He stared at the crew and took his time before speaking. Behind him were the Gorn crest and dark plants. *"Troi, is it?"*

"Yes, Lord," she said. Brisbayne bristled at being ignored but Troi had to keep the conversation going and would make amends with him later.

"We did not expect contact from the Federation at this time."

"No, Lord, but an event of widespread proportions has caused this contact. Are you familiar with the gateways operating in this sector of space?"

"We are," he replied, not moving once. Troi steadied herself in the chair and noticed Liang suppress a shiver. Cold-blooded creatures always seem to have that effect on humans, she knew.

"Have you also been contacted by the Iconians?"

"We might have spoken to them. What of it?" Clearly he was holding information closely, uncertain of what the Federation would want. She perceived that they still felt some obligation to the Federation, and resented it.

"The gateways are active throughout the quadrant

and pose a threat while they peddle the technology like fabric. We are suspicious of their motives and Captain Picard is assembling a representative fleet to approach their leader and demand details and a shutdown of the devices before an interstellar incident occurs."

Slessshh remained impassive, taking in the translation and considering it. There did not seem to be anyone else in the room with him, she noted. This would entirely be up to the Lord and this boded well considering the personal contact he shared with both her and Picard. At least she hoped so; the stakes were too high for this to fail. Without unity, the approach would appear comic, not authoritative.

"For Picard, I will trust this mission. I grant you four ships," he said slowly. *"They will be there for unity but may not necessarily participate."*

"We appreciate the Gorn's support," Troi warmly said.

"Our obligation to the Federation is a heavy one," the Gorn said. *"We dislike it but recognize the need for this mission. Go."* And the screen snapped back to the stars.

"Gorn patrol ship moving off at high warp," the tactical officer said.

"Fine," Brisbayne said. "Stand down from red alert. Double A, let's get ready to lead four recalcitrant Gorn."

"Aye," the duo said in unison. It made her smile and relax for just a moment.

"And Counselor," Brisbayne said, "when making diplomatic contact with a potentially hostile world, it would help if the captain is allowed to speak for the ship. My neck is on the line for my crew, not a visitor's. This could just as easily gone poorly and then we'd have no ships for Picard's convoy."

She nodded and decided the time for amends would wait.

Oliv seemed to mean business, Riker concluded, feeling the tension return to his shoulders. He'd need a good massage when this was over, and found himself looking forward even more to Deanna's return. The Deltan moved his sleek silvery ship incrementally closer, adjusting position with mere thrusters, but clearly encroaching on the Carreon ships. Leaning forward in the command chair, Riker studied the tactical readout. The last few hours had dragged as he spoke with first Oliv, then Landik Mel Rosa, trying to get them to power down their weapons or open a dialogue. He thought he used every trick in the book. All he got in return was rhetoric and a stiff neck.

"Mr. Data, opinion."

The android turned toward the commander and moved his head at an angle, considering his answer. "Captain Oliv seems perfectly content with this standoff while Landik Mel Rosa seems to be losing his patience. If one were to open fire first, I would think it would be him."

Riker nodded. "Lieutenant Vale, keep a targeting lock on the Carreon but weapons stay off line."

"Aye, sir."

Riker liked this less by the minute. He had Data monitoring reports from throughout the Federation and knew the gateways were causing more havoc than help. Starfleet, in their infinite wisdom, summoned his captain and his *imzadi* to Earth and then flung them back out among the stars, but nowhere near the *Enterprise*. He felt understaffed and more than a little ill-equipped to deal with people determined to get into a fight. A part of him wanted to just let them strike out, but he suspected Command would frown on the tactic. Another part of him wanted to be away from this petty problem and use the *Enterprise* for some good, helping those people in dire need because of the Iconian "gift."

Determined to get them moving, get the hostile races speaking, Riker had a thought. "Riker to engineering."

"La Forge here, Commander."

"Geordi, can we punch a transporter beam through the Deltan shields or disrupt them?"

"Sure, I can think of three ways before I blink."

"What about the Carreon?"

"We know a lot less about them, but what works for one should work for the other."

"Okay. Rig the systems with whichever plan you think has the best chance. Out. Lieutenant Vale, send security teams to Transporter Rooms Two and Five. We'll be having company shortly and I want them escorted to the observation lounge."

"Aye, sir."

Data looked at his friend with a puzzled expression. "Is this course wise?"

Riker grinned and shook his head. "Maybe not, Data, but if they won't use the com system, locking them in a room with me might get the dialogue a little further along. Besides, it has the benefit of not having been tried."

A sharp sound behind him made Riker snap around, further straining his muscles. He suppressed a sound and looked at the petite security chief.

"Multiple warp signatures approaching from 474 mark 6. And the Deltans are now moving toward the Carreon at one-half impulse."

"Red alert!" Riker snapped. "Perim, move the *Enterprise* between those ships! No one is going to fight unless I say so. Vale, what do you make of the signatures?"

"They're showing as Deltan, sir. I make out seven, same class. All coming in hard and fast, weapons ready."

"Fourteen against three is overkill in anyone's book," Riker said.

From the conn position, Ensign Kell Perim said, "We're in position, Commander."

"Sir," Data added, "those seven ships will make it impossible for the *Enterprise* to prevent fighting from breaking out."

"It'll be a slaughter at those odds," Vale said. Riker knew it, but had to hear the words.

Leaning back in the command chair, the acting captain let out a deep breath. It didn't help. "Terrific. What next?"

Chapter Four

"YOUR POSITION is not logical."

"But it is my position, Ambassador Lojal."

The Vulcan ambassador stiffened at the tone. Usually the translators could not convey emotion, but this time the message was clear. Lojal had been dispatched to make contact with the Tholians, since they were isolated from the stops being made by Picard, Troi, and Ross. An experienced diplomat, he found himself looking forward to the experience, having never dealt with the enigmatic people before. The meeting was proving to be short and fruitless.

"Erask, I must ask," Lojal said, trying a different tactic. "Are there no gateways in Tholian space?"

The current leader of the Tholian Assembly stood his ground, his features unreadable. The brightness of the

Tholian being irritated Lojal's eyes, despite them being used to the harsh Vulcan sun. While he was used to the glare from his homeworld's deserts, these were garish, bright colors that seemed to shift across Erask's skin. The two men were alone in an antechamber, with the Tholians showing little in the way of customary diplomatic finery. Lojal did not always see the point of elaborate customs but, coming from a world with a plethora of its own rituals and mores, he had come to accept them and their infinite variety. The almost total lack of them here should have been refreshing, but he found them troublesome.

"There are, Lojal. And we are dealing with the intrusion into our sovereign space."

"Of course," the ambassador said. "However, if you sit idly by and let another race gain control of the technology, it would not end these intrusions. They might increase."

Lojal watched the colors shifting, trying to discern patterns, read into them emotions or communications. So little was known of these aggressive, private people that he could not help but be intrigued by them. They were, though, vexing in their inability to see his point. "I should further point out, Erask, that if you exclude the Tholians from this mission to the Iconian base ship, then you lose the tactical advantage of knowledge."

The oranges grew over more of the Tholian's body than the reds, and the yellows were almost nonexistent. Lojal was beginning to form a hypothesis over how the color worked but he was more surprised by Erask's sudden movement forward. He planted his feet firmly and stood his ground, ignoring the violation of personal space. "You would not share with your diplomatic neighbors?"

"Erask, the Tholians have followed their own code of conduct in the years we have known you," he patiently explained. "Rather than share the burden of opposing an invading race, you signed a nonaggression pact with the Dominion. Had the war gone in their favor, you would be feeling their encroachment on your space. The Federation had hoped you would see this problem in a similar light and agree to help us before the gateway problem grew to galactic proportions."

"Ambassador Lojal, we consider ourselves an isolated race and prefer it that way. We cannot ignore the races that surround our space, but we prefer to pursue our own agenda. It does not include risking our ships in this foolhardy mission."

The Vulcan nodded, recognizing the end of the meeting. Since there were no formalities to observe, he would not tarry. He would simply return to his transport, filing a disappointing report with the Federation. Clasping his hands to his chest, he deeply bowed, saying, "As you wish, Erask."

As the ambassador turned to leave the room, Erask spoke up one final time. "Know this, Vulcan, we could afford to bid and own this technology. But it would invite more dealings with other governments. That is not our current interest. We will not be making an offer."

Lojal nodded once in acknowledgment. While not gaining an ally, at least he could report that they had not gained a potential threat, either. Sometimes, that was the best an ambassador could hope for and he would have to content himself with that. Touching his communicator medallion, he asked to return to the ship and a swift journey home.

"Landik Mel Rosa, I give you one hour to turn your ships around and go home. At that time, if you are still here, we will fire," Oliv ordered.

Riker shook his head in amazement. There was no possible way the *Enterprise* could stop the Deltans from firing, no way to prevent a war from breaking out between worlds. This mission had certainly changed his thinking about the Deltan people.

"Vale, any options occur to you?"

The security chief thought for a moment, eyes straining at her station. "Without additional firepower, we're right now sitting in the potential crossfire. Too many ships, spread out in a classic pattern, and everyone's hot to shoot first. We're out of luck, sir."

Riker nodded in agreement and continued to pace the bridge. Walking eased some of the strain, but not enough of it. The standoff was growing tenser and the addition of more Deltan vessels spoiled any hope of a diplomatic solution. Starfleet had not responded to his last communiqué and the Diplomatic Corps was equally nonresponsive. He did not have the authority to contact the Deltan homeworld directly and he wasn't even sure if he should bother. Oliv was determined to gain possession of this dead rock, for whatever good it would do the Deltan people.

He wasn't sure what to do next: make popcorn to watch the inevitable fight or pray for Q to turn up.

Worf stood at the entrance to the bridge of the *Chargh*, taking in the activity. It was, as usual, darker than Federation starships and the officers were in a ring, behind the captain. Commanding the ship was Grekor, tall, overweight, and given to fastidious habits such as even fingernails and well-groomed hair. The hair itself was starting to streak with gray and the full beard was already more salt than pepper in color.

Grekor sat, filling the chair, his arms hanging over the sides, well-manicured fingers nervously tapping at the sides. He seemed a bundle of energy, barely contained, and intolerant of the slightest error. However, Worf noted, he was quick with his tongue, not his fists. Most Klingon commanders ruled with such power, but inspired little in the way of loyalty. This one, though, had an equally aging crew and he suspected they had served together a long time.

"Ambassador Worf, son of Mogh," he announced.

Before the words were finished, Grekor was on his feet and nodded to the ambassador. "Grekor, son of Krad," he replied. "Welcome to the *Chargh.*"

Worf heard an eagerness in the tone that did not seem directed to the battle. He knew the House of Krad had fallen on hard times and that Grekor was one of the senior members. No doubt, he saw this mission as a chance to advance his position. Grekor continued to bark orders, dressing down the engineer, Kliv, for not being warp-ready yet. When all seemed to his satisfaction, Grekor finally turned once more toward the ambassador.

"How may I help the esteemed ambassador?"

Worf now recognized the solicitous tone and was unhappy. Right after settling on Qo'noS, he heard it all too often as people came to his office and asked favors.

"We remain in orbit around Qo'noS," Worf said. "I

came to make sure you understood the parameters of our mission."

"Once more we ally ourselves with the Federation, each grasping for some victory against the Iconians," Grekor answered.

"You are to follow Captain Picard's orders without question," Worf said, the tone allowing no interruption. "Yes, we are allies but we are also there to find the truth. If there is to be a fight, then we will fight our way to *Sto-Vo-Kor,* but under the *Enterprise*'s direction. Initiative is not a requirement at this time."

"But of course, Ambassador. The *Chargh*'s history is nowhere near as illustrious as the *Enterprise*'s. I hope to learn much from Picard's dealings with these people."

Worf winced at the unctious tone, but concluded Grekor would be an irritant, not a complication.

"Very well," he replied. "We leave within minutes. Be ready." He left the bridge, hoping to maintain his distance from the captain.

Picard felt refreshed as he entered the turbolift at the beginning of the alpha shift. The *Chargh* and the *Qob* were matching speed and causing no trouble. Before going to sleep hours before, he received Counselor Troi's message that the Gorn had agreed to join the mission. He was already figuring out flight patterns and communications systems to keep everyone linked.

As he strode onto the small—too small if you asked him—bridge, First Officer Davison smartly relinquished the command seat. It was a by-the-book bridge crew, Picard thought approvingly. He might have been hasty in thinking the Academy was churning out too many replacement personnel with insufficient preparation. Chan, Hol, and Rosario all were at their posts.

"Status, Commander?"

"En route to the Iconian ships."

Hol called out from ops, one hand cupped to the receiver in his oversized ear. "I'm receiving a long-distance signal on a wavelength not used by the Federation."

Picard frowned. "Point of origin?"

Hol studied a readout, then turned to the captain. "Off the starboard bow, about seventy-five thousand kilometers away. It's moving so I think it's a ship."

Picard stood and Rosario at tactical snapped on the yellow alert signal. Picard walked around and leaned over the small, light-haired man's shoulder. "I didn't order yellow alert. We don't know enough to be worried."

The tactical officer swallowed twice and keyed off the alert. Picard noted he knew his station fluently, but was nervous, not something a captain wants in the person with his finger on the trigger. He noted to himself to be precise in his orders. Picard pointed to a readout on the left side of the console and Rosario's head bobbed up and down twice—he seemed to do everything twice, Picard noticed.

"They're too far away to fire on us, and we can't tell if they even have their weapons powered. But do note their course and speed. Ensign Chan, take the feed from Lieutenant Rosario and project backwards. Let's figure out where they came from."

Davison joined Picard at the station and flanked Rosario. The trio studied the monitor and when no new information presented itself, the captain moved on, completing a circuit of the bridge, still getting a feel for the space. He had been spoiled by both *Enterprises,* luxuriating in their size, forgetting his days aboard smaller craft such as the *Stargazer.* Picard imagined it granted the crew easier camaraderie, but also made for close quarters when things grew tense.

After another moment, the conn officer announced, "They're projected as coming from uncharted space."

"Excuse me, Ensign?"

"Well, sir, there are no Federation or even M-class planets anywhere along the path. I've projected a straight-line and it originates in no known system."

Picard nodded and retook his seat. Davison joined him and the two leaned in together as she said, "A hostile?"

He shook his head and gazed off for a moment, analyzing the scant data and checking his instincts. Nothing definite occurred to him so he let the nod be his answer. The two sat silently as the starship continued on its course, with an unknown coming toward them. The captain noted that Rosario had regained his composure and was whispering with Hol. He spoke up, "Something to share, gentlemen?"

Hol looked up, the light reflecting off his bald brow. He seemed surprised to having been caught but had nowhere to turn while the younger tactical officer retreated to his station. "Actually, Captain, we were speculating."

"On the intruder?"

"Yes, sir. Ah, Mr. Rosario and I just placed a wager on the origin of the ship."

Picard nodded and looked expectantly. The science officer seemed dumbfounded for a moment but then realized the captain was expecting more information. Picard held the gaze, measuring the Tiburonian, and hoping he would volunteer the information. He disliked feeling distanced from the crew and was using this opportunity to open things up.

"I was hypothesizing a Breen attack ship and Johnny, that is, Mr. Roasrio thought it might be from the Klingons."

"I think you will both lose the wager, Mr. Rosario," Picard said. "Chancellor Martok promised two ships so it's unlikely we'll have more. The Breen, well, they're a long shot, Mr. Hol."

"Everyone loses," Davison said. She had moved toward the flight control station and was checking the readouts. "We're about to make some new friends . . . at least I hope they're friends. Their configuration is new to me and sensors show differing energy emissions."

Picard nodded in approval, awaiting more detail from the crew.

"They've definitely spotted us," Hol said, caution in his voice. "Slowing to sublight."

"If they have weapons, they're not showing on my screen," Rosario added. "I'm matching their modulation for a hailing call."

"Excellent," the captain said, hoping it would help ease some of the mounting tension. "Helm, go to sublight and let's allow them to catch up easily. Commander Davison, notify Captain Grekor. Distance?"

"Fifty-three thousand kilometers and closing."

"Let's hail them, Mr. Rosario."

"Channel open" was the reply.

Picard stood, adjusted his duty jacket, cleared his throat, and then began his usual greeting. He had certainly handled enough first contacts. However, to make one now during the Iconian troubles seemed odd and out of place. Unless . . . he finished his greeting, awaiting a response, and received only audio.

"Federation? We know of you!"

Picard was surprised by the reply, coming without the matching formality. "And how do you know of us? Where do you hail from?"

"You call it the Delta Quadrant."

The announcement surprised the entire bridge complement. Rosario and Hol shared a glance, Picard noted, both officers having lost their bet. Davison seemed intrigued and Chan was visibly startled. Picard would need to hold them together as he assessed the situation. Looking again at Rosario, the tactical officer checked his station, rechecked it, and shook his head: no sign of weapons being active.

"How do you know of us? And to whom am I speaking?"

"Sorry, my name is Taleen and I met your Voyager."

Voyager! Picard knew Starfleet had only verified they had survived a few weeks earlier and were trapped tens of thousands of light-years from home. In fact, Reginald Barclay, one of his former officers, had managed to establish the first significant contact with the missing starship. Troi had worked alongside him, making sure this was not another of his fantasies gone haywire, but it proved to be the genuine article. Had a gateway network existed there, too? If so, and this ship came through it, there might be hope yet for the starship to come back during Captain Janeway's lifetime. He made a mental note to review the report form Command on that ship.

"Welcome to the Alpha Quadrant, Taleen. How did you find us?"

"We were performing routine patrols and then sud-

denly we detected unusual activity in an asteroid field. Upon investigation we saw this giant spinning window. The pilot steered us too close and we got caught in its energy field, I guess, and we wound up here. Well, not here but back there, where the window let us out."

"Do you have injured or need assistance?"

"Actually, Captain, we have a minimal crew. It was a short-run patrol and our captain was not even aboard. I guess I'm the acting commander."

"Have you tried going back through the window . . . which is actually called a gateway?"

"Well, Captain Picard, the gateway spins so fast, showing differing destinations, we haven't dared try to make our way through fearing we'd get further lost."

Picard nodded to himself; aware of the dilemma posed by an aperture large enough to fit a starship. "Taleen, you and your ship are welcome to join us. Our small group of ships are on our way to meet the gateway's owners and have, shall we say, a little talk?"

"Truth to tell, Captain, we're very unsure of ourselves right about now. I liked Janeway and think I can trust you."

Picard looked once more at Rosario, who shrugged: no weapons he could detect. He wished Troi was with him now, to guide his actions. His own instincts would have to suffice.

"Of course you can. Once we're under way, my first officer will be in touch regarding matching our technologies so we can stay in contact. Perhaps you'll even have a chance to tour our ship."

"Thank you, thank you, Captain. I wasn't certain what we'd find once we got under way, but we didn't

want to stay just in case nastier ships followed us through."

"I understand completely. Stand by for instructions. Picard out. Commander, begin working out the necessary details. Mr. Rosario, keep an eye out just in case we're being fooled. You too, Mr. Hol. I want a full sensor report within the hour. Meantime, I'll be in the ready room."

As he rose, the others acknowledged the commands. Picard stopped at the science station and attracted Hol's attention. In a low voice he said, "If you're a betting man, we can try cards later. On the other hand, this is the bridge where we need to remain focused on the business at hand."

A chorus of "Aye, sirs" immediately followed and Picard nodded in approval. Yes, they would come around and act accordingly.

The captain stared from his viewing station, shaking his head at the sight before him. Huge mountains, tall and craggy, flanked his shipping vessel. He estimated them to be several kilometers higher than any mountain he knew at home. Wrapping his muffler tighter around his neck, the captain couldn't stop shivering. For the last hour, the temperature had dropped several dozen degrees and the crew was ill equipped for the adverse conditions. If it kept plummeting, he expected to find icebergs and wasn't sure how well they'd handle them.

What started out as a three-hour fishing cruise had turned into a nightmare. Belowdecks, fifty wealthy passengers had paid for the tour and a chance to catch the red *gapi,* which was in season. They were among the more easily caught fish, the captain knew, but it made the people happy and they tipped nicely.

Everything seemed fine as they set out from port but about half an hour into the trip, they were caught in a strong current, which pulled them toward something he had never seen before. The archway spanned the entire inlet, embedded in the rock. Within its center, light swirled fast and showed images like a giant screen. He had no idea what it was and his ship's equipment had trouble measuring its output. Worse, the engineer reported the current was gaining strength and pulling the fishing ship toward the thing. He tried every trick he knew but they were headed for the spinning crystal, as he named it, and couldn't stop.

With surprise, the ship simply entered and passed through the crystal. The captain felt nothing, nor did his crew. His fishing passengers, still inside the vessel, had no clue what had happened, not that he knew much more. The wheelwright noted a change in the horizon line and then commented the sun had moved. Moved and grown larger and darker.

Choking back panic, the captain quickly checked his maps and couldn't match shorelines. Worse, his radioman couldn't raise anyone, receiving only static on their normal bands. The only good news came from the engineer, who said the passage through the crystal left the ship undamaged.

An old hand on the water, the captain was reassured by the tang of salt in the air. For a brief moment he considered what kind of sea life might lurk below.

They continued to sail, hoping to find a populated landmass or another ship, but after several hours their hopes grew dim. By then, it became clear to all that they were no longer on their homeworld of Prakal II and none had any clue as to what planet they were now visiting. The wheelwright had suggested reversing course and going through the crystal again, but the captain remained uncertain. Many of the wealthy passengers didn't want to chance it, being fearful of winding up in an even worse location.

On the fifth hour, the navigator found a landmass. It was large and appeared to be a continent. The captain had them radio once more but received no reply. He then directed the ship to parallel the coastline and drift closer along the way. He wasn't sure what else there was to do.

And now mountains—cold mountains which defied logic and his own senses. The captain couldn't imagine how they managed to get between such masses without warning but here they were. He directed the wheelwright to make a steady line between them, praying to the goddess for success.

For eighteen minutes they passed between the mountains, which blotted out the sun and made things that much colder. Except for his crew, everyone was confined to the party rooms within. No doubt they had raided the wine casks, but the captain didn't much care right about now.

Suddenly, directly before them rose a third mountain range, even more immense. Panic gripped the crew and the ship wheeled about, searching for any safe passage. The captain had scopes to his eyes looking for life or hope and found neither. He did feel the sea swell against the hull and the ship started to lose its path. The swells grew and the ship foundered, as the wheelwright tried to keep a steady path toward the narrow space between the mountains to their left and directly before the ship.

Wheeling hard about, the ship tried to avoid the

mountains before them and instead rode a swell that brought them perilously close to the mountains on their side. The swells grew into waves and the ship was battered back and forth, now just going with the flow, no longer able to chart its own course.

The captain gritted his teeth, seeing the gray, featureless land come ever closer. The hull scraped against rocks jutting out of the water, knocking the navigator off his feet. Another swell and another moment of contact but this one had a sound of metal bending.

Could he abandon ship? Did it even make sense to send out the lifecraft with waters getting rougher by the moment?

As one giant wave smacked the boat into the land, puncturing three different parts of the hull, the captain's eyes grew wide in amazement. The mountains before him and to the right were gone, just open sea.

Sunlight played off the churning water and, frozen with confusion, the captain couldn't understand what was happening.

What he would never know was that the sinking ship was another victim of the hypnotic tides on Balosnee VI, a world the captain and passengers had never heard of.

Deep Space Station K-7 had seen better days. It was once a thriving place of business allowing traders to use it as a hub. It was well placed when originally constructed, just a parsec from the Klingon border. Members of both the Federation and the Klingon Empire used it for trading, meetings, and clandestine rendezvous.

It was also immortalized in the several dozen songs the Klingons sang about their nemesis, the tribbles.

Over time, the location became less vital, and as relations thawed between the governments, K-7 remained a resupply station, but no longer of interest. Its clientele deteriorated until it became a place thieves brought their goods to find fences. The station's bar served rumor along with illegal Romulan ale and information was the coin of the realm.

Although still managed by the United Federation of Planets, it allowed establishments within to be licensed and run by, well, just about anyone.

Hovan knew none of that when he woke up. All he knew was that his mouth was filled with dust from the steel deck and the smell in the air made him dizzy. He naturally thought he had too much to drink.

No, that wasn't right. He forced himself to sit up, spit some of the grit from his mouth, and concentrated. After a meeting with his minister, Hovan was walking home when a bright light momentarily blinded him, causing him to trip and sending him into the light.

When he stopped falling, by hitting the hard metal deck of the space station, Hovan had no idea where his home went. The air was different, the sounds were alien to him, and the smells were offensive. Naturally, Hovan presumed the Kes kidnapped him, or maybe another party. Whoever had him would regret it, he concluded. Within his bodysuit was his defensive stunner and he now gripped it tightly in his right hand.

He looked around the dim corridor and finally noticed the rotund form nearby. He was old and had some sort of uniform on complete with weapons belt. Hovan had concluded he was kidnapped, but for what reason? The man was not of Kesprytt III, so the answer was another party, but which one? Ever since the Kes petitioned the Federation for membership, all manner of unwanted people tried to visit their world. Hovan was among the more active members of the Prytt, shunning off-worlders and prohibiting trade whenever possible. He felt it his duty and moral right to remain isolated from the other races and remained offended that the Kes opened their arms like a lowly whore.

Hovan leapt forward, placing the stunner below the left ear of the surprised figure.

"Where am I?" Hovan hissed.

The man's body language indicated he did not understand Hovan's words. So, he was not of Kesprytt, which only confused matters more. Their conflict was strictly an internal one, so who would interfere and why would they bring him to this offensive place? Slowly, the man raised his hands, leaving his sidearm attached to the thick belt. Hovan reached around and grabbed it, not recognizing the manufacture but knowing it to be a weapon. Suspicious of its use, he tossed it far behind him.

"I asked: Where am I?"

The fat man tried to answer but it sounded nonsensical to Hovan and he sneered. Gutter language perhaps. Certainly not something he could imagine understanding, so he spun the guard around and placed the stunner at eye level. The scared figure was sweating, making his scalp glisten beneath the thinning black hair. His very appearance bothered Hovan but he would need someone to get him home and this creature was elected. But what to do next? Without knowing where he was he couldn't begin to figure out how to get home.

With his arm stiff, he gestured with the stunner for the guard to start walking again. The two proceeded several yards in silence until they came upon a viewport. Hovan made the guard stop and together they looked out to the stars. The Kesprytt couldn't recognize any patterns, being a carpenter, not a scientist. He spoke again, and this time the man shrugged.

Nervous, frustrated, and annoyed to be relying on an alien for help, Hovan balled his left hand into a fist and struck out. The punch went deep, given how out of shape the humanoid was, knocking the breath out of him. A second blow made the guard go to one knee and Hovan kept asking where he was and every time there was no response, he struck again. After nearly a dozen blows, Hovan noticed the human had stopped trying to move or protect himself. He just lay there, breathing with difficulty. Hovan looked at the form, spat on his back, and proceeded deeper into the station, hoping to find the elusive way home.

Jerolk liked the market at midweek. It was full of spices and baked scents; he could tell from one whiff of the heavy air who had come to sell and who was missing. For four decades he had come to the market, first with his father and now with his own son. The trip took all morning, so by the time they arrived, atop a wagon full of *setch,* a spud-like tuber, the first thought was not of selling their harvest but of lunch.

Werq's was the place to go, he knew. Old Man Werq served the hottest, spiciest stew in the valley, filling your bowl before you could even sit down. Jerolk's son, Panni, didn't like the spice and sopped it up with hot bread, hoping to cut the sharpness. It rarely worked and his eyes watered, making his father laugh. After all, he was much the same, and the continuity pleased him. Plant after the last snow, harvest when the trees were at their fullest, and every midweek come to the market, dining at Werq's.

The eatery was filled, as usual, but the air seemed different. He sniffed once, twice, and registered stronger, sweatier smells than normal. The tables were also more crowded, making it difficult to navigate. He held tight to Panni's small hand, not wanting to lose him in the crowd. People were grumbling, he noted, not sounding at all pleased.

"It's been like this all week . . ."

". . . he hands me two bars, tells me to get lost . . ."

". . . didn't have my order this week, might not next . . ."

". . . credit wasn't good enough . . ."

". . . sold out faster than ever . . ."

". . . stopped the fight for the last one . . ."

Two large, burly men stood from a corner table and Jerolk grew nervous. They were bigger than normal farmers, clothes blackened and repeatedly patched. These were the source of the stench, and their darker skins meant they weren't native to Cadmon. While this was not unusual, the valley tended not to have many off-world visitors. He grew to like being in this little oasis, away from starports and intergalactic trade. Call him old-fashioned, but this is how he liked his life.

Panni slipped from his father's grasp and ducked under one fellow farmer, reaching the table first, and claiming the two seats. His father smiled with pride and took the opposite chair. The youth didn't notice or at least didn't mention anything wrong, instead looking at the tabletop.

"What's wrong, sprout?"

"Nothing, Dad," he replied. "Just not used to seeing the table without our bowl and stew."

True enough, the wait staff could not maneuver swiftly enough to handle the customers, which contributed to the foul mood permeating the room. Jerolk wanted to eat and begin selling his *setch* so they could start home before dark. There were chores awaiting them both, along with a warm and loving wife. Finally, Meloth, one of the regular staff, showed up with an unhappy look.

"No stew. All gone."

Jerolk was stunned. "This never happened before. What's going on?"

Meloth offered a bowl of bread ends, which the younger man snatched at, causing his father to chuckle. "Miners, lots of them, come to buy supplies."

"Okay, this happens now and again, but all the stew?"

"Been like this all week, Jer," the waiter replied. "They showed up two days ago, started buying up supplies, offering raw ore worth a fortune, and discovered Werq's. We've never been so busy . . . or so strapped for supplies."

"Eh?"

"Well, they buy everything, plus you've got your regulars, Jer. Folk like you. Unexpected demand, same supply, it just means we run out of everything. Werq himself can't get enough to keep the larder full, and the miners still come in and demand food. It's what you might call a situation."

Helping himself to a crust, Jerolk seemed thoughtful.

"Raw ore, you say?"

"Purest stuff I've ever seen. Should bring a fortune

when processed. Wish I were farming instead of working off me debts."

Jerolk puzzled over the situation. If the miners wanted *setch,* he'd sell the lot instead of the two-thirds or three-quarters he normally sold. In fact, he might even charge a higher price to the miners, getting that ore. After all, there'd be tuition, tithing, and a new set of tools he'd need coming up. The ore, if Meloth was right, would help. His stomach rumbled, reminding him of their hunger. "Who might have something hot left?"

The waiter shook his head sadly. "If it's like the last two days, no one. That's the problem, none of us can keep stocked to meet the demand."

"I'll put aside a bag or two extra for Werq," Jerolk said absently. "Couldn't do to make the cook starve, just doesn't seem right. Raw ore from the mines . . . how far away did they come?"

Meloth shook his head once more. "That's the thing of it, Jer. They're from Harod IV, not from here. And the ore is silver, something they've got lots of and we've got precious little."

The news shocked the farmer. Harod IV was nowhere near Cadmon, and they never had any formal trading. Yet there they were, in the valley, buying up everything in sight.

Selling the *setch* would bring him a great price, but if everyone had silver ore, what would its market value be in a day or week? And if they took all the supplies, what would the people have? Short-term, this looked too good to be true. Looking beyond the week, Jerolk didn't like the possibilities.

Not at all.

* * *

"Time's up, Mel Rosa. You're still here."

"Did he have to be so punctual?" Riker asked no one in particular.

Undaunted, Data commented, "He is actually early by thirty-five seconds."

"Swell. Status, Lieutenant Vale?"

"He's a man of his word," Vale replied. "Weapons charged, locking on targets directly ahead."

Riker leaned forward, resting his boot on the side of Data's console. "Perim, get us in the line of fire. Vale, more power to the forward shields."

As the Trill got the ship moving, the lead Deltan vessel unleashed a crimson beam that erupted in a shower of sparks on the *Enterprise*'s defensive screens. The larger starship was a little rattled but maintained its position between the Carreon and the Deltan craft.

Even though the *Enterprise* took the shot meant for Landik Mel Rosa's ship, the Carreon fired back. Two other Deltan ships returned that volley and within moments, the Federation starship was caught in a horrible fight. Shots glanced off the shields, shaking the ship, but it took no direct hits.

On the bridge, Riker had a tactical display put on the forward viewer. He and Data approached the display and studied the positioning of the ships. The Deltan ships were well spaced, requiring little movement, while the fewer Carreon vessels scrambled fire and move, fire and move. Those last seven Deltan ships had hung back—score one for Riker.

"Vale, I want half the phaser banks locked on to the Deltans, the other half on the Carreons—I don't care which ship or how many. On my signal, I want a simultaneous burst. Maybe that'll knock some sense into them."

"Aye, sir. Targeting now."

"Commander," Data asked, "what do you hope to accomplish with this action?"

Riker glanced at his control screen, tapped in some commands, and considered his response. It was surely a question the brass would ask of him when this was over. "I want to make them wonder if I'm willing to fire on a Federation member, whose side am I really on."

Data looked at him intently.

"Something else, Data?"

"Which side *are* you on, sir?"

Riker grinned. "The right one." He turned to Vale, standing tautly over her station. "Ready, Lieutenant?"

She nodded.

"Fire."

Riker could hear the phasers from all around him and was satisfied the starship was performing as expected. He had grown to like the Sovereign-class version of the *Enterprise,* although he still had warm feelings for its predecessor. Still, one needs to keep up with the times and the time was now for this ship to perform.

"Direct hits on four ships, three Deltan and one Carreon. Shields faltering, no other systems impaired."

"Nice firing, Vale. Ready another volley."

Just then, the tactical display started to shimmer as ships from all points began to move. Riker didn't like the pattern and liked it less when he was proven right. All the ships converged and fired on the *Enterprise,* buffeting it. Riker stumbled, tripping on the command platform, and fell to the carpeted deck below.

Picking himself up, Riker coughed once and looked around as damage control teams arrived to work on shorted circuits and burned-out isolinear chips. He noted that everyone else remained seated, so he took his place in the command chair and asked for reports. So far they remained relatively unscathed but Riker didn't like the idea of defending himself against so many ships.

"Okay, maybe the side of the right was overstating things a bit."

Captain Picard liked to consider himself an open-minded individual, so he could make himself equally comfortable sharing drinks with Chancellor Martok or spelunking on Risa. But he didn't like Cardassia.

He had plenty of reason to personally dislike the Cardassians, having battled against them and been tortured quite thoroughly by one of them. Their willingness to sell their souls to the Dominion brought about a war that would leave its mark on the quadrant for at least another generation.

As the *Marco Polo* approached, he could see a gray ball. Cardassia always seemed to have a miasma around it from centuries of exploitation. It was a resource-poor world when life took hold, and remained such, which may have fueled the Cardassians' desire to grow beyond their solar system. Picard's ancestors faced similar problems but managed to find ways to generate the power they needed to grow, without destroying the ecosystems. It was a lesson the Cardassians never learned.

Now, though, the miasma was more of a shroud; the result of the Dominion's final, brutal attack on the planet before their surrender which left untold thousands of Cardassians dead, their cities in ruins.

They would certainly have the desire to gain control

of the gateways, Picard mused, but would they have the ability to pay for it?

"Dingy," Chan said, breaking Picard's thoughts.

"Dirty," Rosario agreed. Chan looked over to him with bright eyes.

"No, I go with dingy," Davison added to the discussion, as Cardassia grew larger on the screen.

"That's two dingies to one dirty," Chan noted. "What do you think, Kal?"

The Tiburonian looked up from his studies, glanced at the screen, and offered, "Unsuccessful."

Picard nodded at that observation and stood. Everyone grew silent, which bothered the captain. He had hoped to find himself growing more comfortable with the young and eager officers, but it wasn't coming easily. The experiences aboard the *Enterprise* might have spoiled him more than he realized.

"I'll do this from the ready room, Commander. You have the bridge. Let's make sure our Klingon friends remain on this system's edge. There might still be raw feelings on both sides."

"Aye, sir."

The captain walked from the bridge, noting that the debate over the planet's appearance had started up again. Had anyone bothered to ask him, he would have suggested "disappointing."

Seated at his small desk in the ready room, he personally opened the channel to Cardassia's government. The planet and its ruling Detapa Council lay in ruin. A ruling body had formed, with representatives from around the planet. A touch of democracy, he thought, something foreign to the Cardassian Union for many centuries. Gone was the joint rule of the military, in the form of Central Command, and the shadowy spy network of the Obsidian Order; gone was the iron hand of the Dominion.

The new government had readily accepted Federation aid, working around the clock to rebuild their devastated homes. They appeared sincere in their efforts to start afresh, which Picard applauded, but he privately wondered if there was too little left to salvage. The Cardassian people were so accustomed to reaping the resources of their conquered holdings that they turned scant attention to rebuilding their own world's ability to sustain life.

Picard also knew that all was not harmonious on the world. People remained loyal to the Detapa ideals or even had served in the now-obliterated Obsidian Order. Accepting Federation assistance would be anathema to them and they might even go so far as to sabotage the rebuilding efforts.

Still, they had ships and officers and might be willing to help as a return for the quadrant's generosity.

The small desk screen came to life and the benign features of a Cardassian greeted him. The man was your typical native, pale gray-green skin with the thick ridges running down the sides of his neck. Picard found he could not read the man's expression.

"This is Captain Jean-Luc Picard of the Federation starship *Marco Polo*," he began.

Unexpectedly, the man's face brightened. *"Ah, the famous* Enterprise *captain."*

"Have we met?" Picard asked cautiously.

"Not at all. Until recently, I owned a humble tailor's shop on Deep Space 9 and I don't think you ever paid me a visit."

"I see," Picard said neutrally.

"But word does spread; some ships have such won-derful reputations and storied adventures. I daresay most Cardassians are familiar with you and your ship."

"I don't know whether to be flattered or alarmed, Mister . . ."

"I am Garak."

"Do you have a title, sir?"

"Just plain, simple Garak will suffice. How can we help you today?" His unctuous voice sounded like that of a salesman, someone used to serving. Picard, however, had read the reports and knew of Garak's involvement on DS9, and how he helped Captain Sisko on numerous occasions during the war. Now, Garak was something like a world leader, holding power on a world with very little power to offer.

"I would think, rather, you would anticipate us coming after your meeting with the Iconians."

Garak thought a moment, and Picard realized that he couldn't read the man's expressions. He masked them quite well, but the eyes were bright and he seemed interested in talking. *"Well, then, it's no secret they paid us a call,"* he said. *"I'm told they visited many governments, hm?"*

"Yes, which is why I am here."

"Not to bring us more supplies, as I had hoped." He genuinely seemed disappointed.

The captain nodded and waited, deciding to let this Garak prattle on until they could get serious. To his surprise, though, Garak affably waited as well and the silence grew. He didn't dare look away, suddenly recognizing the game this had become. Finally, though, when the time seemed interminable, he gave in and said, "Mr. Garak, I am assembling a fleet of ships, representing many cultures, hoping to force the Iconians to reveal their true plans for the technology and why they have chosen to return now."

"A humanitarian mission for the good of the Alpha Quadrant? Very noble of the Federation, Captain. Your altruism has always impressed me. I keep expecting it to be your downfall and I remain disappointed." Garak kept his voice well modulated, giving nothing away but Picard thought there was a mocking tone coming through.

"We had hoped to include a representative from your government as well."

Garak's eyes opened a bit and he took a shallow breath. *"Now that's very interesting, Captain. Why would we expend our resources on such a venture?"*

"The gateways are causing all manner of havoc throughout known space, reaching as far as the Delta Quadrant." He noticed a change in the Cardassian's eyes. The tailor lived up to the briefings, Picard concluded. Dr. Julian Bashir had noted how wonderfully absorbant Garak's mind was and how good he was at misdirection and subterfuge. The mind was processing this new information, weighing it against a decision he suspected had already been made.

"Do you expect this to become a battle, explaining K'tinga-class vessels rather than smaller birds-of-prey?"

Picard grunted, wondering how good their sensor array was. Now he knew, and it wasn't like Garak to give something away unless he thought it was payment for the previous information. It was like trading with a Ferengi, without looking for the trick.

"I accepted what the chancellor offered, as I will from your government."

"Very good of you, Captain. Having those gateways would certainly allow us to rebuild our trade with other cultures a lot faster, wouldn't you say?"

Picard grew silent, not rising to the bait.

"Marvelous technology. It's a shame, really, that they don't exist anywhere within light-years of our world. Imagine how it could make us all one large neighborhood."

With Cardassia so close to Bajor and the wormhole, it should have occurred to Command that the Cardassians might not be approached. And if they weren't approached or had easy access to even a single gateway, the conclusion was inevitable.

"Indeed," Picard said. "I'm not going to receive any assistance from your government, am I?"

The game over, Garak shook his head slowly. *"I'm afraid not, Captain. But I must say it was a privilege to have a chance to speak with you."*

With that, the screen faded to black and Picard sat back in his chair. The trip had been a waste of time, he concluded. Precious time gone by. There was little likelihood the Cardassians would ever agree to such a mission and Ross, of all people, should have known that. Intriguing as Garak was, Picard did not need to spend time in pursuit of a quarry preferring its current isolation.

He signaled the bridge, asking the *Marco Polo* to leave dirty, dingy, unsuccessful Cardassia behind and continue on their way.

Chapter Five

THUNDER CRACKED OVERHEAD as Troi materialized in the Grand Nagus's antechamber. She had already argued with Brisbayne that a meeting like this needed to be one-on-one and she would be fine on her own. His coarse manner grated on her nerves and she felt he wouldn't handle the Ferengi well at all. The Ferengi could be devious, even dangerous on occasion, but the current ruler, Rom, was reported to be a different sort of man. He had actually worked alongside Starfleet for a few years as an engineer for Chief O'Brien on Deep Space 9 before Grand Nagus Zek retired and named Rom his successor. Still, Troi was uncertain of how fast things might have changed under Rom's leadership. Certainly some of the attitudes had been altered, including the role for women, something she applauded. To be safe and respectful of the long-standing culture, she needed to operate under the laws as she knew them.

A short man with a smile showing well-sharpened teeth awaited her and nodded as she stepped forward. "I am Grinj," he said. "I am to bring you to the Nagus."

Grinj led Troi through ornate double doors and into a chamber where Grand Nagus Rom sat. On one side of the room sat a series of clerks, working at high tables, clearly calculating income. There was a constant, almost rhythmic, tapping from them. On the opposite side, under a small window, sat an older woman beside a gorgeous, lithe Bajoran woman, which surprised the counselor—especially since both women were clothed. Given the four-lobed construction of Ferengi brains, she could not sense anything from them, which always vexed her. However, from the Bajoran woman she sensed a certain confidence, and a kind of nervous pride.

"Welcome, Counselor," Rom said, standing up. As nervous as the Bajoran was, Rom's body language showed that he was much more so, very much unlike Zek, his predecessor. Most Ferengi were strong-willed, scheming types, usually with nerves of steel.

"I greet you, Grand Nagus, on behalf of the Federation." She put her wrists together, hands out, fingers curled, for the traditional Ferengi greeting, her combadge cupped in one hand.

"Ah . . . thank you . . . Counselor." He stammered a moment more, returned the gesture, and then seemed lost in thought.

"Is there a problem?" Troi asked.

"Not at all . . . it's just, well . . . here." He jumped

from the dais where his large chair was and moved to the far side of the room. From a peg, he took down a large green, orange, brown, and purple robe, seemingly made from different fabrics. He walked over to the counselor and presented her the item.

Now Troi was perplexed and said so. "Have I offended you, Grand Nagus?"

"No, not at all," he stammered out. "It was very considerate of you, but, ah, I think you'd find it more comfortable wearing this."

With a shrug, Troi accepted the robe, and then suppressed a snicker when she spotted a large ad across the back for a transportation service. The robe proved to be very short–cut for a non-Ferengi physique—but certainly warmer than presenting herself in the manner of most Ferengi women. Her show of honor and respect seemed not to have worked.

"You're a good boy, Rom," the older woman said.

Rom beamed at the praise, started back to his chair, and then turned around again, looking comical in the process. "Ah, Counselor Troi, I would like you to meet Ishka, my Moo . . . mother. And this is Leeta, my wife."

Both smiled at her but remained where they were, probably so as not to annoy the Ferengi men who sat on the opposite side of the chamber. They did not look like a happy lot, mostly whispering back and forth among them, pretending to be working over the accounts. Troi found it interesting that the leader of the Ferengi people had married someone from off world. She would like to have learned more but needed to stick to the matters most pressing.

"Grand Nagus . . ." she began.

"Rom will do, please," he said. With a wave of his left hand, he gestured her to a chair before the dais. While she'd have to look up, at least it'd be more comfortable this way.

"As you please. May I ask if the Iconians have come to visit?"

"Yes, with that amazing technology," Rom said, warming to the topic. "I had heard about the gateways from when the *Defiant* encountered one in the Gamma Quadrant, and couldn't begin to imagine how they could work. Before they came, one was found on another continent and I flew to see it. I wish I had the time to look under the paneling."

Troi didn't need her skills to see his enthusiasm. "What did the Iconians offer?"

"They said we could own the technology, be able to trade across the four quadrants. Brunt thinks it's a trick but Moogie, that is, my mother thinks we should make an offer."

Troi smiled at that, seeing the nagus was actually a man willing to listen to others. Of course, as a former engineer, he also had an appreciation for the technology. Troi found herself growing to like him and his unassuming way. Most of her experiences with the Ferengi had been unpleasant, most notably the time she and her mother were kidnapped off the *Enterprise* and were scheduled for slavery, so this was a welcome change.

"Did you make an offer yet?"

"Not that I know of, Rom," she truthfully replied. "In fact, I am here because we are growing concerned that the gateways, left active as they are, pose a great danger. To be honest, we suspect their motives."

Rom nodded enthusiastically, as if her point proved him right. "That's the Seventh Rule of Acquisition: Always keep your ears open." He seemed pleased and once more, Troi had to suppress another chuckle, imagining how the Ferengi could ever close their enormous ears. "What do you know of the Iconians, Counselor?"

"Very little, actually. My commanding officer, Captain Picard, has made a great study of the scant information found. He has a great respect for them so we're proceeding cautiously. May I ask if you have made an offer?"

Rom opened his mouth, but one of the men, a dour-looking sort, cleared his throat theatrically and Rom's lips slammed shut. The nagus and the men exchanged looks and Troi watched in fascination, not being able to fully discern the obvious power play going on.

"We are talking with them," Rom said finally and without much conviction.

"I see. Well, we're assembling a convoy of ships from different governments in the hopes we can get more information, and more honesty from the Iconians." If the Ferengi weren't going to offer up the complete truth, she wouldn't share the Federation's deeper suspicions.

Rom looked at his mother, then his wife, and then slowly turned his large head toward the men. He was clearly torn in making the decision but she couldn't tell which way he was leaning himself.

"I think it would be wise if we sent someone with you," Rom said. "We can still talk with their representative, protecting our individual interests, while participating in this."

Troi smiled at the nagus and he looked pleased. She

did see him check for reactions around the room and was surprised at how little support he seemed to be getting from the men. Leeta seemed proud and Ishka just nodded to herself. "I think that's very wise of you, Nagus," she said formally. "Our ships will leave within the hour. We'll send coordinates for your team."

"Ah . . . Counselor, if you like the robe, it's yours. Just ten slips of latinum."

Troi fingered the garish garment and sighed. "Thank you, Rom, but I really am not in a shopping mood right now."

Rom shook his head sadly. "I understand."

"Report, Counselor," Picard said from the viewscreen.

"The good news is we have four Gorn ships meeting with us in just under two hours."

The captain nodded solemnly. *"And the bad news?"*

Troi shrugged, back in her own quarters, and sipping tea. She acquired the habit after countless meetings with Picard and his beloved Earl Grey. It was too strong for her, and she was experimenting with milder blends, searching for one to call her own. She was dressed in her uniform again, which she much preferred to the ill-fitting robe, and the *Mercury* was already en route to the rendezvous point.

"Not bad news actually," she admitted, thoughtful. "We're bringing along a Ferengi Marauder as well. I gather they are negotiating already, or have made an offer. I don't think the nagus really wants to own it, just tinker with the technology. He's not at all what I expected."

Picard nodded. *"On the other hand, the Cardassians are not interested in helping us. There are no gateways near them to exploit and Command should have antici-pated that."*

"No doubt they're overwhelmed," she said, sounding apologetic when she had nothing to do with the decision.

"We still wasted time when there is none to waste," he muttered, clearly perturbed.

"It's in the past; we need to stay focused on the future," she said.

"The Tholians have also rejected our offer. Admiral Ross has also said there are no traces of the Melkots. We're beginning to head for the rendezvous ourselves. Oh, and Counselor . . . it's a lot emptier here without you. Picard out."

Troi looked at the Starfleet delta on her screen, sipped her tea, and considered the burdens of command. Picard's admission was not one she would have heard only a few years ago. She liked much of the responsibility that came with command but recognized the stress factor was one thing to study, another to experience. Something to consider as the *Sabre*-class vessel traveled at high warp.

Picard turned away from the screen and pondered his own frustrations. Everything pointed to the Iconians playing at a larger game, not just selling the technology. Once more he mentally reviewed the mysterious race that flourished throughout the quadrant and beyond. They devised wondrous technology, and left on several worlds an influence that survived over two hundred millennia. Why come back now, why offer to sell their greatest achievement? And if these weren't the Iconians, how did they get their hands on the technology, and why were *they* selling it?

Shaking those thoughts from his mind, he picked up a padd and added in the Gorn complement to his flight plans. With the *Enterprise* at the head, he could put the Klingons on the right flank and Gorn to the left. He still didn't know what to make of the Nyrians, so he felt putting them in the middle was safest, with the Ferengi Marauder closer to the Klingons. *Mercury* and *Marco Polo* he put directly behind. Four races might not be enough to make the impact Starfleet had hoped, but it would have to suffice.

Picard began recording a log entry, but was immediately interrupted by a summons from Davison. He stopped recording and strode quickly to the bridge.

"We have two warp signatures coming from 323 mark 37, approaching at warp five," Davison said, as Picard took his chair.

"Mr. Rosario?"

"The power signature makes them to be Romulans."

He raised his eyebrows at the announcement. Admiral Ross was to deal with the Romulan Senate and wasn't scheduled to be there yet. The ships must have been patrol vessels, although they were on the wrong side of the border. With the relaxation of postures on both sides, strict enforcement of the boundaries had been lessened. Two were certainly not enough to be an invasion force taking advantage of the gateway chaos.

"Go to yellow alert," Picard ordered. "Contact the *Chargh* and *Qob*, have them standby. I want no overt actions on their part. Time to contact?"

"Under an hour, Captain," Hol said from science.

"Both Klingons acknowledge, but they didn't sound happy," Rosario said.

"That's a surprise," Davison added dryly. Picard just gave her a glance.

"Klingons rarely sound happy," he said. "It's all in how you listen to them. Commander Davison, let's keep an eye on them. Also, let's summon Ambassador Worf to the bridge. The enmity between the two races has not lessened at all despite our work together during the war. Helm, change course to intercept, let's do this with our eyes wide open."

Everyone acknowledged and set about their tasks. With a little time, Picard prepared a personal dispatch to Admiral Ross and sent it, making it clear he felt the Romulans could either bolster the plan or compromise it. Unlike his crew, he did not feel like making a wager.

Worf arrived, eyes alert, face impassive. He immediately stood beside Picard's chair and ignored the sidelong glances given him by the crew.

"Warbirds," he said.

"Nice to see you haven't lost your keen observational prowess," Picard said with a grin. Worf merely stared at him.

"They are not an attack force," Worf continued. Picard nodded.

"They're also ahead of the admiral's schedule so they were not sent to us," the captain added. "Will Grekor follow our lead?"

"His House has never betrayed the Council," Worf began. "Grekor is old, a loyalist, and eager to serve for future considerations. He will obey."

"Good to hear," Picard noted. He gestured for Worf to sit and wait with the bridge crew.

The hour passed quickly, and as the enormous

warbirds came closer, Picard initiated contact. Almost immediately, a young woman appeared on the screen.

"I am Commander Desan, of the Romulan ship Glory."

"What brings you out this way, Commander?" Picard asked.

"There have been disturbances in the Empire and we are seeking reasons."

"Have you found anything?" Picard didn't mind fishing for information, fully expecting Romulan reticence.

"It's an internal matter," the woman replied.

"And these disturbances, do they have anything to do with the gateways operating in your Empire?"

She eyed him carefully, without a quick, prepared response. *"That's not for me to say, Captain."*

Worf shifted in his seat and caught Picard's eye. He slightly nodded, giving approval, though strictly speaking Worf didn't need it. Picard suspected the years of serving under the captain led Worf to defer to him out of habit.

"I am Ambassador Worf from the Federation," he said.

"How interesting," she said disdainfully.

"Commander, Federation representatives are on their way now to Romulus requesting support for this mission. Perhaps we can help each other."

"I am listening, Ambassador," she said. Picard sat back, content with Worf handling the woman, giving him a chance to observe.

"I can surmise that if the Klingon government and the Federation Council were approached by the Iconians, then so too did they visit your leaders."

She remained silent, listening intently.

"The Federation suspects these people and we are putting together a representative fleet to find out more from them. Having the Romulans beside us will give us strength."

"My government likes to remain up to date on all matters of such import." She seemed confident, almost arrogant in the response. Her hair was long, lighter than most Romulans,' and was pulled back, exposing a smooth face. She wore large dangling earrings in geometric patterns that glittered in the light. Picard took her presence to mean that somehow, their secret police, the Tal Shiar, had managed to learn of the Federation's plans—no doubt as soon as they were announced during the holoconference. Despite increased security, and a measure of paranoia, Starfleet Command still could not stop the spying.

"Captain, Ambassador, we approached with the truce beacon on and it remains so. My Praetor feels we have a mutual interest in this situation. Our patrols were in hopes of finding Iconians for further ... discussion."

Picard recalled the old adage: "Keep your friends close and your enemies closer." With the war over, it was unclear which category the Romulans fell into, but either way, it couldn't get much closer than this. He also drew confidence from the presence of the Klingon ships, which helped even the numbers should a problem arise. Of course, he knew, the Klingons would object to their presence, old animosities being very tough to bury.

"Do you acknowledge that the Federation is taking the lead in this mission?" Picard asked in his most authoritative tone. "Anyone accompanying us does so under my direction. I will not abide rogue ships causing a problem during these sensitive talks."

Desan's eyes flared for the briefest of moments, betraying her true feelings. Good, Picard thought, honest emotion. Now he knew her better. *"Once we hear what the Iconians have to say, we will decide our own course of action."*

"Agreed," Picard replied. "Obviously, I will ask you take the left flank, apart from the Klingons."

This time Desan's face twisted into a frown of disgust. *"We would have done so in any case, Captain. Glory out."*

Unsettled by the turn of events, Picard sat in thought as his crew busied themselves around him. Worf stared at the screen and Picard could imagine what was running through the warrior's mind. Although Worf had improved his attitude toward the Romulans, he retained some suspicion and it was understandable. Their dealings throughout the years built up a body of experience that forced such suspicion. Davison had already taken it upon herself to begin positioning the ships as Picard outlined. Chatter remained formal, but he barely paid attention. He absorbed the new facts and poured them into his mental paradigm, considering the consequences of each act. The first order of business would be to keep the peace among the fleet and to accomplish that, he needed Worf.

"I will not serve with petaQ!"

"Captain, the chancellor assigned you to this mission, to follow Captain Picard. Who else accompanies us is not of your concern." Worf was standing by the tactical station, holding the conversation with the captain while Rosario stepped back.

"Actually, Ambassador, it is," Grekor said with a surly tone. *"I no more want to see our people attacked than you do. I think Picard has the heart of a warrior and I do not object to his being in command. But we will be exposing our backs to a people known for their treachery, and that I cannot abide."*

Worf steeled himself, trying to find a persuasive argument to convince the captain that remaining was better than trying to force the Romulans to leave. Worf certainly had no love for the Romulans, but for this mission every little bit would help.

"We cannot force the Romulans to leave without provoking a fight," Worf noted. "That would waste time and resources. And there is no honor in provoking such a fight just because they share the same space with us. They are our allies and have been since the war—why not travel alongside them now?"

Grekor considered that, eyes barely wavering from the screen, which showed the beak-like head of the Romulan ship. Dull green light filled the bridge since the captain ordered the alert and Worf knew the disruptors were already trained on both ships.

"They are not to be trusted," Grekor repeated. *"What sort of commander would I be were I to lead my men into a Romulan ambush?"*

"A dead one," Worf replied, not intending any humor.

"True, but there is no pleasure in it this way."

"But," Worf persisted, "Captain Picard has also faced these people. He will not allow such a situation to arise. He has Martok's trust, why not yours?"

Grekor forced the breath from his body and took a moment. He seemed to be forcing himself to relax and

Worf was surprised to see a smile on the captain's face. *"You, I will trust, Ambassador. Your accomplishments have earned that. In fact, when this is over I would like to discuss ways to bring our Houses closer."*

Worf turned his head away from the corpulent captain and rolled his eyes.

Chapter Six

"We're taking damage, Commander," La Forge called from engineering. *"I can't guarantee how long before shields fail."*

"Another volley coming from port," Vale said from behind Riker.

"Deltan ships three, five, and six are coming at us, one-quarter impulse," Data added.

"We're in over our heads," Riker muttered. It wasn't the most brilliant observation he had ever made, but it was essentially accurate. For the last hour, the combined Deltan and Carreon forces had managed to put aside their differences and took on the *Enterprise* as a common enemy. Both captains had stopped accepting the commander's hails and he now considered his last stratagem a spectacular failure.

He had tried to avoid direct shots, merely phaser blasts that would divert the ships away from the hulking starship. Rather than move the battle, he kept the vessel in its position, avoiding complicating the targeting process by being constantly in motion. The other ships were not as courteous and darted through space like angry bees. And they were going for direct strikes wherever they could. Vale had reported no contact between the races, so they weren't sharing information. At least it gave him some hope for getting out of this mess intact.

The ship shuddered under the current round of pounding as Vale fired back, picking off what she could, missing on occasion. Riker noted that damage-control teams were on over half the decks and Dr. Crusher was already complaining about the increasing number of injured.

Vale looked at him with concern. "We're hitting the sixty percent mark on torpedoes, shields down to fifty-four percent."

It was long past time to put an end to the fighting. He just didn't have an idea that would get the Deltans' and Carreons' attention.

"Data, time to get out of here," Riker began.

"Agreed."

"Ensign Perim, Z minus fifty thousand kilometers, as soon as we're clear, engage at warp one. Plot us a circular course that will bring us back as quickly as possible."

Perim nodded in acknowledgment and set about her station.

"Vale, open a channel to Starfleet." He heard the telltale beep and began, "This is the *Enterprise*. Situation has grown out of hand. Request backup from whichever vessels are closest to this position."

The *Enterprise* began dropping as instructed, but two Deltan craft dropped with it, firing continuously. Riker, with little choice, instructed that both ships be disabled. Concentrated ruby light struck from the ship's under-hull, making contact first with one ship, then the other.

On the bridge, Riker saw the hits register on the tactical display and congratulated Vale. He saw the ship continue to lower, putting enough distance between them to form the warp bubble required to leave the area.

Two more ships, one Deltan, one Carreon, replaced the injured vessels and renewed the attack. Once more, the *Enterprise* struck back; a great wounded animal fighting to escape. It was not a pretty situation for the commander, one he was unused to. It grated against him and already regretted the report he would have to make when Picard returned. He had barely thought about his friend's own mission, not allowing himself to worry about things he could not change.

"Distance," he asked.

"Thirty-seven thousand kilometers," Data answered.

"Geordi, what's the minimum safety for going to warp?"

"You're right about there, Commander, but it's going to be tough with them still firing."

"Understood, out." He turned to Data, prepared to give the order, feeling like he was running away from a fight he started. Before he could issue the order, Vale interrupted.

"Signal coming in, Commander, it's the captain!"

"Will, what in hell is going on there?"

Riker grinned at the tone, glad if someone had to come haul his butt out of trouble, it was his friend. "My strategy backfired, Captain. How far away are you?"

"We've pushed it to warp eight, Number One. We should be there in minutes."

"Four minutes, thirty-seven seconds," Data offered cheerfully.

"I missed that precision, Mr. Data," Picard said.

"Captain, we'll send you complete tactical reports so you know what you're getting yourself into."

"Try not to lose my ship until then, Commander. Picard out."

This time, when Riker took his place in the command chair, it didn't feel so burdensome. "Perim, evasive course, full impulse. Make us a moving target and let's get some distance between us and that damned planet."

The Trill ensign began piloting the starship in an erratic pattern that seemed to confuse the smaller ships. Not that they stopped firing, but they were missing more than they were making contact. As a result, Riker could hear reports coming in a little faster as repairs were finished. Even La Forge said the shields were finally holding steady, back toward the seventy-five percent mark. Riker let out a deep breath, forcing himself to calm down and not get too excited about his captain coming to the rescue.

"We have visual, Captain," Chan announced.

Picard put the fuel consumption report down and saw the image of his starship moving like a drunken boxer, having taken one shot too many. Its flight pattern seemed evasive and they were not firing back at the ships, which kept dipping in and around the vessel. From the tactical report sent by his crew, Picard figured out that Riker somehow made the *Enterprise* the focal point of all hostilities. While questioning the strategy, he did note no ships had been lost.

"Red alert. Captain Picard to Captain Grekor," Picard called out.

"Grekor here," a rough voice replied on the audio system.

"I'm transmitting a pattern I would like your two ships to follow. I'm asking the others to hang back and give us room to maneuver. You are to shoot only if fired upon, and shoot to disable, am I clear?"

"Bah, that's not a battle, it's target practice."

"Still, our mission is to preserve the peace, not let the gateways sow unnecessary trouble."

"*Chargh* out."

Despite a few decades of peaceful coexistence, Picard thought, few truly understood the complex warrior culture that dominated the Klingon people. After being thrust directly into it, and as a duty to Worf, Picard had immersed himself in its intricacies. Their codes and mores were fascinating reading, and he understood how they united under an ideal. Some of their conquered worlds went unwillingly, but an equal number liked the way of life and were proud to be a part of the Empire.

"Chargh and *Qob* in position," Chan reported.

"Mr. Rosario, we're going in at full impulse. Target the ships closest to the *Enterprise*. Let's move them off while our friends start pushing the two sides apart. They just might think twice when staring down several phaser banks and disruptor turrets."

"Understood, sir."

"Engage," Picard said and then took a sharp breath, readying his mind, from diplomacy to battle.

Dropping out of warp, the three ships seemed to materialize from nowhere and immediately went about their business. With precision phaser shots, Carreon craft were moved away from the *Enterprise*'s nacelles while the Klingon ships bracketed Deltan ships with fire, giving them only one course to take.

On the bridge, Picard watched his adopted crew perform and was impressed. They took little joy in the battle but did as they were told and kept the usual side comments to a minimum. Even through the red haze of combat lighting, he could tell from the tactical displays that the plan was working. The sudden arrival of so much firepower scared off the much smaller ships and they easily scattered to two clusters, far from the Federation starships.

In all, it was over in five minutes.

"Go to yellow alert, stand down from firing. Mr. Rosario, patch me through to captains of those lead ships. Link the *Enterprise* so they can listen."

"Aye, sir, it'll take a moment," the curly-haired man replied.

While waiting, Picard once more sought to adopt the more placid tones of a diplomat, a role he had played more and more often these last few years. During the Dominion War he was either soldier or diplomat and had come to miss the exploration aspect of his mission. Even this Iconian situation cried out for an explorer but first he had to be a fighter. It just didn't seem fair.

"On screen, Captain. The Deltan is Captain Oliv and the Carreon is Landik Mel Rosa."

"Thank you," Picard replied.

Both captains appeared on the screen and Picard could tell at a glance that neither one looked happy to see the Federation's best-known defender. Oliv had a smug look, one born out of superior numbers, while his counterpart's eyes spoke of his devotion to the fight.

"I expect all defensive weapons placed on standby while we sort this out."

There was no question that they had to comply. Powerful as they were, neither side wished to anger the superior firepower represented by more than one Federation starship, not to mention the Klingon battle cruisers. He saw both captains nod to off-camera personnel and he spared just a glance backward to tactical. He got a double nod and smile from the relieved lieutenant.

"You both traveled through gateways to arrive in this disputed area. While I recognize the risks inherent in using them to return, I urge you both to go home. Your disputes may be legitimate, but are minor compared to the bigger issue facing us all. If you wish, once this is over, the Federation can dispatch a mediator to settle this once and for all."

Before either captain could react, Picard forged ahead. "This problem will only escalate, which is why I am trying to ascertain exactly what the Iconians really want. If I accomplish nothing else, I want them to close the gateways to prevent further bloodshed. To demonstrate our peaceful intentions, I am assembling a representative fleet. I would welcome one or more ships from the Carreon to join us. An equal number of Delta craft could join if it makes Captain Oliv feel better about your problems.

"We're moving out, meeting with other ships. You can coordinate with Lieutenant Rosario and Commander Davison. You have ten minutes, Picard out." With a hand gesture, he signaled to cut the signal.

"Didn't give them a moment to breathe," Davison observed.

"Absolutely not," Picard said, relaxing just a little. "We don't have time for posturing or arguments over a dead world. There are times, Commander, when having a reputation can be put to good use."

"And," she added, with a smile, "having two Klingons for emphasis never hurts."

"Never," Worf agreed.

"Mark me," Picard concluded, "there will be two of each and we can go to warp on time."

"I'll take that bet," Chan said, clearly happy order had been restored. A stern look from Picard reminded her to stay focused on her duty.

To anyone looking at the warp signatures, they would have scratched their heads in wonderment. Why would there be a Federation starship, flanked by two Klingon vessels and two Romulan ships, followed by two ships from Delta IV and two ships from the Carreon, then a ship with an unrecognized signature, and followed by a smaller Federation ship? These eleven vessels were streaking through space, forming a fleet that few would dare challenge.

Picard suppressed a small smile at the accomplishment, having four (or five, counting the Nyrians) governments represented before even arriving at the rendezvous point with Counselor Troi. The smile was also due, in no small part, to his return to the *Enterprise*. With the mission complete and now under way, he could leave the *Marco Polo* under Davison's watch and assume his rightful place on his ship.

Riker was waiting for him as he materialized in

the transporter room. He looked worn, the captain thought.

"Will, exactly what have you done to my ship?" he demanded with a smile.

The first officer shook his head, but couldn't keep the twinkle from his eyes. At least he hadn't lost his good nature, Picard noted. They strode off at a brisk pace, heading for the nearest turbolift. "Actually sir, a lot less damage than the last time I was left in command this long."

"Oh, so I still have a warp core?"

"Absolutely, sir. Wouldn't leave the sector without it."

"Excellent idea. Damage report."

"Minor structural damage, but Geordi says it won't slow us down. He's also got crews replacing blown circuits. One ODN is still giving him trouble, but it'll keep him occupied and happy."

"Very good." They stepped into the lift and headed straight for the bridge. Riker had already assigned crew to retrieve Picard's belongings from the other ship.

"Miss us?"

"Maybe," Picard said. "Not a bad ship, the *Marco Polo*. Smaller crew, fewer headaches."

"Less glamorous assignments," Riker added.

Picard nodded. "For a patchwork crew, they performed well, which gives me hope. We'll need them. But, I don't quite know about leaving Davison in command. She's logged very few hours in such a position and I'd rather have someone with more experience."

"I see you picked up a stray or two," the first officer added.

"The Romulans happened to be on the way, which adds import to our group, but also some complications."

"Such as keeping the Klingons from firing."

"I have no doubt Captain Grekor will maintain order, and having Worf aboard the *Marco Polo* will be an additional asset."

Riker raised his eyebrows at the news that an old friend was coming along for the mission. Before he could follow up on this, Picard succinctly filled him in on the Nyrians, the Cardassians, and the lack of success Ambassador Lojal had with the Tholians. There was little time to waste, he felt. By then, they had left the lift and taken their customary places on the bridge. He was pleased to see his alpha shift in position, his most trusted officers ready for the dangers ahead. And he knew all their names.

"There's always Data," Riker suggested as they each picked up a padd and began catching up on reports.

Picard shook his head. "I will need him when we deal with the Iconians. If he were to be in command, I'd scarcely let him off that bridge."

"Spoken like a true first officer," Riker quipped.

Picard gave him a small smile, then handed two padds to a young officer. "Ensign, these reports should be routed to the quartermaster before coming to me." The younger man nodded and hurried off.

"And that leaves Dr. Crusher out, in case this turns into a fight," Riker observed.

Staring at another padd, from an engineer, he double-checked some figures, then added his thumbprint for approval. "Very true. I suppose Geordi could handle it," Picard said.

Riker handed the padd to a waiting officer and looked at his commander. "Same argument as with the doctor. There's always Deanna."

"Number One, I thought you said we shouldn't give her another command after she crashed the *Enterprise-D*." Picard tried to look overly shocked at the suggestion but couldn't keep the small grin from his face.

Riker put on a look of mock surprise. "Me? Couldn't imagine saying something like that about a capable Starfleet officer."

Picard cocked an eyebrow and let the comment go without rejoinder. In many ways, having Troi command the other ship made sense and she would still be close enough to offer guidance. She certainly had proven her ability with people and there was plenty of support, in case of trouble.

"Let's make it so," he said finally.

As Riker busied himself, Picard spotted Crusher entering the bridge. He stood to greet her and she seemed pleased to have him back but also a little worn. Her hands were tucked into her jacket pockets and her reddish hair looked unkempt.

"Good to have you back, Captain. Your first officer seemed determined to fight like a Klingon."

"I'm sure Commander Riker's experience aboard their ships gives him a rather unique perspective on interstellar politics," he replied seriously. "Any serious injuries?"

"Nothing I couldn't fix although they were starting to stand in the halls with all the shaking going on," she continued, looking determinedly at Riker. He ignored her, consulting with Data on something, and this amused Picard.

"I'll try and keep things under control for the duration," Picard said.

"Thanks. A meal later?"

He looked into her green eyes, feeling warmed by her smile. "Absolutely," he promised.

As the two continued talking, Riker had Vale put a tactical chart on the screen, showing the fleet and the rendezvous point. From there, he and Picard busied themselves with contingency plans, trying to anticipate how to move so many ships should trouble occur. Picard also had Data assemble a report on further troubles caused by the gateways and also asked for an update from Captain Solok's attempts to create a map. As the crew busied themselves and he lost himself in the planning, a part of Picard's mind noted the comfort and ease he had with his crew. They had served together longer than most command crews and that gave Picard the confidence to take them further than he might with another crew, such as that of the *Marco Polo*. Yes, he was spoiled, but he took full advantage of that which kept him and the *Enterprise* in the forefront of the Federation's exploration and defense.

"Ambassador, I wish to consult you on the tactical planning."

"That is between you and Captain Picard," Worf replied, bristling. He sat in his quarters, staring at the viewscreen and the obsequious captain.

Grekor was hunched over a table, studying the flowing diagrams that charted possible battle scenarios. Grekor and Krong, the first officer, were trying to see how quickly the two Klingon battle cruisers could pivot and fire cleanly, without placing any other ship in the crossfire. When the two disagreed, they turned to Worf for his input.

"Ambassador," Grekor began slowly, *"we merely*

plan our defense in case of treachery. There's little you can offer when the disruptors begin firing."

Worf gritted his teeth, frustrated by wanting to offer complete help with his extensive experience but needing to remember his role as the ambassador. "Actually, Captain," he said as casually as possible, "if they do break formation in this manner, you can take the first shot between the Nyrian and the *Marco Polo* because a ship of that nature can react faster than you. The Federation craft will, by routine, rise, opening an opportunity."

Grekor studied the board a moment, then nodded as an officer reprogrammed the simulation, watching as the purple blip representing the *Marco Polo* moved as Worf suggested. Sure enough, there was a clear shot awaiting the fastest ship. Armed with this knowledge, Grekor could strike first, and Worf hoped, respect what he had to offer.

"Excellent, Ambassador. That's the kind of thinking we need more of."

Worf stalked his room, not caring if he moved away from the camera. While he liked things spare, the ambassador did wish to have room for a holocube so he could look at rotating pictures of his son Alexander, his now-dead wife Jadzia, and a recent portrait of his adoptive parents. Still, he hadn't packed for a vacation but a vital mission.

He wished for the luxury of a holodeck, but *Sabre*-class vessels didn't have room. His alternative was to find a sparring partner and use a workout chamber, but he did not know any of the *Marco Polo* crew well enough to share such an experience.

"Ambassador, your help has been immense. We will

be better prepared thanks to you," Grekor said by way of signoff. Worf felt his frustration mounting.

Before he could indulge himself and put a fist into the bulkhead, his communication terminal beeped. The Klingon letters crawling across the screen indicated it was from the *Enterprise*. Hastily, he stabbed the activation button. Riker's perpetually cheery face awaited him.

"Ambassador, how good of you to make time for a lowly commander."

Worf nodded and replied, "Ambassadors are trained to speak with the high . . . as well as the low."

Riker winced at the barb, continuing to smile.

"It's good to have you with us," the human said, bringing a feeling of calm to Worf. *"You know enough of the Iconian situation to recognize the more experienced hands the better. How's the diplomat business treating you?"*

"As one might expect."

"I see," Riker replied knowingly. *"If that's the case, maybe I should arrange a small reception in honor of our ambassador."*

"Thank you, no . . . Will," Worf replied, still trying to get used to using the first name. "The last one was sufficient." Then, with sudden inspiration, he looked intently at the screen. "Actually, Commander, allow me to entertain you. We shall re-create the battle of Malkir, readying our limbs for the battle ahead."

Riker looked at his friend and Worf could tell he was being read like an open book. Try as he might, he could rarely keep from such scrutiny by those who knew him well. Finally, the first officer smiled and replied, *"Sure thing. If I recall the battle, it was two against a dozen, over an active hot steam geyser. Did you bring one?"*

"We shall improvise," Worf added and cut the signal.

Twenty minutes later, the two men were on an *Enterprise* holodeck, stripped to the waist, their skins slick with sweat. All around them were swords and *bat'leths,* some still attached to their opponents' hands. The dead around them might have been holograms, but there was a joy pounding in Worf's chest. It had been too long, he realized, since he had the chance to cut loose like this.

Riker was grinning, which Worf found annoying more often than not. Still, Riker comported himself well and could display any emotion he wanted.

"Guess ambassadors don't get to do this too often, even on Qo'noS, eh, Worf?" Riker ducked and swung his sword, one-handed, to his left, keeping an attacker at bay.

"Indeed." Worf jumped right over the geyser, ignoring the stinging steam, and punched an attacker in the side of the head. It seemed to only stagger him and as he whirled about, Worf butted him again, this time with his *bat'leth,* which forced him to his three knees.

The first officer lunged low, aiming the sword up, and the rushing attacker impaled himself on the tips.

Riker stepped closer, wiping his twin-tipped sword on the pant leg of a fallen foe. "You're enjoying this almost too much so I know something's on your mind."

Worf leaped high, avoided a swipe from an attacker, then landed. With both hands gripping the *bat'leth,* he thrust it so one end was in the enemy's forehead and the other point in his abdomen. Removing the weapon, he watched the figure fall in a heap, atop two other bodies.

Riker's question remained unanswered. While he was able to share many of his concerns with Wu these last few months, he and Riker had endured so much together, even going so far as to love the same woman. While his heart mourned for Jadzia, it was also glad to see Troi and Riker back where they belonged: together. His friends aboard the *Enterprise* were always getting him to open up, something he did with reluctance. And yet . . . and yet it usually did help.

"My name, my accomplishments . . . they are a matter of public record, yet Grekor sees me as nothing but a career opportunity." He whirled as the final two attackers rushed him. He held the weapon horizontal, ready for the final movement.

Riker ran toward Worf, jumped onto one pile of bodies, and sprang from it so he could swing his sword from a high angle, cleaving one of the final enemies almost in two. The action provided sufficient distraction so Worf needed just one swing from his blade to decapitate the final one. The battle was over.

"Most commanders have a natural dislike for diplomats, comes with the territory." Riker was thoughtful for a moment then added, "You're just not used to being the center of attention. And, you're a man of action so sitting on the sidelines hurts."

Worf nodded in silence, staring at the ichor dripping from his *bat'leth*, recognizing the words' validity.

"I'm impressed, though," Riker offered. "To put aside those warrior tendencies to take on an even greater mission for both your people takes quite a man. I don't know if I could have done it. Martok's lucky to have you close at hand on Quo'noS."

Although the commander had said nothing Worf did not already know, hearing it from a trusted compatriot did take some of the sting out of the mission. He let out a deep breath and nodded once in appreciation.

"Now," Riker said, reaching for his uniform jacket, "I want to know something about the *Qob*'s captain, Tarnan. The captain and I need to make sure he won't take the opportunity to gut a Romulan during all this."

The next hour slid by as the two talked ships, armaments, and strategy. Worf hadn't felt this good in a long time.

Picard turned command over to Data and left the bridge for his ready room. As the android took the center seat, Geordi La Forge strode across the wide space to join him. To La Forge, Data seemed a little off his game, reacting to orders just a little slower than usual.

"Something wrong?"

Data looked at him, paused and turned his head to stare into space, and less than twenty seconds later replied, "Internal diagnostics show everything performing within optimal guidelines."

La Forge chuckled and shook his head, knowing he should have been more specific with the question. "No, Data, you seem distracted."

His mechanical friend looked at him with some concern.

"It's okay, if you have other things on your mind. Happens to everyone."

"I am not everyone," Data said. "But you are right. In addition to the mission, I have allocated portions of my brain to continue working on long-standing issues. You might be happy to know I am almost done with my latest poem."

La Forge rolled his eyes, recalling the last poem was over one hundred stanzas long and involved a most technical explanation of a sunset. He put a sympathetic hand on Data's shoulder and walked off, heading back to his console. On the way, though, he looked over his shoulder and sure enough, Data seemed to be staring off into space, not at the status reports coming through to his station.

He'd have to keep an eye on his friend.

Picard watched Taleen appear on the transporter pad and smiled as she looked around in wonder. She wore a hat that covered much of her dark hair and tapered several inches higher. Her uniform tunic was of a similar shade of brown, which went down to her thighs, with matching brown pants. She seemed to be in her mid-thirties with a wide-eyed expression. Clearly she remained rattled by her ship's arrival in the Alpha Quadrant and the captain wanted to make certain they were able to operate as part of the fleet.

"Welcome, Taleen, I am Captain Jean-Luc Picard," he said by way of welcome.

"Thank you for having me to the meeting," she said. He noted her voice was rather pleasant but betrayed a lack of experience as one in command.

"I have invited all the captains," he said as he escorted her from the room.

"I still don't feel like much of a commander," she said with a sigh. "I wasn't trained for it and this was never supposed to happen."

Picard pointed out some of his ship's features to her as they walked along the curving corridor. He watched as she took everything in with round eyes, but also noted how intently she stared at anything technological.

"You will find, as have some of my crew, that extreme situations can bring out the best in a person, crew, or ship," Picard said encouragingly.

"Or the worst," she countered.

"The Federation tends to be on the optimistic side of things."

"Captain Janeway certainly never gave up," she said.

"So tell me, how did you encounter *Voyager?*"

Picard saw her hesitate, clearly reviewing the incident, and finding the best way to explain it. She certainly didn't look happy about it.

"My people tried to, well, that is, we were trying to relocate the *Voyager* crew and use the ship."

The captain looked at her with some alarm, worrying that he might have misread the woman and her intentions. Still, she seemed genuinely abashed by the mere mention of the incident. She went on to explain how their people took other ships for their own use, finding a proper place for the crews to live. Janeway and her people had managed the rare feat of escaping and negotiated not only the return of *Voyager,* but also the freedom for the other races in similar captivity. Picard was once more impressed with the growing legend of Kathryn Janeway.

Finally, they found themselves at a pair of doors, which he explained was the turbolift, which would bring them to deck twelve and the briefing room. "With so many people, I felt it best to use a larger room," he explained as they stepped in.

As they emerged, Riker was waiting for them and the captain made quick introductions as they walked to the room a short distance away. It had been just an hour since the *Mercury* and the Ferengi Marauder *Kreechta* arrived, followed by the four Gorn ships. Seventeen ships meant just as many captains plus an ambassador.

He decided to bring aboard the primary leaders from each government.

In attendance were Captain Oliv of the Deltans, Landik Mel Rosa from the Carreon, Commander Desan for the Romulans, Captains Grekor and Tarnan for the Klingons, DaiMon Bractor from the Ferengi Alliance, Ralwisssh from the Gorn Hegemony, Taleen—who seemed woefully out of place—and the Federation's Brisbayne, Troi, and Riker. Ambassador Worf had a seat near Picard and he sat there, speaking with Troi in hushed tones.

Before speaking, he took a moment to truly look at this polyglot of races, all with one goal: get to the truth. An undercurrent to all that remained keeping the hostile factions—Deltan vs. Carreon, Klingon vs. Romulan— from open warfare. Still, he remained suffused with pride that this many different worlds willingly came together.

It took a few moments, but all eyes finally settled on the Picard. He was not the tallest or broadest in the room, but it was unmistakable who was in command. He prided himself on how he comported himself and felt he could not give in to any pettiness.

"For everyone's benefit, let me sum up our situation: the Tholians, Breen, and Cardassians have rejected our offer. Our Romulan friends have joined us. So much the better," Picard began. "Essentially, all the major Alpha Quadrant governments have been asked to be a part of this mission. Now we must move forward, in unison."

"Tell me, Picard," Mel Rosa said, interrupting. He was not terribly tall, with dusky skin, bright blue eyes and a frame that seemed totally out of human propotion so the head seemed smaller than it actually was. Picard noted, though, that the man wore a bright, crisp uniform with signals of his command running up the center flap of the jacket. He didn't know much of the Carreon, having rarely encountered them, so he tried to retain an open mind despite their belligerent tendencies. "Why don't you just blow up these portals?"

"There's no profit in that," Bractor, said. He was the shortest of the captains, clad in a formfitting monochromatic gray uniform with just gold circles at his sleeves, denoting his rank. Picard personally met him in the transporter room a little while earlier. The conversation was tense at first since the last time they had seen each other, the DaiMon was trying to blow up a Federation starship during a training exercise. Along the way, he had dealt the *Enterprise*-D some severe damage, all the result of a serious misunderstanding.

"Because, Captain," Picard interrupted, ignoring Bractor's comment, "they all seem to possess defensive fields that dampen weapons." He tried to keep the annoyance out of his voice.

"It's true enough," Grekor agreed. "We fired torpedoes at one and their guidance systems failed. Disruptors were also rendered useless at close range."

"What are they? Magicians?" Mel Rosa asked.

Briefly, Picard sketched out what was known about the Iconians, and asked for his guests to compare experiences of dealing with the Iconian representatives. He watched as Troi made herself some notes and was curious for her analysis when they were once again under way.

"Actually, Captain," Desan began, "my Praetor has already made two offers. One several days ago and another within the last few hours. It seems the Orions are bidding aggressively through an agent of theirs."

"Are you here, then, to insure the Iconians are treating your offer seriously?"

"Captain, I am here to make certain that what they have to offer is genuine and that they deal fairly with one and all. I think we're agreed, should the Orions or Kreel get it, none of us will be safe."

"Sooner the Pakleds than them," Grekor said with a sneer.

"As if our worlds would be safe if you obtain it?" Desan questioned.

"Or our worlds," Mel Rosa interrupted. That earned him an annoyed look from Oliv, the Deltan captain who had tried to snatch a world away from the Carreon. Picard watched carefully, wanting to avoid a fistifght.

So many agendas, most public but some still hidden. One baits another, more out of habit than anything else, which earns a rebuke. The task Ross gave him was feeling heavier by the minute.

"We've run the simulations," Bractor said, catching people's attention. "If any one government gains control of the gateways, all the spacelanes will have to be redrawn, avoiding floating apertures and potential tolls. The cost of either is immeasurable." For a Ferengi to say that, meant it was serious to all.

"No one will be safe if just one government has control," Taleen said, her small voice almost lost among the rumblings.

"Go on, Commander," Troi said in an encouraging tone.

"You're all worried about species against species here," she continued. The others began to look at her intently. "I'm from the other side of the galaxy. If the Hirogen find their way here, the damage could be insurmountable. Or if your more aggressive races, these Orions I suppose, come to my world, we wouldn't have the first clue as to how we can defend ourselves. Captain Picard, no one government should ever control this much power."

The captain nodded in understanding. He looked at the others, watching each consider what might happen if the others in the room were to gain the gateway technology. All had their own fantasies, all looked extremely uncomfortable.

Good. It would help keep them working in unison.

"It's a damned big universe," Brisbayne said. "There are dangers everywhere. Friends become enemies, enemies become allies, and then the unknown creeps up to bite you. Anyone getting this for themselves will invite as much trouble as they cause."

"The Federation has done much to maintain the peace," Oliv said. He was, Picard imagined, an older Deltan, the skin a little less perfect, crow's feet forming around the eyes. It struck Picard that this was an experienced space commander but, as he was also a member of the Federation, pledged to support their goals. "It was the Federation who first began mobilizing all of us against the Borg threat, or once more pulled us together to oppose the Dominion. But even they should not be allowed sole access to this much power. What we need is a way to make a pact within ourselves and with the Iconians so the technology is shared."

"Words," Ralwisssh said. His translated tones focused attention on him. "We need to know everything about the technology, how it works, how it has lasted this long. When they tell us that, then we can find a price worth paying."

"Should an enemy government get the device, the Cardassians say," Grekor said, "nothing will stop us from annihilating them before they could attack us. Self-defense is a universal right."

"And so it seems, is starting a needless war," Ralwisssh said slowly. "You say you are a people of honor. Attacking because you are a sore loser is not honorable."

"The Klingons would attack in the name of self-defense which is their right, but to start a war that may involve us all, is not," Desan said coolly.

"We have no interest in supporting something so disruptive to our neighbors," Bractor added, a tone of salesmanship in his voice.

Worf leaned forward, wearing his ambassadorial robes, and waited for attention. He saw Grekor gesture to stop Oliv from making a comment. His eyes were bright, and his great brow furrowed. Clearly, Picard saw, the ambassador had something to say but felt the weight of so many counting on his wisdom.

"Klingons do not fight wars just to fight," he began. "We save that for after. Romulans rarely allow themselves to get dragged into something so messy as a war. The Gorn fight to protect what is theirs, but they do not provoke others. The Ferengi may have armed those seeking war, but have never declared it themselves. *All* of that might change should one government acquire this technology.

"Clearly, that cannot happen. One race cannot and should never dictate terms to other races. The Federation has asked you all to come together and seek nothing more than the truth. Together we can keep the peace, be allowed to pursue our own destinies. That is the way it has been and should always be."

Picard watched the emotional temperature change in the room. He could have said those words and it would have meant one thing. But for a Klingon to say them, one who represented not Qo'noS but the Federation, that had a much stronger impact.

Finally, the Carreon captain broke the silence. "These Iconians of yours, Picard, are they real?" This from Mel Rosa, strategically located away from Oliv, seated between Taleen and Troi.

He looked across the room for a moment, making sure he had their attention. "Oh they are real," he said. "They ruled here with a reach we have yet to fully chart. Two hundred millennia after they were last seen, their equipment still works and is plentiful. Those we are negotiating with claim to be their descendants. And that is what we are here to discover while restoring the peace.

"We're to set out for the Iconian ships in two hours. Commander Riker has already transmitted flight patterns to your crews. In order to avoid internal conflict, and to best protect one another, do not deviate from this. Additionally, I am asking that all ships maintain an open channel to the *Enterprise.* We need to make absolutely certain we can react instantly to any adversity."

There were some mumbled comments from Mel Rosa and Ralwisssh, but he let them pass.

Looking over the table once more, he added, "Since I will be taking command of the *Enterprise* once more, the *Marco Polo* will need a mission commander. For your information, I am temporarily reassigning Counselor Troi to that position."

She looked surprised and couldn't hide the reaction. The Betazoid looked at Riker, who merely grinned, and then back at Picard. "Of course, sir," she stammered. "I'll make you proud."

"I expect so, Counselor. Report to your ship and be ready to move out. Unless there are any other questions, we're done."

"Just one, Captain." All heads swiveled to the scaly visage of Ralwissh. "We're a mighty force, but what if these Iconians, in addition to superior technology, also have superior weapons?"

Picard stared hard at the Gorn and didn't have an answer. The question did, though, make him stifle a shiver.

Chapter Seven

"GREEN."

"Veridian IV. Purple and diamond."

"Eminiar VII. Naked."

"Easy, Betazed."

"Really? I was kidding." Chan turned around in her chair and looked at Rosario. He bobbed his head twice, making the curls wave.

The tactical officer grinned back at her. "Yeah, but trust me, those are wedding holos you don't want to see."

"Where were we?"

"I guessed right. My turn: Orange."

As Chan tugged her ear in concentration, Troi appeared on the bridge and caught the end of the conversation. She smiled at how well the younger crew members were getting along just as Picard described.

With a glance, she saw that despite himself, Hol was following the game. She had quickly studied the crew manifests, and got snapshot descriptions from Picard as she rushed through packing a travel case. Things were moving very quickly for her, but she channeled the adrenaline to keep her moving rather than let her anxiety take hold of her. She hoped there'd be time for some meditation en route to the Iconian ships.

Picard had escorted her to the transporter room, trying to convey additional information about the *Marco Polo* crew. She had smiled, realizing he had come to appreciate them fairly quickly, something he wouldn't have done a decade earlier. Troi was proud of him.

Riker had remained on the bridge, coordinating ship-to-ship activities, and couldn't spare a moment to wish her well. It hurt a little but she recognized there was little time to waste.

Finally reaching the transporter room, Picard had summed up, "They're more green than not, but they will follow your commands." She had nodded and placed her case on the pad beside her. The captain had stepped toward the console and held out his hand to the transporter chief.

He, in turn, had reached down and handed the captain a helmet of some sort. Troi hadn't recognized it and couldn't understand why it was here.

"Commander Riker was busy, but he did ask that we present this to you for your new command," Picard had said with a grin.

"And this is?"

"An old-fashioned helmet, used by the early fliers on Earth. Will thought you might need it in case . . ."

". . . I crash another ship. Very funny. Thank you,

Captain. Will you please tell the commander that I will show my appreciation when I return to the *Enterprise*."

His grin had widened. "Of course, Counselor. Good luck. Although I'm sure you won't be needing it."

As the transporter beam had caught her, Troi suddenly realized how it was going to look when she arrived on the smaller vessel carrying a crash helmet. Oh yes, Will would see just how much she liked the gift.

Davison was waiting for her and sure enough, gave her a quizzical expression, but chose not to ask. She merely had a yeoman take the case and helmet to the captain's quarters and escorted Troi to the bridge. Troi realized they were young and eager, some a little scared, but their emotions were bolstering. They all wanted the mission to go well and were thrilled to be a part of it.

She hoped they would not come to regret the notion.

"I'm stumped," Chan finally admitted.

"Altair IV, Imsk, or Korugar," Hol said from the science station.

"Let me guess," Troi said, making her presence known, "colors for weddings?"

"Captain Troi!" Chan exclaimed. All heads swiveled toward the turbolift doors and the counselor. She had forgotten for a moment that the commanding officer of any vessel automatically gained the title of captain for the mission's duration. It would certainly take getting used to, she noted. On the other hand, she idly wondered if this would finally allow her to ascertain the veracity of the legendary Captain's Table pub.

"As you were," she simply said. With purpose, she strode to her command chair and settled in. It felt good and comfortable, she realized. Davison sat beside her, watching in silent amusement.

"We do this to stay sharp," Rosario said from tactical. "Passes the time, you know?"

"Indeed I do," Troi replied. "On my first assignment, we would try and name all the Federation worlds and when they joined. We've grown a bit so it's tougher now."

"Which is good, right?" Chan asked brightly.

Troi nodded in agreement. "We're moving out in fifteen minutes. Status reports please." And a flood of information came from around the bridge. Davison went last, reporting on the readiness belowdecks from sickbay to the quartermaster. Troi absorbed things as best she could and found new appreciation for how Picard and Riker could manage the larger amount of data presented them on the *Enterprise*.

"Ready to move out on Captain Picard's signal," Troi said finally.

"Aye, Captain," replied Chan.

Troi broke into a smile, deciding that she could get used to that.

"Hold tight, Jenny!"

The class teacher, Chuma Chukwu, tried to keep his group clustered together. There were ten of them, but it was hard to see them all. Sure, there had been sandstorms on Mars, but usually seen from a distance, through a wall of transparent aluminum. Never had the teacher or the students been caught in one.

"What happened, Mr. Chukwu?"

"That, Marisa, is a very good question," he shouted over the wind to be heard. All Chukwu knew was that during a break from their field trip to the first Martian park a ball had rolled away from the group. Three of the students chased it and called the others. Before the teacher knew it, all ten of his charges had gone through the thick, leafy bushes to see the discovery. After a few more minutes, he decided to corral them and continue their prescribed path.

As he pushed the branches aside, Chukwu was greeted with the sight of a gateway, its archway bright and inviting. The students were in a semicircle looking at it and trying to identify the changing scenes.

"It's Paris!"

"That's Tellar . . . no Vulcan!"

"And that's us! How?"

"How indeed," Chukwu repeated. He stepped closer, fascinated. "Darleen, that is neither Tellar or Vulcan but I believe Beta Proxima. See the cloud formations? Too fast for you?"

Thinking back, he wasn't sure who darted through first, Bruce or Darleen, but once one went in, the others followed with glee and curiosity. With no choice, Chukwu went through, feeling neither glee or curiosity. It was fear and trepidation, lightened only a little when he realized all ten had wound up in the same place.

He scolded them for taking the risk but that quickly gave way to figuring out where they were. It was sandy, like portions of Earth and Mars. The sky was blue and the temperature was hot, perhaps hotter than they were used to. There was no sign of a city or structure in any direction and the sun's position meant it was late afternoon, not early morning. Chukwu reached into his shoulder bag and withdrew the padd he used for lesson plans. He had hoped to find some distinguishing feature but saw little out of the ordinary.

"Mr. Chukwu, do you see that?"

He looked up from the padd, turning his head to follow Angela's voice, and saw the dark forms on the horizon. They were moving closer and growing bigger at the same time, darkening the horizon, and it became apparent to him that it was a sandstorm.

"We have nowhere to go, children. We must huddle together and hope it passes quickly. Hold on to your partner, link arms. We'll form a ball too big to be moved." As the children did as instructed, he hoped his words were prophetic. He heard a few whimpers and one, Bruce maybe, call them crybabies. What did Bruce expect from his fellow seven-year-olds? Chukwu wondered.

As the storm approached, Chukwu avoided joining the human ball, but punched in the planet's characteristics to see if he could narrow things down. He presumed they were somewhere else not somewhen else, but he'd heard enough stories in the media not to be too surprised. Within moments, the padd beeped and he started scrolling through the dozens of planets that fit the broad definition. He peered at the lists, not noticing the arrival of the storm until the padd was ripped from his hand and he went tumbling.

The ball of children was similarly moved, but not as far. They were farther away though, Chukwu realized by listening to their cries. It tore at his heart to hear them in distress but he didn't have long to think about that as the storm picked him up and sent him tumbling for nearly a minute. Sand got into every crevice of his body and he kept spitting to clear his mouth. After a short while, it proved fruitless.

There was little light and he kept his eyes closed, relying only on his hearing to discern where the children were. This proved difficult as the roar of the wind and grating sand never lessened their volume. After a time, he couldn't hear them at all and didn't dare open his mouth to try calling to them. Instead, he got on his hands and knees, hoping to survive the storm. He noted the sand piling around him, rising past his elbows. It even began to feel cooler, away from the direct sunlight.

Chukwu's plan worked, the children survived the buffeting by linking up. His prayers were similarly answered and the storm proved to be relatively brief, or brief by the standards of Nimbus III, the planet they had journeyed to. It lasted almost twenty minutes but that was enough to change the topography of the landscape and forge new pathways for the planet's people to use until the next storm.

Jenny and Darleen were the first to stand up, shaking sand from their hair and clothes. Bruce succumbed to terror and had joined in the crying before, but now he resumed his tough-guy stance. The three called out for Mr. Chukwu and grew desperate with each passing call and lack of response. Marisa was the one to find his body, mostly buried in the sand, an arm and leg barely visible and only because of the bright red suit he had worn that morning.

Whimpering, the ten children dug out their teacher, none daring to ask what would become of them now.

"Give me the readings!"

"Blood pressure nonexistent, heart rate twelve, superficial wounds to the face and arms."

"Was she conscious?"

"Not when we arrived."

"Never seen clothes like this. They've got to go—

bag and tag them. Give me an injector with cocamine, ten units."

"Doctor, when she's awake we must question her."

"If she wakes up. She's not doing much breathing, could be brain damage. Better order a model done."

"But Doctor, she's not from here and poses a security risk."

"Cocamine's working, blood pressure to two and rising. Heart's at eighteen."

"Have you matched the blood type?"

"Alien in origin, Doctor, we have the computer running a diagnostic now."

"Prepare oxygen ventilation. If she rouses, it'll help."

"Really Doctor, I must insist that I speak with her the moment she's conscious."

"Actually, officer, if that happens, first we'll do a medical history so we know how to keep her alive. If, by the Lord's will, she pulls through, you can ask her anything you want."

"Doctor, computer matches the blood to one of four worlds: Kavis Alpha, Kaelon II, Cor Caroli V, and Lysia."

"Lysia! Have the computer scan the sample and match against our blood."

"Doctor, what's wrong?"

"Officer, Lysia had an outbreak of Vegan choriomeningitis only a year ago. If the disease is in her blood there could be an outbreak."

"Heart rate and respiration are reaching safety norms."

"Ready to scan for the brain model."

"Computer analysis confirms the disease is in her blood, Doctor."

"Grife. Hold on the model. Okay, we're now going

to quarantine protocol one. Officer, whoever was there when she wandered through that doorway has to be brought to this installation—now!"

"There's a cure for this chorio . . . whatever, right?"

"Known Federation treatments do not work on our systems. If there's an outbreak, we're going to have a lot of dead Troyians before we can find a cure."

The man was scared. That much was obvious to his inquisitors. His green skin, sloping brow, and long hair made them almost as nervous. Whatever came out of his mouth made no sense to them and the metallic adornments on his clothing gave them concern. They had never seen anything like it.

He had wandered into their village, dusty, tired, and obviously thirsty. The man stumbled by the well, helping himself to cool water while the villagers scattered, calling for the Protectors. They weren't sure what to do with a green-skinned man and in turn summoned the Clerics.

Wrapped in their gray robes, allowing only their eyes to be seen, the women came from their secluded church and studied the stranger. They whispered among themselves while the Protectors kept the man surrounded. Parents kept their children indoors but the windows were filled with round, young faces looking anyway.

When he first spoke, everyone took a step back. Some felt he was a demon pronouncing a curse but cooler heads prevailed and realized he was attempting to communicate. One Protector, an older man, stepped forward and gestured. The man repeated the gesture, proving there was intelligence behind those frightened eyes. The stranger made any number of hand motions to suggest the direction he had come from and then pointed to their setting sun and held up two fingers.

He had walked for two suns, they concluded. No wonder he was thirsty. Quickly they estimated how far two days' walk would get a stranger, where could he have possibly come from. There were no other enclaves in that direction, it was the wrong time of the year for the nomadic tribes to be in the area, and that left them one conclusion: he had been cast out of heaven. The Protectors turned to the Clerics, who continued to silently watch.

When they shared the news, the lead Cleric reached within the robe and extracted a small object and plucked its center. The sharp, high note reverberated through the now-silent village and made the stranger wince.

Shortly, three colossal, robed figures came forward. Their robes were not gray but brown, and they carried coils of rope with them. The Cleric gestured toward the stranger and the men surrounded him, quickly binding his hands and feet. Two then hauled him on their shoulders and carried him toward the church.

None of the Protectors accompanied them, instead bowing deeply toward their spiritual leaders. The women ignored the obeisance and followed their Inquisitors to their home and the beginning of their study.

Now the stranger screamed in gibberish and the women watched in silence. One of the Clerics had retrieved scrolls from the catacombs under the church, wiping the dust from them with a scarlet cloth. She unfurled them on a wooden table and two others joined her as they scanned the texts. They had always known that God cast out the ill behaved but the last such known instance predated the village's existence. The Clerics did not know what to do with such a Holy

Criminal so they had to ask him. And he did not know the answers.

The hot coals of the fire, providing scant warmth to the chamber, glowed orange and red as an Inquisitor stirred them with a stick. It caught fire, adding additional illumination to the room. The stranger's eyes bulged in fright and anticipated pain. He babbled, going on and on in long strings of words that made no sense to the Clerics or the Inquisitors.

With detached interest, the Clerics watched as the green skin on his left arm began to blacken after being prodded by the stick. When the skin cracked and peeled, they were more than a little surprised to find that the blood matched their own: red. Studying this cast-out demon would prove more interesting than any other devotions the Clerics had carried out since their ordination.

One sat at the table, dipped a pen in a bowl of ink, and began inscribing a new incident for the texts.

The stranger's screams, she later wrote, stopped after the third day.

Geordi La Forge and Data were on an *Enterprise* holodeck, looking at a re-creation of the one Iconian gateway they had encountered years earlier. Over time, the Federation had managed to decipher exceptionally little of the language, not nearly enough to attempt manipulating the controls.

Using a handheld probe, La Forge took careful measurements of the re-created gateway and then peered at it with his enhanced eyes. The size was designed for taller people, maybe wider but definitely one at a time. Data had already accessed the files regarding the larger gateway encountered on Vandros IV by the *Defiant,* as well as another, previously classified mission on Alexandra's Planet. La Forge used those measurements to estimate the size required for starships and shook his head.

"Is something wrong, Geordi?"

"Not at all, Data. I was just wondering why the Iconians would have built themselves gateways that would allow starships. Why would they need something so large?"

Data walked around the simulation and came closer to his companion. "Modes of transport and the needs of their people were no doubt very different two hundred millennia ago. It is not useful to waste time wondering when we have more pressing issues."

"Yes, Mom."

"I am not your mother," the android replied.

"Of course not, Data, you just sound like her." La Forge chuckled and closed the device. "Have you studied the reports from Admiral Ross?"

"Yes," Data answered, not looking away from the control console. "The person-to-person gateways all appear to be approximately the same size, though some have frames, as the one on Vandros IV, and others, such as the one we discovered on the homeworld, do not. Those with control stations all have similar designs. Starfleet has determined that they range in age from two hundred millennia old to 200.237 millennia old. That now gives us a better understanding of their rise and fall."

He fell silent and La Forge waited, hoping to get more information or even supposition from his friend. Instead, all Data seemed to be doing was looking at the console.

"Something wrong?"

Data didn't reply at first. "The Iconians have demonstrated, long after their civilization existed, superior technological skills. Their probes caused the *Yamato*'s destruction. These are a formidable people, Geordi."

"Right. Makes me still wonder why they are willing to sell the technology. If they keep it, they become major players in the quadrant."

The two stood quietly for another moment and La Forge watched his friend. Clearly, something was troubling him but La Forge couldn't quite tell. "Captain Picard is right, Geordi. This seems most unlike the people who built these devices. The questions remain unanswered about where they have been, why are they coming back now, and why sell their prized possession."

"Okay, so we're agreed this mission makes sense."

"The Iconians did not seem to keep records. We have not found any and now have more places to look. Why do you think that is?"

"I don't know, Data. Maybe to keep their privacy."

"But in those records would be the keys we seek now."

La Forge thought back to the original mission, over ten years ago, and suddenly the pieces fit together. "Are you troubled over encountering their computers again?"

Data finally turned toward the engineer and nodded once. "I was nearly reprogrammed by them, losing memory engrams in the process. Everything that I have become was almost wiped clean."

"And you're scared?"

"With my emotion chip now in place, I recognize how close I came to ceasing to function. Yes, Geordi, I think I am a little scared of dealing with this technology." He made a small laughing sound, which sounded very artificial to La Forge, though much less so than past attempts. "Silly, is it not?"

"Not at all, Data. You and I, we've both had technology turned against us. Sometimes intentionally, sometimes not. It makes us protect ourselves a little better, but not once has it made either of us crawl into a shell. And you're not alone, Data. We'll be right beside you. We saved you once, and know what to do should this happen again."

Geordi touched Data's arm in the spirit of friendship and was a little surprised when the android's other hand crossed over and held the gesture a moment longer. With nothing left to say, they exited the holodeck and returned to the bridge.

The aroma of her hot food made Troi realize how much she missed her last meal, skipped because she got involved with a sensor overload. Without trying to micromanage everything, she did want to stay atop of the ship's performance since she expected to call upon it to perform in the heat of battle. Something deep within her warned that the outcome was not to be a diplomatic one. Were these the real Iconians, she knew, there might have been a chance, but if they were impostors, as Starfleet and Picard feared, the situation might well get ugly. Taking a seat, she forced her mind clear and wanted to simply enjoy the Heshballa curry, with its four varieties of meats and seventeen spices. Two mouthfuls into the tangy meal, though, she saw Mia Chan hovering nearby, holding her tray.

"Please, come join me," Troi said. Before the words were done, Chan had already settled in to Troi's right.

The counselor broke into a broad grin, noting the enthusiasm Chan brought to everything.

"Sorry to intrude, Captain," Chan began but Troi waved her silent.

"Forget it," she said.

"I never imagined we'd get to stay for the fleet and see the action close up," Chan admitted before beginning her soup. "I just thought we'd be Captain Picard's taxi and get dismissed, but this is so much better. Don't you think?"

"Well, since this allows me my first command, I would think we all benefit," Troi said cheerfully.

"Very true. We couldn't begin to guess who would command us when we learned the *Marco Polo* was staying. . . ."

"So no betting, eh?"

Chan shook her head in silent laughter. They ate in silence for a few moments before the conn officer spoke up. "I should admit to you, before we go into battle that is, that I have feelings for Johnny Rosario. Not that I think it will interfere with my work, since after all, my back will be to him and . . ."

Troi looked up with mild surprise. She suspected with a crew thrown together and the excitement of the mission, something like this might develop. It was perfectly natural but Chan's freely admitting it was different. "Does he know?"

"He'd be blind not to, but he's not saying much. You're an empath, can you tell anything?"

Troi shook her head before resuming her meal. "I wasn't really looking for any clues, Ensign. After all, with so many life-forms nearby, I'm doing my best to screen out the conflicting sensations."

"That's got to be so hard," Chan said, ignoring her food.

"It can be difficult but when you've been trained from birth, well, you get pretty good at these things."

"And having a human father, did that make things harder or easier?"

Once more, Troi looked at Chan in surprise. "How did you know that?"

"Well," Chan admitted while staring at her soup, "I looked up your service record when we got the posting from *Enterprise.*"

"That's actually good thinking, just caught me a little by surprise," Troi said. She stared thoughtfully at her half-full bowl. "Not being a full telepath made it a little difficult, growing up, since my friends had trouble adjusting to my . . . limitations."

"So, you haven't noticed anything?"

"About Lieutenant Rosario? Whether or not he has feelings for you?" Troi laughed, which felt good, and she smiled at the eager young officer. "If he has them, they will be pretty clear to one and all. Then you can act accordingly."

Chan finished her soup in quiet thought, allowing Troi to work on her curry and bread. The change in topic was a nice break. Having recently renewed her relationship with Riker, she wanted to see everyone find happiness. Especially the young like Chan and Rosario or those who had lost much like Worf.

Grekor strode onto the bridge and took his seat toward the front of the room. As officers from behind sounded out status reports, it was confirmed the *Chargh* was battle worthy.

"Did the meeting go well, Captain?"

The captain settled uncomfortably into his chair, grimacing at the bulk that his stomach had become. He hadn't noticed it before the conference, but compared with the trim forms of his peers—even the Ferengi was thin—he had let himself go. It was unbecoming a warrior.

"Eh? Yes, yes it did," he said to his gunner, Daroq.

"What do you make of Picard?" the younger, healthier officer asked.

"Picard looks your ordinary, pampered human," Grekor replied. "But there's rock beneath the veneer. I can see why K'mpec liked him." Indeed, Picard was impressive and not once did he mind serving under such a commander. The captain knew Worf's history with Picard and felt if he performed well during this mission; the word would go from Picard to Worf and from Worf to Martok. There could be much glory for his House, needed after years of misfortune and ignominy. The House of Krad had long ago joined an alliance against K'mpec and failed, losing their seat at the Council. An entire generation before Grekor's suffered for it and only now, through years of hard work and hard-forged alliances, did any member of the House earn glory. This very mission meant much to the aging Klingon, perhaps a last chance for honor and redemption for his father's father.

"Maltin," the commander snapped.

"Your Lordship," the man said.

"Contact the homeworld. See if my sister is at home. If so, I would speak with her," he commanded. The officer snapped to and moved away, letting Grekor sit in the too-tight chair and mull over hopes and dreams.

* * *

"Picard is as hew-mon as they come," Bractor explained. "Soft-looking, but deceptive. There's a banker's brain in there."

His trusted officers sat around the table, sharing a bottle, enjoying what they knew might be a final moment of peace before the mission began.

"And the *Enterprise,* is she everything they say she is?"

"That and more, Clax," the captain said. "I'd love to have seen more of it, understand its propulsion and those wondrous quantum torpedoes but there was no time. By the Grand Exchequer, it will be a treat to fight along side such a beauty."

Four other Ferengi sat at the table, all younger than Bractor, who was considered one of the finest pilots in the Ferengi fleet. He had parlayed his victories for lucrative contracts that fattened an off-world account, insuring a safe retirement. The thrill of adventure, though, forestalled any thought of leaving the service. He did not live to make deals, although he was more than adept at the practice. No, he owed a debt to his people and found tremendous satisfaction in his duty. Few others among his people could say that, which always made Bractor feel smug.

"Why would the nagus send us to fight," Clax asked. He was clearly not seeing the bigger picture and the Ferengi captain felt sorry for him.

"Knowledge is power. It's such an old phrase but so true," Bractor said. "If the hew-mons are right and these are not Iconians, then we need to know. And if someone else gets the power, then we stand by an alliance that can do more to protect our accounts than we could ever hope to do alone. They may say Grand

Nagus Rom is an idiot, but . . ." He paused, raising the glass high in the air.

Together the crew joined in. "He's our idiot!"

"Ah, Mr. Data," Picard began when the two returned to the bridge. "We have a new report from Starfleet. Captain Solok is making excellent time in creating a map. Please review the information and let me know if this affects our current plan."

The android accepted the padd and looked it over from his station. Picard sat back and asked Vale to put a tactical situation on the main screen. With a mixture of pride and concern, he saw the seventeen starships moving toward the Iconian position. Each ship was marked with their government's crest and the mélange looked a little odd, but appropriate for the moment. According to the read-outs below the images, they were going to be in position to begin long-range sensor sweeps within the hour, and at the Iconian position in four hours twenty-seven minutes.

He felt the mounting tension, which was tinged with anxiety, a volatile mixture and one he couldn't quell. Picard would have to trust his people.

"Everything looks steady," Riker said. Perhaps he, too, sensed the emotional state of the crew.

"Yes, Number One. Would that it remain so."

Riker grinned at his commander and sat back, forcing himself into a relaxed posture. "We're getting close enough to see them, it's incentive enough to keep even the Romulans in line."

Picard nodded and continued to think and rethink the situation.

"How do you think Deanna's doing on the *Marco Polo?*"

"Oh, she'll have them eating out of her hands, Number One. They're eager to please and she'll respond to that. Pretty bright crew on that ship."

"Well, that's good. Sometimes I wonder about the number of cadets being pumped out of the Academy."

"As do I," Picard admitted, taking his eyes from the screen. "Of course, I seem to recall saying that around the time your class was graduating."

Riker leaned over, a look of surprise on his face. "My class in particular?"

"I was guest lecturing at the Academy around then," he explained. "It was shortly after the loss of the *Stargazer,* and a few years before the *Enterprise* was built. Starfleet had given me numerous assignments, but in between them, I spent time at the Academy." Time well spent, he reflected, although all he recalled of those days was a restlessness to be back in space.

"Many in the faculty thought growing the number of cadets around that time lowered our standards. Starfleet was building bigger ships back then, anticipating the start of the *Galaxy* class. Bigger ships required more crew. And although the Romulans had been quiet, Command was growing concerned about the Cardassians."

"So, it wasn't just my class?"

"Not really, no. But, everyone felt the cadets might not be seasoned enough. After all, there weren't enough ships available to give them the same number of star hours as in my day."

"I'd like to think Geordi and I did just fine."

Picard smiled warmly at his friend. "After tempering some of that youthful inexperience under my command."

Riker chuckled.

"Captain," Vale called out. "Admiral Ross is trying to gain contact."

"On screen," he said, and assumed his customary command posture.

Ross looked even more tired than he did at the conference, dark marks under his eyes, hair less than perfect. Picard acknowledged his presence.

"Captain, I apparently journeyed to the Neutral Zone in error."

"Because I already have their support, yes," Picard replied.

"The Praetor assures me Commander Desan will serve honorably. I'm headed back for Earth and coordinating the activities."

"How goes the defense?" Picard asked.

Ross frowned before answering. *"They've started keeping a death toll at Command. People in the wrong place at the wrong time, cultural shock, some religious conflicts, you name it. We're stretched tight and can't keep up with the activity, to be honest."*

"Any word from our allies and how they're handling the events?"

"Chancellor Martok is concentrating on his borders and most of the others are too busy to chat," Ross said glumly.

"Admiral, this has stretched beyond the Alpha and Gamma Quadrants. We've added a ship from the Delta Quadrant."

"I know," Ross said. *"The* Defiant *has reported that the gateway that's endangering Europa Nova opens on the Delta Quadrant."*

Picard nodded. "We have encountered a ship belonging to a race known as the Nyrians and they've encountered *Voyager*. In fact, they came to join us as a result of that experience. We seem to have earned their trust."

The life in Ross's face dissipated quickly and he seemed more than a little lost. Times like this, Picard was just as content not to have any admiral's responsibilities. He liked and trusted Ross and hoped things would turn out well in the end.

"Our fleet is making contact shortly," the captain said, to keep the conversation going.

"Tread carefully, Jean-Luc," Ross said. *"Everything tells me this stinks."*

"Your instincts haven't failed the fleet yet, Admiral, we'll keep your thoughts in mind. Picard out."

"He seemed troubled," La Forge said, standing beside Vale at tactical.

"In many ways, this is a much worse threat than the Dominion War," Picard said.

"Indeed," Data said. "The prospects of any one culture gaining instantaneous access to the rest of the galaxy would cause massive chaos. Benevolent races might share it while others would hoard it, threatening others to accede to their terms in matters of trade, commerce, and holdings."

Picard stood, looking out among his friends and officers. Slowly, he walked the bridge, surveying control readouts and once more studying the tactical positions of the fleet. "The Federation alone is trying to protect the sovereign rights of billions upon billions of people," he began softly, more to himself than any one officer. "The Carreon have their own people to protect as do the Ferengi and Romulans. The stakes seem to be raised each time we venture out, but the goal remains the same. Protecting the lives and ways of life for each world, making no judgment on how they conduct themselves. Counting on allies or making new alliances to get the job done, asking nothing in return."

Vale leaned over to La Forge and whispered, "That man is at warp speed." He nodded in agreement. Picard turned toward them, having heard the casual comment, but chose to say nothing. The captain didn't even offer them a grin.

Picard continued to walk the bridge, not noticing the silence. Everyone had turned his or her attention toward him, listening closely. "We cherish these privileges and protect them, risking our lives because it's the right thing to do. We are also explorers and today we must be both. Who is out there and what do they really want? Can we prevent a galactic tragedy and stem the loss of lives?"

"We have before and can again," Riker said quietly.

"We must, Will," Picard said. "Our oaths must be more than words and our actions must convey the strength behind them."

"Captain," Vale interrupted, "we're making contact with the Iconian ships. Long-range sensors have gone on line."

The bridge suddenly burst into frenzied activity as people began sifting through the first readouts as they arrived. Picard settled back in the command chair, letting the organized cacophony wash over him.

"We are counting at least five dozen ships, smaller than us," Data said.

"Hard to get a count at this distance since they're all in motion," Vale added.

"Traces of ions and neutrinos, warp plasma . . ." La Forge said. "Can't imagine what propulsion they use."

"No return scans from them as yet," Data added.

"Shields up, Captain?"

"No, Lieutenant," Picard instructed Vale. "We're on friendly terms so far."

"We are too far away to get any life-sign readings," Data said.

"Feed the signal to Dr. Crusher," Picard said. "She can begin studying them as soon as distance allows."

"Captain, extremely strong sensor probes have been launched by the Carreon ships. Small, self-propelled. No weaponry aboard."

"Keep track of them," Picard ordered Vale.

"Message from the Romulans," she said in turn.

"On screen," Picard instructed.

Desan's calculating face appeared immediately and without preamble she began. *"Odd, don't you think, that there are no gateways active in this region?"*

Picard hadn't stopped to note that and stole a glance at La Forge, who nodded in confirmation. He should have thought to ask that of his crew.

"It could be why they settled here to begin negotiations," he replied.

"Read a star map, Captain," she said harshly. *"If you arrived in this region of space and wanted to contact Romulans, Klingons, Ferengi, Cardassians, even Orions and Breen . . ."*

"And humans," Riker interjected.

"This is far from the ideal spot," she continued, ignoring him and letting the omission hang as an insult. *"It must be the lack of gateways."*

"We'll know more soon enough, Commander," Picard replied evenly. He refused to let his annoyance at her attitude interfere. No doubt there will be plenty of strong emotions being suppressed as the mission progressed.

The screen winked off and the telemetry reports continued to flow in. Riker was taking the various reports and having them assembled into one master analysis for Picard's review. They were moving, the Iconian ships, but not any closer. The fleet remained in formation so things were progressing as well as one could expect. There were still three hours before they could make direct contact, so Picard chose to visit his ready room, enjoy a cup of tea, and await Riker's initial analytical report. He suspected it would be his last chance to relax for some time.

He was, of course, quite right.

The door chimed almost three hours later and Picard welcomed Riker and Worf into his ready room, comrades in arms, readying themselves for either diplomacy or battle. Picard suspected a little of both and was comforted by being surrounded with Starfleet's finest technology—and officers.

"Report," he said.

"Sir, we are coming within hailing range. So far, we have mapped their movements and can't find a pattern that makes sense. Additionally, the level of comm traffic between their ships is surprisingly minimal."

Picard nodded, digesting the information. "Your opinion, Number One?"

"They must know we're coming by now. Their silence may be a waiting game, forcing us to make the first move."

"Do we?"

"Not yet," rumbled Worf. "We cannot provide a provocation that would weigh their thinking against any race here."

"These people came to our portion of the galaxy,

selling us their wares. They've been in touch with the significant races so I see the silence as a ploy. Maybe some form of negotiation tactic. I say wait them out."

"Spoken like a true poker player," Picard commented with a tight grin.

"Captain, you seem more than a little preoccupied," Riker said softly.

"Am I, Number One? It's just that I expected something . . . more from a race as great as the Iconians were. If these are truly they, then I am deeply saddened. If they are not, they still may hold the key to what became of the civilization."

"So, you don't believe the Iconians are extinct?" Worf prompted.

"Not at all, Ambassador," Picard admitted. "The gateways alone tell me they could be elsewhere, another galaxy perhaps. That their technology has survived all these millennia tells me they built things to last. This was not a culture that just withered and died out like so many others."

Riker nodded and Picard rose from his desk, snapping off the desktop screen. It had been reports from their first visit to Iconia, which he continued to pore over in the hopes of learning their secrets. He needed to push those thoughts to the back of his mind and concentrate on the here and now.

"Is everyone alert?"

"Absolutely. Geordi's been over the weapons and defensive systems while Vale has been figuring out strategies now that we know how many of them there are. We're rested and more than a little anxious to see what's really going on."

Picard turned to his friend, placed a hand on his arm

and said softly, "Ambassador, I can't ask you to do anything more than observe. You're welcome on the bridge, of course, but leave the fighting—if any—to us."

They stepped on to the bridge and the bustle of activity made the captain glad. When on duty, he wanted to be accomplishing something and his chance had arrived. Taking their seats, the command team surveyed the crew and was satisfied.

"We have sixty-three Iconian craft identified, sir," Vale said from tactical.

"Readings show an odd propulsion system, among other anamolies," Geordi began, "but they seem to be moving little better than three-quarter impulse."

"The formations they are making seem not to be defensive, but more like coming close to share information or supplies and then moving on. All of the ships are involved," Data said.

"Ugly little things," Riker said quietly.

"Number One?" Picard inquired.

"Their ships, not designed for attractiveness."

"Hmm, I see." Picard asked Vale to show up a close-up view of one such ship and although their hull cameras had trouble keeping up with the darting vehicles, he got a good look. The ships were long and with huge exhaust ports for the engines. They tapered in the middle and then flared out into a cured front section that seemed to have sensors and weapons exposed. They were built for speed, he surmised. Yet, there were odd patterns to the hull, a crazy-quilt kind of look, and it nagged at Picard. After all, the Iconians wrote graceful—albeit powerful—software and the design of the gateways had an elegance about them.

The crew continued to study the vessels, making

guesses and sharing readouts as the fleet drew closer. Nothing in the Iconians' behavior indicated anything was amiss. They, in fact, seemed to be ignoring the incoming ships. That action more than mildly irritated Picard, who disliked this sort of game-playing. He could only imagine how the other captains must feel.

"Captain, message coming from Captain Grekor." Now he'd know.

"On screen, Lieutenant."

Yes, he confirmed, the Klingon captain seemed less than thrilled to be ignored. *"Picard, are we just going to keep approaching until we ram them? Interesting negotiating ploy."*

"Actually, Captain, I am trying to force them to speak first, allowing us a better sense of their attitude toward us." Picard stopped for a moment, then added, "After all, they may not be happy to have their potential clients teaming up."

Grekor snorted in disgust, letting the captain know exactly how he felt about whatever it was the Iconians were thinking. *"As you see fit. This is your mission but I am already weary of these people."*

"I share your opinion, Captain," Picard said mildly, no doubt annoying his counterpart. "Still, I suspect this will get us the fairest gauge of their true nature."

The screen winked off as Grekor cut the signal and Picard noticed how much closer they were to the Iconian ships. He was reminded of the old boyhood games of chicken, daring one another to commit some crazed act, waiting to see who would blink and stop first. He didn't consider himself to be as good at it as his brother, Robert, but he felt he had learned a few tricks over the years.

"Captain," La Forge interrupted. "I'm reading fifteen separate types of propulsion being employed."

Picard's eyebrows went up at the news. He studied the screen a bit closer and remarked, "The pattern on the hulls isn't a design—those must be patchwork ships."

"Confirmed, Captain," Data said. "We note the hulls have a mix of composite elements, no two ships with the exact same construction."

"Weapons seem to vary from phasers to quantum torpedoes," Vale added. "I'm sure there's more to them because I'm getting energy readings I've never seen before."

"Steady, Lieutenant," Picard said. These were the damnedest Iconians he ever imagined meeting, and with each passing moment he grew firmer in his belief that Starfleet was right all along. These weren't the Iconians at all.

"Captain, the Iconian communications have increased," Data said.

"Can we understand it?" Riker asked.

"Not at this time," the android replied. "However, if their emotional tenor was similar to human norms, I would say our presence was making them excited."

"That's something," the first officer noted.

Just then, the ships all moved, their random meandering suddenly taking form, clearly putting the Iconians on the defensive.

"How do you read it, Number One?" Picard asked.

"Groups of six, spread out, almost forming a globe shape. Haven't seen defense like that before."

"Agreed. Anything further on the communications, Data?"

"There was a spike in traffic, but it has since died

down to almost nothing, sir. I should point out, Commander Riker is correct. There are ten clusters of six ships each, but within the center is a smaller cluster with the three remaining ships. I have triangulated the communications and have determined the smaller cluster as the central one."

"Perfectly protected by the others," Vale offered.

"Change our flight pattern, Captain?" Riker asked.

"Not yet. Now we can make them sweat a little," Picard replied.

"Captain Grekor sends his compliments," the security chief noted.

"Well, that's one Klingon who knows how to acknowledge the game," Riker commented. "I think I like him."

"You haven't spent much time with him in person, have you?" Worf asked.

Riker shot him an amused look but before he could say anything, he was interrupted.

"I certainly feel safer with Romulans and Klingons at our flanks," Ensign Perim said at the conn.

"The last thing we need is a free-for-all, Ensign," Riker admonished.

"Actually, Number One," Picard said, "with the Klingons, Romulans, and Gorn at our side, we know what to expect. If there's a battle to be fought, I like the odds."

The moments ticked away as the fleet drew closer and the Iconian ships remained in formation. Sensors stopped revealing new information and Picard had his crew began preparing their analysis. He had Riker check in with the other Federation ships and all remained ready for whatever came next.

"Slow to one-quarter impulse," Picard commanded.

"The last thing we want to do is be at point-blank range should something happen."

"Are they forcing our hand?"

"Not yet, Number One. Just prudence on our part."

"A standoff like this usually will wear on someone's nerves. Should they have an itchy trigger finger . . ."

". . . or someone aboard a Romulan ship," La Forge added.

"Understood, gentlemen. Picard to Troi."

"Go ahead, Captain."

"Do you sense anything?"

"Actually, given my position and the high number of differing life-forms in the vicinity, no. Lots of anxiety, some anger, but I can't determine if it's our side or the Iconians. I do suggest, though, as the customer, we may want to hail them."

"Thank you, Captain Troi," Picard said, and watched Riker's double take at the title. He smiled, despite the moment.

"A very short message just came from the central cluster to all vessels," Data said. "Content unknown, we still have not managed to decipher their communications code."

"All ships, be alert," Picard commanded.

And as the words left his mouth, the Iconian ships opened fire. A brilliant flare of pale pink light filled the viewscreen and the *Enterprise* shuddered as it took the brunt of the onslaught. Everyone remained in his or her chair, but the com system immediately filled with damage reports.

"Do not return fire," Picard shouted, as much to Vale behind him as to the fifteen other ships.

"Shields holding," La Forge called. "Looks like directed energy similar to phasers. I'm heading down to engineering just in case."

"No serious damage," Riker reported.

Picard looked at the main screen and saw the vessels rotate, growing the sphere a little larger. He couldn't fully understand the tactic and desperately needed more information.

"Captain," Grekor's voice filled the speaker. *"They've blinked. Why do we not fight back?"*

"We may have scared them or there may be a misunderstanding. However, I will politely ask for an explanation before this turns into a war."

Picard turned to tactical and saw Vale's eyes gleam in anticipation. There was a ferocity in her slender form that, when unleashed, made her as dangerous a fighter as Worf. "Lieutenant Vale, target the two ships closest to us but stand by. Open hailing frequencies, make sure our other ships can hear me."

She quickly stabbed at several keys, never taking her eyes off the viewscreen, and Picard admired her skill. No question, she was an admirable replacement for Worf— the thought of his friend behind him was also comforting.

"This is Captain Jean-Luc Picard of the *U.S.S. Enterprise.* I wish to understand why you fired upon us. Our reason for being here is entirely benevolent."

Silence greeted his words as the Iconian ships continued to rotate their position.

"I ask again," Picard continued. "Why fire upon us when we are potentially going to negotiate with you for the gateway technology?"

The Iconian ships continued to rotate position. Picard swallowed, a sudden suspicion forming in his mind.

"All ships, scatter plan Omega, execute!"

The seventeen ships began to move, appearing to randomly split formation and go their own ways, but each following a carefully laid-out course. Riker had devised the plan hours earlier and he was glad it had been loaded at every helm post.

The *Enterprise* surged forward, taking hits but not stopping. Worf's fingers began to move in the air, pantomiming activating first phasers and then a spread of quantum torpedoes. Catching himself, he balled the fingers into fists and stood still, watching the unfolding battle. Already snippets of a poem occurred to him, although it was not his place to compose one—he was an observer and that honor was reserved for actual combatants. The pain in his heart was not new, but still unwelcome.

Just as the ships began moving, the Iconians, still in motion, opened up with sustaining fire. The raw energy filled the space where the ships had been, their rotation allowing them to cover a wider portion of space than if they were stationary. The move was carefully coordinated and the captain nearly underestimated them.

"All ships, defensive fire only. *Mercury,* when an opening presents itself, try and penetrate the sphere. That central cluster is our objective."

"Acknowledged," came Brisbayne's rough voice on the com channel.

"Ensign Perim, swing us about, let's try and scatter the sphere," Picard instructed his pilot.

"Aye, sir," the young Trill ensign replied. Perim, Worf knew, could handle her task. She had performed well under fire against the Bak'u last year when Worf had temporarily rejoined his old comrades in the Briar Patch.

Riker had already had a tactical display flashed onto a screen to their left. The ambassador saw the fleet in their proper positions, holding their fire, with the *Enterprise* moving toward the first cluster of six ships.

"Data, any hope of cracking their communications?" Riker asked.

"Negative, Commander." Data studied readouts from his operations console and input new commands.

Just then, the cluster before the starship opened fire once more. The forward shields deflected the attack, but not before the *Enterprise* shuddered once more.

Aboard the *Chargh*, Grekor grinned with glee at the prospect of a battle. His hands gripped the command chair, whitening his knuckles. His crew was efficient, the captain knew.

"Bring us about, 217 mark 38, full impulse," Grekor said.

The ship moved and managed to avoid a burst of blue light. The officer at the science post stood over her viewer and finally said, "Unknown energy, Captain."

"Can it hurt us?"

"I can't say with surety," she said.

"Helm, 218 mark 23, keep us dancing," Grekor instructed. He turned to the officer, who seemed to shrink from his glare. He turned to Daroq, who shook his head—out of weapons range.

"Tell me about the energy!" demanded the captain.

"It was pulsating photons, changing in frequency every second," she said, holding her ground.

"If it hits this ship, what happens?" Grekor stopped looking at her and returned his gaze to the viewscreen.

"The very pulsations might cause our shield harmonics to be disrupted" was the answer.

"Potentially lethal," he muttered. "Bring us within range. Weapons, aim at the ship on the starboard side. Target that large propulsion tank!"

It took several long seconds for the ship to be in position, but once it was, everyone straightened up, ready for battle.

"Target locked."

"Fire!"

The battle cruiser's phaser barrage pierced the ship's shielding and struck the hull. The impact knocked the ship's position, sending it spinning counterclockwise. Sparks from the remains of the shields showed it vulnerable and Grekor smiled in victory.

"Fire!"

The next phaser barrage struck the same spot with deadly accuracy, blistering the hull, then breaching it. The engines sparked in the naked vacuum of space and then they died out, leaving the ship a hulk of metal.

"Excellent" was all Grekor said, as much to himself as to his gunner.

"Do we go for the kill?" the officer asked.

Grekor hesitated a moment and then said, "Picard wants none of them killed and for now, we will do this his way."

"The *Kreechta* is using their plasma weapon on the cluster," the gunner called out. Grekor turned to watch the smaller screen and saw that the highly effective Ferengi weapon practically obliterated one of the enemy ships. His brow knit in thought and then he said, "I always underestimate those sneaky accountants. But then

I see them fight and remember why we haven't conquered them yet."

Grekor continued to watch in satisfaction as the battle continued to unfold. The five ships that remained of the cluster scattered, breaking the formation. The captain ordered another blast, trying to force one ship into another, a calculated risk. It failed and the commander's curse was barely audible. Instead, he had a torpedo launched at the nearest ship and disruptors fire at the farthest.

"The *Chargh* opened up the sphere!"

"Lucky bastards," Captain Brisbayne said. He saw the larger ship pursuing two of the smaller ships and directed Liang to move the ship through the hole.

"Engineering, shore up the forward shields," Srivastava called.

"Doing what I can, but we're already straining the EPS outputs," Solly said from below.

The *Mercury* darted forward, avoiding blasts from two different directions, and returned fire at the one below them. The shot grazed a shield and did no damage, so the small ship remained caught between two Iconian ships from the sphere to their port side. As a captain, Brisbayne had never really been on the front lines much, even during the recent war. He had his skirmishes with pirates and even traded shots once with a Romulan border ship that "accidentally" crossed the Neutral Zone, but his career lacked the color of officers like Picard. It usually never bothered him, but now he recognized the need for such experience to lend him insight as to how best to proceed.

After forty years of service, he was going to have to rely on his skills and intuition, hoping they did not fail him. None of which, though, kept his stomach from churning.

"Twenty-three thousand kilometers to the center ships," Liang reported.

"Steady as she goes," the captain said. He leaned forward as if it would get him there any faster. "Livingston, rotate phaser fire, upper and lower hulls, forward and aft, keep them guessing."

"Aye, sir." Livingston began the random firing. The captain heard the whine of phaser fire, mentally tracking its tone from one side of the ship to the other, and nodded in approval. If he could keep cluster seven away from him, he might have a chance to reach the goal. Exactly what Picard would have him do once he arrived remained to be seen, but Brisbayne always considered himself a patient man. It got him this far in his career and he expected it to take him just a little bit farther.

The Iconians, though, seemed to have another idea.

The six ships on either side, clusters marked six and seven on the screen, swiveled to turn toward the *Mercury*, and twelve sets of weapons were unleashed simultaneously.

None got through the shields, apparently, as Brisbayne tumbled to the back of the bridge, landing atop another crewman. Smoke was already filling the air and he could tell from feeling the deck plating beneath the carpet that his ship was badly wounded. People coughed, someone was vomiting toward the turbolift doors, and there were moans. He swiped blood from his split lip onto his uniform as he staggered to his feet, taking stock of the pain throughout his body. Pushing that to the side, he helped up the crewman below him, who turned out to be Livingston. He seemed relatively unharmed, just dazed, so Brisbayne guided him back to his station.

"Report!" he bellowed, hoping to get a reply.

Ranjit Srivastava was on his knees, wiping blood from his forehead, a blank look in his eyes. He was not in any shape to answer, probably concussed, Brisbayne concluded. Liang was slumped over the helm, coughing from the smoke. Agbayani was on his feet, his Hawaiian features marred with soot and blood, and he leaned over the engineering board.

"Warp core offline," he shouted, his voice hoarse. "Shields below safe tolerances at eight percent, structural damage to the port nacelle, phasers are offline, torpedos seem fine. . . ." He squinted at the board and Brisbayne turned away and helped Liang settle into her chair. Then he stole a glance at the screen. The ships seemed to hang in space waiting. He didn't like it at all and wanted to swat them away like flies on a summer's day.

"Bridge to sickbay," he called out, and noted how sore his voice sounded.

"Levy here, it's a mess and we're still counting the casualties. I've a medic on his way up."

"Bridge out. Engineering, report."

The silence seemed ominous. Looking around, he pointed to Alan Chafin, still orienting himself at ops. "Get to engineering, find out what's going on down there. We need as much power as possible, shields and environmental systems first."

"Aye, sir" was the reply and the officer rose unsteadily to his feet. Brisbayne took a moment to look at him and was surprised to see the burn marks on his face. The officer seemed uncomfortable being stared at and looked away.

"When you're done there," Brisbayne added, "stop at sickbay and have those burns tended to."

Chafin, dark-haired with a ready smile, nodded and continued unsteadily toward the turbolift, stepping over a body, most likely Alfonzo's, the captain realized.

"Livingston, can you target the torpedoes?"

The man stared at the equipment, stabbing at controls, and finally shook his head.

"Go to manual. We're not going anywhere and they're not getting us without a fight," the captain said.

The two Romulan warbirds were the largest ships in the melee, and this brought Desan some comfort. She anticipated this advantage, knowing they had more people per ship and more weapons than any of the "allies." Still, they were fighting fiercely, since even gnats could sting.

They had managed to disable four Iconian ships in cluster three, one of which was being torn apart by a tractor beam, each piece being carefully scanned. The science department was already speculating as to the nature of the constructs. They peeled apart easily since they were not well constructed. Desan had no feelings for these ships or their people, only contempt for the entire charade.

The Iconians had approached the Praetor. The Tal Shiar, the Empire's vaunted secret police, immediately began investigating their claims. There was nothing to confirm or dispute their claim but the Tal Shiar were a suspicious lot. When word reached them that Starfleet was on alert and there was suspicious activity involving key personnel such as Ross and Picard, they assumed their suspicions were justified. As a result, it was decided that Desan would lead a delegation, as much to learn about the Iconians directly as to keep an eye on the Federation.

Subcommander Jilith interrupted her thoughts. "Commander, we've completed the initial scans and have determined the ship is composed of a metal composite we've never seen before and basic duranium. The propulsion unit is actually an antique, from around the time of the first Romulan-Earth war."

This was interesting. How would a race, from another part of the quadrant, have come across something so old? Her curiosity was piqued.

"Two of the ships are trying to retreat," the helm officer called.

"Let them," Desan replied. "They're not firing. Bring us closer to the core, helm. Half impulse."

"Yes, Commander," he said. The mighty vessel moved forward, leaving the disabled Iconian ships in their wake. Others converged on the green starship, opening up with unusual weapons fire. The particle beams were a veritable rainbow of colors, but all seemed ineffective against the Romulan shields.

On the screen, the two smaller Carreon ships flew by them, pirouetting and concentrating their fire on one of the Iconian ships. She admired their versatility even though she knew very little about the race since they were located far from Romulan borders. She did know them to be aggressive and stubborn, but not annoyingly so, like the Klingons. They tended to keep to themselves but somehow got dragged into the battle, and given their fighting prowess, it was good to have them along.

With their attack a success, the Iconian target hung dark and lifeless in space, so the ships moved on. What neither Carreon seemed to notice, though, was another Iconian ship flying up from below them, firing the bright blue beams. Desan did not warn the allies but instead had the beam analyzed.

She watched with interest as the beam struck one of the ships, flared against its shields, but persisted. Within seconds, the shields sparked off and then the Carreon starship was struck dead-on, a blackening scar appearing near its nacelles. Another few seconds and the beam completed its work, breaching the hull and destroying the ship and all hands.

"The weapon is the most powerful phaser I have ever seen," the science officer reported.

"Interesting," Desan said, watching the other Carreon vessel flee the area while the Iconian ship chased it.

"Torpedo!" called the tactical officer, and that got Desan's attention. They hadn't fired one yet and she thought them without. On the screen she noted it came from a vessel they hadn't bothered with, presuming it out of disruptor range. *An estimate that may prove fatal,* she calmly thought.

It slammed right through the shields, and impacted with a deafening thud on the "neck" of the starship. Everyone fell to the starboard side as the mighty bird pitched with the impact. Desan's last thought, before losing consciousness, was how much the rainbow lights reminded her of home.

"I don't approve of that, Number One," Picard snapped, holding tight to his chair as the *Enterprise* endured a blistering phaser attack from six ships, forming Iconian cluster five.

"Well, you said not to destroy them, nothing about dissecting them," Riker replied, equally holding on for dear life.

"Torpedoes away," Vale called. The ship's quantum torpedoes streaked through space and managed to hit three of the ships, causing all manner of distortion in the area and making them break off the attack.

Seeing the opportunity, Perim had the starship yaw dramatically, trying to squeeze between two clusters at almost warp one. It was a tricky move but Riker assured his captain Perim could handle it. The ensign was gritting her teeth, Picard noted, but otherwise flew his ship just fine.

Now beyond the clusters and heading toward the core of three ships, Picard let out a breath and looked about. His crew was handling the battle admirably, and while he never enjoyed such engagements, he never shied away from them either.

"Captain, the *Mercury*'s been hit bad," Vale said.

"On screen," he snapped.

There, the small ship hung at a steep angle, sparks from one nacelle providing illumination. Its running lights were out and it seemed dead. As Data and La Forge reported in, it was far from dead but in no shape to conduct a battle.

"Number One, order the Deltan ships in to protect the *Mercury* then signal the *Marco Polo* to go for the center."

"The Iconians clearly can outgun the *Marco Polo*," Riker argued.

"We'll set up covering fire from . . . the *Qob* and the

Carreon vessels," Picard said, checking the tactical display.

"I'd sooner have the *Glory* cover Deanna," Riker protested.

Picard realized the struggle Riker was going through, but duty demanded a specific course of action and it needed to be followed. He, too, hoped for Troi's survival, but a diplomatic mission had turned into a battle with no notice and this fleet could not shirk its responsibility. He grasped Riker's arm in reassurance and then stood and moved to the upper deck.

"Send in the *Kreechta* for support," Picard added.

At the rear science station, the captain punched up charts showing how badly hurt the *Mercury* was. So far, they were all acquitting themselves well, but there was going to be damage and it was unfair for the captain to wish it on only the ally ships. He really didn't know Brisbayne, but he felt for the older man, seeing that he was now out of the picture and was going to need protection.

"Picard to Captain Grekor," he suddenly called.

"Go ahead."

"The *Mercury* is hurt. Can you tractor it out of the way?"

"If they can't defend themselves, then we shouldn't risk our ship to help" was the reply.

"That's a Klingon tactic and approach I do not subscribe to, Captain."

Another voice interrupted.

"The Federation requests your assistance, Captain," Worf said from the bridge's rear. "Will you help your allies or not?"

There was a tense moment and then a station chimed.

"Orders sent, Captain," Riker said tightly.

"Thank you, Will," Picard replied. He turned to his left and nodded silent thanks to the ambassador. They resumed their seats as the *Enterprise* moved toward the core, ignoring the fire from all sides. It was far from a smooth ride, but they were making progress, which was more than he could say for any other member of his fleet.

Then, on the screen, he watched a brilliant light show, as Iconian ships began a new form of attack on the *Glory*. It seemed to withstand the onslaught but barely. Then came the torpedo attack and Picard was stricken to see such a proud and powerful ship suddenly stopped dead in its tracks.

"What was that Data?"

"Analyzing telemetry now, sir," the android responded.

"*Glory*'s hurt bad, isn't she," Perim inquired.

"Yes," the captain replied. "And if the Iconians can do that to a Romulan ship, we're all vulnerable. Slow to one-quarter impulse, redirect energy to our shields."

"Aye, sir," Perim replied.

Whatever hopes for diplomacy had been shattered over the last few minutes and Picard had been gearing himself to become a warrior. He preferred such conflicts to be one-on-one matches, disliking commanding so many ships, controlling so many lives. But here he had no choice and he had to fight for every millimeter, and preserve the lives of the fleet. The Iconians needed to be stopped and he also had to assure that they wouldn't be wiped out in a fit of Klingon or Romulan rage.

Riker was standing at the tactical display with Vale, watching the colorful icons moving about at a rapid clip. Picard joined them and they assessed the scene for a moment, trying to think of a way to end the battle.

Those thoughts were interrupted when four ships broke from their positions and as a unit began an approach toward the sphere's top. If they looked like anything, they were small insects buzzing about.

"Ralwisssh," Riker said.

Picard saw the Gorn craft swing above the sphere, out of weapons range, and then angle and aim directly at the top cluster. As their descent began, they fired from every port and the ship glowed on the screen. Grimly, Picard watched the small, but deadly, ships approach the Iconians, narrowing the space. Then, one Iconian ship winked off the screen, followed by two more.

"Captain Ralwisssh, I ordered no lives to be taken," Picard cried.

"The time for that has passed, Picard," the guttural voice replied. *"They have hurt us and now it is time for retribution. If you do not have the stomach for such a fight, we'll cover your retreat."*

The captain, stone-faced, watched three more vessels vanish from the tactical screen. On the one hand, it made their job easier by blowing another hole in the Iconian defense, but he didn't want this to become a slaughter. He would have to act quickly and decisively to remain in control of the fleet. All he needed was a plan.

As he was thinking, he saw Riker step closer to the display. He followed his first officer's gaze and watched the *Marco Polo* complete a complex turn and begin its approach toward the center. Riker pointed to the right of the screen and frowned.

"The circle is closing ranks," he said.

Bractor didn't need to wait for an order from Picard. He was a trained tactician and knew what was required.

With the sphere defense tightening, each hole punctured was being closed. At least one aperture needed to remain open and he decided that was his assignment.

From his command chair, he gave a series of commands to the tactical officers standing before their operational orb. They did their jobs in silence since he rarely liked chatter during an operation. He liked concentrating on the opponent and would tolerate interruption only if it was about the operation.

The *Kreechta* swooped in a wide arc, above the plane of the battle, aiming itself at the space between clusters three and four. Shields had been reinforced fore and aft; weapons aimed at the closest ship in cluster three. He had the engines increased so the velocity was on a gradual increase. As they banked, it forced everyone to hold tight, and Bractor's breath quickened. This was the moment he loved, the instant when he committed his ship beyond the point of no return.

"Fire!" he snapped.

Ferengi energy leapt across the space between ships and smacked against the shields of the Iconian vessel. The shields flared, and as a second volley arrived, the Ferengi Marauder was past them, already firing on the next closest ship. Again and again, the ship fired as it muscled the Iconians aside, keeping the two clusters from merging.

Bractor most certainly loved his job.

"Six Iconian ships down," Davison said, reading the display to her left. "With the three disabled by *Enterprise,* we've opened up the bottom entirely."

Troi nodded and kept her gaze at the main viewscreen. She received her orders from Riker, cut and dried without any hint they were lovers or he was putting her life at stake. While she intellectually understood it, her heart refused to acknowledge the command and was in rebellion.

Mentally, she tried a quick discipline her mother taught her when her mental skills were just developing. It was to control her quick temper at the playground on Betazed and worked more often than not.

It didn't work just now.

All along, she was trying to filter the thousands of emotions, all heightened, from assaulting her psyche. She told Chan she could handle the concentrated emotions but that was before the firefight broke out. Her mental blocks were in place but they were being unintentionally pounded upon and it was giving her the mother of all headaches.

The *Marco Polo* had to escape being caught in a pincer move by two clusters of Iconian ships, taking heavy fire in return. Troi had the ship drop below their approach and then roll to confuse the attackers. Sacker in engineering said it would be twenty minutes before shields were again at full intensity. On the *Enterprise,* if Geordi had said twenty minutes, she could bet on it. Here, she couldn't tell if Sacker was the kind of engineer who exaggerated repair time or not.

"We're clear," Chan said, sounding very relieved.

"Not entirely," Davison commented. "Our path brings us around and straight into the gap, but they'll see us coming."

"I'm reading something unusual," Kal Sur Hol said from ops. He remained rigidly bent over the viewer and his left hand punched in commands. "There's an energy buildup from cluster four, something I've never seen before."

"Rosario, tactical on screen," Troi commanded. The stars became a computer-generated image with each Iconian cluster numbered. She quickly saw that number seven was being approached by the Romulan warbird *Glory*.

"Any analysis?" she inquired.

"Not yet. Something like tachyons but not quite. Whatever it is, I'm very intrigued by its . . ."

His words were cut off as the screen displayed the torpedo assault on the Romulan ship. She never imagined a simple torpedo could do that much harm to something so large. Her bridge grew silent, except for the chirps from the equipment.

"Captain, we're approaching our target," Davison said quietly, breaking the somber tone that gripped the crew.

"Chan, as we discussed, ease us into the gap, like a butterfly finding its branch, float us in," she said as soothingly as she knew how.

The young flight officer acknowledged and eased up on the speed, giving her more maneuverability. The *Marco Polo* had two Iconians fire over their position, caught by the change in motion. The attacking ships were, in turn, fired on by Landik Mel Rosa's ships, keeping the enemy distracted as the Federation ship continued into the sphere.

"Well done, Mia," Troi said with a genuine smile.

"Careful, three Iconian ships have broken off from cluster four and are approaching, weapons hot," Rosario called.

"Increase speed to full impulse," Troi called. "Bring us up the Z-axis fifty thousand kilometers."

"Something that steep, that fast could damage the nacelles," Davison warned.

"No choice," Troi snapped. "Engage."

The *Marco Polo* went into the rapid climb, taxing the inertial dampners and forcing everyone to hold on to their chairs. Two of the three Iconians attackers followed them up, while the third held its position.

"At fifty thousand, break down, sharply, aim us right at the Iconian ship," Troi commanded.

"Ma'am?" Chan said.

"Just do it," Troi said, getting annoyed at being questioned. Still, it was a difficult situation with her in command and a relatively unseasoned crew. They would have to follow those orders blindly to get the job done. Hesitation, in a situation like this, could prove deadly.

The ship shuddered as it reached its zenith and then was pushed straight down, in a tight arc that forced the integrity fields to their limits. As they descended, still at full impulse, Troi could hear the reports coming from engineering and it didn't sound good.

Of the two Iconian ships following them up, only one managed to slow up as the *Marco Polo* flew past them. The other shot farther up and seemed lost. One did slow down, tried to fire, but their targeting was off and the rainbow-hued shot went wide. It continued after them.

"At eight thousand kilometers veer off at 312 mark 8, straight for the center, warp one in a two-second burst," Troi said. If she recalled the Picard Maneuver right, this would be similar but would let the Iconians do all the shooting.

This time there were no questions, just confirming the order and then silence. Utter silence, which gnawed at Troi but she ignored it. Just as she ignored the apprehension from Davison and tinge of fear from Chan which stood front and center from all the other emotions threatening to overwhelm her.

As the ship approached the eight-thousand-kilometer mark, the Iconian ship that remained below her angled itself up, taking aim. The Iconian ship pursuing them from above fired once more and again missed.

"Going to warp," Chan finally announced.

"Inertial dampers are failing," Hol almost immediately called out.

The ship lurched worse than Troi feared, as it straightened itself out and then accelerated into warp space. Hol flipped over his chair and landed with a bone-popping sound. Rosario managed to hold on to the tactical station but that only meant a yeoman smacked right into him, injuring a shoulder. Chan rolled from her chair and backward toward the command chair. Troi, already on one knee, helped her back up and guided her to the station. Bracing herself against the chair, the captain studied the readouts. Even the two-second burst was enough to disrupt all activity on the small starship.

"Who's hurt?" Troi asked.

"Hol's injured," Rosario reported. "Already signaled sickbay."

"Engineering reports dampers reconfigured and back on line," Davison reported.

"Johnny, are you okay?" Chan interrupted.

"Fine, Mia, just fine. You fly the ship safely," he said softly.

With the *Marco Polo* no longer in their sights, the Iconians who chose that moment to unleash a torpedo had no way to call it back. And the ship coming straight down could not move out of the way fast enough, so it took a hit at point blank range. The fifth Iconian cluster ceased to exist.

"Amazing," Riker said, shaking his head.

"That ship has a good pilot," Picard noted.

"We couldn't do something like that," the first officer said.

"No, but a smaller ship could and Captain Troi knew that. She continues to surprise me."

"And me," Riker said with a grin, a twinkle returning to his eyes.

"The *Marco Polo* is now nearing its objective," Data said. "The Iconians in the center have yet to fire."

"Maybe they can't," Vale noted. She bent over the far right portion of her station, straightened up, and shrugged her shoulders. "Then again, maybe they can. We can't get solid readings."

"Too much distortion from the firefight," Riker said.

At that moment, the tactical screen revealed the unusual sight of the Romulan ship *Bloodsword* and the Klingon fighter *Qob* approaching the remains of cluster number four. Disruptors that were more similar in nature than either side would ever admit unleashed their fury as the two ships targeted one small Iconian vessel after another. Within moments, four of them had vanished off the tactical board while the other two scampered away, going to the far side of the sphere's remains.

"Nice shooting," Riker said.

"Indeed," Picard said, since clearly there was nothing left to be said of the carnage. It sickened him.

"Captain, look at this," Vale called.

Picard strolled over to the tactical station and she magnified the readouts. There, the Deltan ships, which had previously been providing cover for the *Marco Polo*, were now under heavy fire from an entire cluster of ships. He noted the power amplification made to the phasers were nothing he had ever seen before and the pounding was getting worse for the Deltas, which were clearly not meant for this style of punishment.

"Who's closest to them?" he asked.

"Maybe the Gorn, but they seem intent on decimating our opponents," she replied.

"Wait, look." He pointed to the bottom of the screen and there, a ship swooped into view, maneuvering through debris and avoiding fire.

"It never occurred to me," he muttered, as the Nyrian ship approached the Deltas.

Coming from underneath and behind the Iconians, they fired once, then again. Their discharges seemed to blossom as they traveled away from the Nyrian ship, crackling with energy and causing damage to the first two Iconian vessels the energy flow touched. With two such ships damaged, the other four spread farther and fired on the Deltas. The distraction provided by the Nyrian ship enabled the two craft to separate, swooping high and avoiding much of the enemy attack.

The Nyrian ship came closer and fired twice more, and once again, the energy discharge did serious damage to the Iconian shields.

"Lieutenant, are you studying the Nyrian weapons output?"

"Recording everything for study later, sir," she said crisply.

"I'd be curious to know how that works."

"Me, too, sir," she said. He noted she was smiling, enjoying the spatial acrobatics and firefight unfolding before them. Truth be told, he was pleased at how well the little ship was contributing to the fleet and found himself anxious to learn more about Taleen and her people.

"Don't you find it amazing, Number One," Picard began, as he returned his chair. "Look at how well our group has persevered. There may be hope for us all, yet."

"Maybe," Riker said. "But right now we have two goals: get to the lead ship and protect the *Glory*."

The brightness in the captain's eyes dimmed as he realized they still did not know a thing about the torpedo that managed to do so much damage to the Romulan warbird. The Iconians might not have been what they appeared to be, but they were no less formidable. He could not lose sight of that.

Not once.

Picard forced himself to slow down and look hard at the tactical display. The defensive sphere's bottom ceased to exist, as did the adjacent cluster. Even as they contracted, the Iconians could not possibly close every gap if they remained in the rigid six-ship-per-cluster formation. That could prove an advantage but he needed to make sure their next moves would not make them vulnerable.

The Carreon had already lost one ship in its defense of the *Mercury*, and the *Glory* was still showing no signs of movement. He had fourteen able ships to the Iconians' forty-nine and it seemed that the Iconians' sole goal was to defend the core three ships. Picard ran the numbers six and three through his mind, matching them against what he knew of the Iconians, and nothing came to mind. More than likely, further evidence these were impostors. That galled him but he fought to contain the anger, saving it for the leader of these people.

"Number One, they will defend the gap here," he began, tapping the wide opening in the sphere formation—thanks to the *Kreechta*. Even as he touched the screen the Iconian markings moved closer—they were continuing to tighten their posture. "Everything else will be spread thin, creating weaknesses between the clusters. I think if we hammer at those points, simultaneously, we just might crack the entire sphere."

Riker was studying the screen and the captain approved of how quickly his first officer was running the possibilities through his mind. In his own career, Riker had seen his share of combat and also had the experience of serving aboard a Klingon ship. This gave him possibly even better insights to the strategy.

"If everyone behaves, it should work, but I'd put the heaviest guns still working on the gap. Maybe *Kreechta* and the Nyrian ship—they seem to pack a wallop."

"Agreed," Picard said a tight smile of approval on his worn face. "The *Chargh* can go here, between nine and six, while the *Qob,* Carreon, and two of the Gorn work between seven and eight. The other Gorn ships can pierce the top, clusters one and two. We'll move the *Bloodsword* to between two and three and send the Deltans to five."

"Makes as much sense to me as anything else," Riker said. With one more glance at the screen, he returned to his position and began tapping in the new commands.

Picard checked ship's status and then stood before his chair. The screen showed a swarm of ships, some from his fleet and some Iconian. Their odd markings and composite forms disturbed the captain. It was clear these impostors were in possession of the gateway technology, and several other marvels, but they had no overriding technological structure. No sense of a cohesive anything—they seemed to be scavengers, which meant they likely knew where to find the real Iconians. That was also a worthy goal and he redoubled his efforts to get to their leader before a crazed Gorn could atomize them or they chose to self-destruct.

"All ships will be in position in ten minutes," Riker said.

"Have them fire while en route, keep the Iconians on the run," Picard said.

Riker nodded and returned to his screen. Vale acknowledged and Picard welcomed the sound of the forward phasers pounding cluster nine as the *Enterprise* moved into its own position. The screen once more filled with bright light as the battle was rejoined by the Iconians. He feared the reappearance of that torpedo but couldn't tell if they all had the weapon or just that one ship. If his scavenger theory prevailed, the latter was actually quite likely.

"Desan to Picard."

"Go ahead, Commander. How is your ship?"

"We're damaged but not dead" was all she would reveal. Sensors showed a degree of the damage but within the huge starship, the extent remained a mystery. *"We will still fight."*

"Stand by," Picard said. "We're trying to crack their defense and then surround the core ships. I hope to force a truce."

"You feel the core ships hold your secrets? It could just as easily be a lure."

"It's a risk I'm willing to take. Join me?"

"Oh, I wouldn't miss this for the world, Captain Picard." Unspoken remained the taunt of a surviving Romulan ship to report the tale back to the Empire. It rattled the captain, but he felt there was little choice.

The remaining minutes ticked by and Picard contented himself with reviewing the status reports coming from the other ships. None had remained unscathed. The Deltan and Gorn ships were terse in their reports, leaving much unsaid. They followed his orders and that would have to be enough. The *Bloodsword* seemed to be the ship with the fewest damages. He fretted the most over the *Mercury,* which might not be able to make enough repairs to sustain life. Starfleet should never have sent out a ship before maintenance was completed. Now there was a price. There was more than enough room to relocate the crew, but Picard hated the loss of any ship, recalling how bitter he felt at losing the *Stargazer* and not even being present when the *Enterprise*-D crashed onto Veridian III.

Finally, he assessed his own ship, consulting with La Forge and Crusher. *"Shields are at full power and I think I can keep them that way,"* La Forge reported from below. *"Of course, if they have any more surprises in their armory then all bets are off."*

"We'll try and wrap this up quickly," Picard assured him. He then contacted sickbay, where Crusher said there were burns, cuts, and a few broken limbs but the total was surprisingly light. *"They certainly built this one to take a beating,"* she observed.

"That they did," Picard replied, with a touch of pride in his voice. The *Sovereign*-class was the finest Starfleet's engineers had to offer, after the recent turn of events, starting with the discovery of the Borg some ten years earlier. The current crop of starships had to be more resilient, more capable of sustaining itself over time and distance.

"Any areas of concern?" he inquired.

"Nothing out of the ordinary, just your usual space fight."

"Well then we'll just wrap it all up and keep things light," he said, forcing himself to sound relaxed and perhaps more confident than he felt.

"Keep it that way," she admonished him, and cut the signal.

"All ships will be in position in one minute. Iconians firing at will," Data said.

Picard wanted to correct him. These weren't the Iconians and he didn't want that once grand name sullied by these interlopers. Still, he couldn't just call the enemy "them," and so let the insult continue.

At the thirty-second mark, Picard watched as one cluster after another suddenly stopped firing. Within another five seconds, the entire defensive alignment went silent and Picard fretted a final assault might be in the offing.

He was about to have his forces scatter when a frantic-sounding Vale interrupted his thoughts.

"Captain, message from Starfleet. The gateways have all closed down!"

Riker punched up the communiqué on his screen and nodded confirmation, not that it was needed. Picard stood still in the bridge's center absorbing the news. Were they giving in? Had they already sold the technology to some other race?

"Communications between the ships has reached an unprecedented rate," Data reported. "We are just beginning to get a sense of their algorithms, but have been unable to crack the language."

"Damn," Picard muttered. "Thoughts, Number One?"

"Same ones as you, I'm afraid."

"Picard to the fleet: approach positions but stand by."

Within seconds, Data reported the ships had achieved the charted positions and were ready to engage. It was now up to Picard, and he turned options and variables over in his mind. Indecision could be just as deadly but he had to factor in the new information. With finality, he straightened himself and asked for a hailing frequency.

"This is Captain Picard. We do not wish to prolong this battle but to reach an understanding. Our ships are now holding their position, but I am bringing the *Enterprise* to your core. We intend to open a dialogue."

His message was greeted once more with silence, so Picard asked Perim to bring the starship forward. They slipped past the ships at cluster nine without incident, giving him confidence.

Riker turned to Picard, a look of concern on his face. "New message from Admiral Ross. The gateways are active once again. Apparently, the folks on Deep Space 9 came up with a way to shut them all down, but it only worked for about ten minutes before the gateways all reset and started working again."

"Troi to Captain Picard."

"Go ahead, Captain."

"Right after the gateways shut down, the level of panic in this region increased dramatically. It has now subsided."

"Timed almost to the moment when the gateways blinked off then on," Picard noted.

"I can't tell you what that means but I would be cautious."

"We always are, Deanna," Riker said.

And the *Enterprise* crept closer to the core ships.

Chapter Eight

MOMENTS AFTER TROI'S MESSAGE, the firing started once more.

None were directed at the *Enterprise* as all the Iconian ships concentrated on those vessels outside the sphere. Vale noted this as a tactical anomaly but was cautioned against pre-emptive fire. From her reports, Picard knew the battle seemed evenly matched with no new surprise weapons being deployed. Shot for shot, there was a startling amount of parity among all the ships engaged in the fight. Picard pushed that mental note far back in his mind for later.

"Ten thousand kilometers to core ships," Perim reported.

"Steady as she goes, Ensign," Riker said.

Picard instructed La Forge to scan the area for any

out-of-the-norm readings, still wondering why they had remained unmolested within the defensive sphere. After several moments the chief engineer admitted to nothing out of the ordinary.

"Fear," Riker said.

"Of us?" Picard asked.

"Could be. We've gotten this far, maybe they think we can take them after all."

"And why not use the same torpedo attack that crippled the *Glory?*"

"Because it was all they had," Riker said, sounding speculative. "They have some second-rate ships with just a few offensive tricks up their sleeves. The piloting is uninspired, this sphere is a joke, and if Deanna's right, they're awfully scared."

"Pay no attention to the man behind the curtain," Picard said quietly.

"Sir?"

Picard smiled his first genuine smile in hours. "An early-twentieth-century bit of literature. A man out of his element used all manner of trickery to make those around him think he was some great and powerful wizard."

"Still, I'd feel better keeping the shields at maximum."

"There's no question."

"Since after all, this wizard behind the curtain may actually have a quantum torpedo."

"Of course."

The *Enterprise* drew closer and the fighting continued around it. The three Iconian ships hung in the center, close enough to potentially share shields. Picard studied their outlines and realized that unlike the other vessels, these were surprisingly uniform. Data confirmed the hulls to be entirely made from the unknown metallic composite and were built for long-distance travel with nearly fifty percent of each vessel dedicated to engines.

"Captain," Data said, "these ships have exterior armaments that appear to be of Breen design."

"Now how on Earth did they acquire that?" Picard's frown etched lines in his handsome face.

"Trade with a friendly Ferengi?" Riker said, clearly trying to keep things light.

"If these people have traded with the Breen before, why have they not dealt them the gateways yet?"

"The Breen are not an especially rich people," Data replied, "particularly after the losses they sustained in the Dominion War. It could be they could not meet the price."

"And it'll be some price," Riker noted.

"Sir, the Breen use type-three disruptors, which at this range, might cause trouble," Vale said.

"Thank you, Lieutenant," Picard said with a nod.

At that moment, the Deltan ships broke through their position, entering the sphere and scattering the remaining Iconian ships near them. The Nyrian ship followed, unleashing their unique weapon, which widened the gap.

Vale let out a short whoop in admiration of the action, which earned her a surprised look from Riker and a stern one from the captain. She returned her gaze to her station and told Picard, "The *Qob* and *Marco Polo* have punched through. The entire bottom of the sphere is compromised."

"The counselor is never going to let you forget this," Picard whispered to Riker. It elicited a chuckle from his friend. Then he said in a louder voice, "All ships within the sphere, one hundred eighty degrees about face and cover us." But once more, as the ships entered the sphere's shape, the Iconian vessels ceased fire.

"They are protecting the core ships," Data suggested.

"It's something valuable, not a trap," Picard said.

"Ensign, hold us at five thousand kilometers," Riker told Perim.

"Aye, sir."

"What did the wizard want?" Riker asked Picard.

The captain let out a small laugh. "He liked helping these people, but all he really wanted to do was go home."

Feeling emboldened by the huge amount of firepower at his back, Picard stared at the three Iconian ships before him. All manner of communication had been rebuffed and he couldn't tell why. His next actions would prove to be either the key to the mission or his downfall. Standing beside Riker, the two looked at the three ships, their dark colors and minimal running lights making them little better than silhouettes on the screen.

"Number One, I'm bringing the other ships in, closer to us. It should make us safe. When they're in position, I want you to lead a boarding party. They don't answer so we'll have to find them and ask them our questions in person."

"Aren't we violating some accord somewhere?"

"None that I can recall," Worf said. He had kept his silence, which Picard imagined had to have been hard. The Klingon also seemed remarkably unfazed by the battle. Picard had considered including Worf in the tactical discussions, but he knew that if the ambassador had had any contributions, he would not have hesitated to make them. Obviously, the former *Enterprise* security chief thought Picard's tactics to be sound for the nonce.

Picard shook his head in firm agreement with Worf's statement. "We don't know these people and they fired without provocation. I feel that gives me a tremendous amount of latitude. Take Vale and let's invite our Klingon allies to beam their own team aboard. We'll share our information with the others, but I can't trust the Carreon at this time."

"And the Nyrians?"

"We can share our data," Picard noted. "They're lost people, Will. Whatever we can do to return them home will remain a priority."

"Be nice to get *Voyager* back the same way," Riker said.

"Captain!"

Picard turned and looked at the viewscreen to see the disgruntled visage of DaiMon Bractor.

"I am most displeased I am not allowed to board the ship. Space salvage rights clearly give us an equal opportunity to participate. You'll be giving the others a clear advantage over my people."

Picard knew the *Kreechta* acquitted itself well in the just concluded battle, and he was pleased there seemed to be no lingering grudges from their first meeting. However, he disliked the pushy nature of the Ferengi, who seemed to think diplomacy was just another sales tool.

"DaiMon, I am trying to control a volatile situation. I should point out that space salvage involves derelicts and abandoned ships, not those still crewed."

"You're hiding something!"

"You've thought that of me before," Picard said as mildly as possible. "I wasn't then nor am I now. I've shared all of our telemetry to date and will continue to do so. Please stand by." He signaled for the message to be cut.

Turning to Worf, Picard continued, the Ferengi already forgotten. "Ambassador, I'd like you on the ship with the away team."

"Of course, Captain," Worf said, practically bursting in anticipation of doing something useful.

Picard turned the other way, looking at Riker. "Assemble your teams, full armaments, and you'd better bring a medic with you, just in case."

"Dr. Crusher will insist it be her," Riker said with his customary grin.

"I have no doubt," Picard replied.

Finally, some action.

It was all Riker could think about as the turbolift brought him, Worf, and Vale below to the transporter room. Picard controlled the space battle as well as any commander could have under the circumstances, but the first officer was definitely feeling the itch to do . . . something. Picard was content to analyze, study, and pore through ancient Iconian artifacts, while Riker preferred activities that involved movement—either his cooking, or his music, for example.

That was one of the main appeals to remaining first officer: the ability to be usually the first one down to a planet, meeting the unknown face-to-face. It was one thing to study them with sensors and probes and another to share a room with them, picking up on all the subtle clues you couldn't detect with instruments, no matter how sophisticated.

They stopped at the armory and were met by the rest

of the team, which consisted of Vale's security people. There was Iol, a Bolian woman who recently signed aboard; Rutger VonBraun, who was Vale's number two; and Patrice Ribero, a five-year veteran. Fine choices, in his mind, as he accepted his hand phaser. Vale couldn't keep the gleam of anticipation from her eyes and he appreciated that they shared the same enthusiasm for any mission.

Down the corridor was Transporter Room Three and as the solemn sextet strode in, he noted the absence of chatter. It was just as well, since he wasn't sure the level of danger inherent in this contact. Already inside was engineer Tomas DeSanto, who handed the first officer a tricorder, matching his own. With approval, Riker nodded at the hand phaser tucked into DeSanto's hip pocket.

Following behind them was a breathless Beverly Crusher. She had her medical bag slung over one shoulder and she too had a phaser in sight.

The instructions he gave were fairly simple: board and find the Iconian leader, learning as much without causing any loss of life.

"The *Chargh* is beaming aboard her own team," Vale warned her officers. "Knowing them, they will be even more heavily armed and without any medical support. Captain Grekor intends to place them on the opposite side of the ship since we can't tell where their command center might be."

Riker remained impressed with Vale's hard-nosed demeanor, commanding respect not only by her actions but how she carried herself. Her addition to the crew could never replace Worf or even Tasha Yar, but she was more than capable and was even willing to sample his cooking. A glance over to the ambassador showed a nod of approval on his part. She knew how to brave unknown territory.

"Which ship do we board?" DeSanto, built like a security officer but one of the gentler souls aboard the *Enterprise,* asked.

"The center one," Riker replied. "Data managed to triangulate the bulk of the communications to that ship." With that, everyone took their positions and the transporter chief sent them to the Iconian vessel.

As expected, the gravity and atmosphere were close enough to human norms that they couldn't even detect a difference. The transport brought them to an empty corridor at the prow of the ship, which suited Riker just fine. It was not as well lit as the *Enterprise,* but he could make out doors with signs in an alien script, and a dark red and brown color scheme that contrasted with his own ship. There was the tinge of an odor in the air, not offensive but clearly marking the ship as alien. The decks had bare metal floors and not much in the way of decoration. He did spot several computer interfaces down the lengthy, empty corridor.

Flipping open his tricorder, Riker scanned the area and was satisfied to see no life signs in the vicinity. With his free hand, he gestured DeSanto forward. The first officer was surprised by the bulky man's agility, but he moved quickly to the first interface and scanned it with his tricorder.

DeSanto frowned, which bothered Riker. To date, they had not been successful at piercing the Iconian communications or computer systems. Still, the engineer tapped in commands, trying to coax the Iconian computer to open up its secrets.

"Commander, we're being scanned," Vale said, holding her own tricorder up toward the ceiling.

"They know we're here, then." Riker was not at all surprised. He signaled for the engineer to return to the group. Now he had to pick a course. The lack of activity implied command was elsewhere, so he pointed with the tricorder to a juncture about fifty meters before them. In a tight group, they moved down the hall.

With several meters left, doors on either side of the corridor opened, disgorging a large number of Iconians. Riker barely had time to absorb their appearance but he noticed their yellowish skin and his last thought was of Data's own golden skin when a fist doubled him over. Okay, he admitted, they had strength.

The phaser rifles would do the team no good although Iol wielded hers as a club, taking down two Iconians with one swing. Riker's own fist connected with a chest, pushing his attack off him.

With a brief glance, Riker saw that, robes or not, the ambassador was Klingon-born and was not going to stand by idly. Instead, he hefted an Iconian over his head and tossed him down the corridor.

They were outnumbered at least two to one and he had no idea how long Crusher and DeSanto could hold on with such odds. As with their ships, the Iconians seemed to believe in numbers being a deciding factor. He also spotted that the doors remained open and seemed to reveal turbolifts.

"Vale, can you handle these goons?"

"POC," she said.

"POC?" he asked as he lashed out with his left leg, staggering an opponent.

"Piece of cake, go!"

"Commander, I will help the lieutenant and join up with you," Worf shouted, as he elbowed an attacker trying to attack from behind.

Grinning, Riker hauled one Iconian headfirst into another, freeing Crusher for a moment. He stepped over a fallen body and twisted to avoid another one being thrown by VonBraun. Finally, he stepped into the small cabin and prayed he could get the door closed. A quick study of the single control panel showed nothing intuitive, so he began pressing buttons at random until one finally snapped the door closed with a resounding clang.

Three buttons later, the lift began to move, sideways and then down. A preprogrammed destination, he suspected. As the lift moved him, Riker caught his breath and began to think about the Iconians. They appeared approximately human norm in size and shape although these had rather bland faces. Chins, Riker thought, as he focused on the details. They had little in the way of chin and their eyes seemed ill formed, as if a sculptor had not completed his work. They certainly didn't match any species he could recall and he was not terribly surprised to find them bipeds. A suspiciously high percentage of all four quadrants were designed that way.

Riker noticed the lift slowing, estimating he must have descended to the final deck of the ship.

Taking out his hand phaser, Riker touched the door stud and sure enough, it slid open, making the same racket. No sense of surprise now, he thought. He crouched low and peered out the doorway, first right then left. Another dim corridor, but this one had Iconians lined up one-third of the way. One turned his way and pointed, sounding an alarm in clear Federation Standard. That alone made Riker hesitate, but what really caught his attention was that several of these Iconians seemed to have Klingon forehead ridges. He quickly recovered and fired the phaser toward the ceiling, hoping to scatter the crowd. He turned about only to discover the lift had closed and moved on.

Scatter they did and Riker bolted in the other direction, turning left at the first opportunity, searching for either another lift or some place to hide until he could figure things out. He ran quickly, hearing sounds of pursuit, and he realized he had no idea what sort of hand weapons they possessed. So much for journeying into the unknown.

Ten meters down the new corridor, Riker heard the sound of metal grating on metal and saw an Iconian figure fly through an open doorway. This one had a Romulan brow, and pointed ears but the same yellowish skin. He then heard a sound that made him smile and he ventured toward the battle.

As expected, the Klingon landing party was having their hands full of rushing Iconians. Even outnumbered three to one, Riker could tell there wasn't even a contest. One Klingon, Captain Grekor himself, spotted Riker and grinned.

"Come, I can save one for you!"

"If it's all the same, I'm still looking for the command center," Riker replied.

Grekor hefted an Iconian over his head, the alien's arms pinwheeling in fright, and tossed him to the far side of the room. "As you wish, Commander."

Riker watched the toss and tried to figure out the room's purpose. There were control panels and miniature monitors everywhere. Of course, the writing still made no sense to him, nor did the readouts. He saluted the Klingon with his phaser, shouted *"Qapla'!"* and continued down the corridor.

The dimness bothered Riker, reminding him of how tired he was. There had been little opportunity to rest, let alone sleep. Still, he knew he was in good shape and had the endurance to go for hours more. He was hungry, though, and thought about the rations Crusher kept in her medical bag. She was nowhere nearby so he banished the idea from his mind, concentrating on negotiating his way through the alien ship.

As he turned another red and brown corner, Riker heard footsteps approach. He tried to step back but the Iconian spotted him. This one, oddly enough, looked more human than others, complete with well-groomed hair in a current Federation style. His clothes also seemed like the style of leisure wear one wore on Argelius, all bright colors and patterns, certainly going against everything he had witnessed aboard this ship to date. The Iconian's face turned angry as he spotted the Federation officer and he pulled out his own hand weapon, which seemed to glow as it touched his skin.

Riker dove forward into a shoulder roll, and then extended his form so he was practically eye to eye with the alien, too close for him to fire. The move surprised the Iconian and suddenly, Riker had him by the shirt collar, the phaser at his temple.

"Do you speak Standard?"

"Y-yes," the man stammered.

"The command center, bridge, whatever you call it, where is it?"

The man seemed to consider his options and when he took too long, Riker dug the phaser's emitter a little more into the man's temple. He noted there seemed to be a lot of loose skin there. Something to share with Crusher later.

"Two decks up, one-quarter of the way forward," he finally said in a slightly frantic tone.

Score one for diplomacy, Riker mused. He used his free hand to punch the oval control panel set into the nearest door. It opened loudly and Riker shoved the man in and fired near his feet. It did the trick, freezing him into position until the door cycled shut. One burst from the phaser fused the circuit panel, trapping the man.

Finally, some progress, he thought. Still, something was wildly amiss and Riker tried fitting the pieces together, forming a profile of the Iconians, and it was far from complete. Why were the Iconians looking like Klingons, Romulans, and humans?

He found another lift, finally beginning to recognize that their door shapes were slightly different in style than the others. Not being able to read their writing was bothersome, but he was beginning to get the hang of the technology. It only took four attempts to find the "up" toggle and he managed to stop the lift after two decks. One-quarter forward was not exactly precise, but Riker figured the closer to the command center he got, the more "helpful" Iconians he would encounter.

The door opened, Riker once more peeked out and stepped forward, phaser thrust forward. He stepped gingerly, toward the Iconians walking away from him. By following, he had hoped to locate the bridge. What he didn't expect was a pair of hands reaching him from behind and hauling him around a corner. Riker was spun against the wall and was surrounded by five men, probably one more than he could confidently handle.

Three of the five were human in appearance, like the

one he left below; the other two were the tallest Ferengi he'd ever seen. These, too, seemed in leisure clothes but armed with the same sort of hand weapons. Once again, though, Riker was too close for them to be of much use. He held his ground, hoping to learn from them. No doubt they had questions of their own.

They spoke among themselves in their native tongue; then, finally, the one on Riker's extreme left spoke to him. The voice was smooth, with almost a melodic quality that was actually pleasing to the ear.

"Why are you here?"

"I'll explain that to your leader. Where can I find him?"

"Why are you here?" This from the pseudo-Ferengi in the center.

"We've tried peaceful contact, but you ignored us. We approach and you fire on us. I think you owe my captain some explanations." Riker looked them right in the eye, which they seemed unused to. They looked away, at one another and then back at Riker's chest.

"You invade our ship and will have to pay the price." The two on his right stepped closer and reached for Riker, who was held tight. However, they ignored his legs so he kicked up, grabbing the alien in the center with a scissors hold. The five struggled, not used to fighting apparently, which Riker turned to his advantage.

With his legs, he pulled the alien toward him, forcing all five off-balance. He twisted and knocked one Ferengi down, tripping up another human-lookalike. They couldn't maintain a solid grip so Riker struggled free for a moment. One of the fallen men grabbed a leg while another reached for his weapon.

Once more, the first officer ducked down and rolled,

kicking the downed alien with his free leg. He began to rise when someone reached from behind and smacked his head into the hard metal corridor wall. Momentarily, bright lights flashed before Riker's eyes and he couldn't tell where his assailants were. His left arm swung lazily, hoping to make contact with something. Instead, it got grabbed and twisted behind his back while another hand reached for the phaser, now on the ground.

From his right, an alien kicked viciously and Riker's ribs protested and he let out a grunt. Another kick, this from the other side, and Riker knew he had to move to survive. Balling himself up to protect his body, he tried to roll forward and moved a foot or two. He then did a backward sweep kick, which managed to knock down one alien, and Riker pounced. The two struggled, rolling on the ground, each holding on to articles of clothing. The action seemed to keep the other four at bay.

But only for a moment, as two of them reached down and grabbed Riker's arms, this time keeping away from his legs. The punches began, all over his body and weakening the first officer. He started to sag, losing hold on consciousness, and began to find his mind drifting, thinking of Deanna, safely away from the battle, or of a piece of music he had been trying to master for a week.

He felt himself slip to the ground, no longer being held, but he was winded and couldn't focus. Idly, Riker wondered what became of the hitting. It seemed to have stopped. He shook his head, trying to regain his senses, find the alertness that had wandered away.

Blood had stung his eyes as he blinked repeatedly but he was pretty certain some larger figure was pummeling an Iconian. Maybe two. When he heard the battle cry, he broke into a broad smile.

"Ambassador Worf, my hero," he cracked, looking at the Klingon warrior standing atop a heap made from the five bodies.

"Will, you are injured," Worf said in that deep, welcome voice of his.

"Nothing the doctor can't cure," he replied.

Worf stepped forward and helped the commander to his feet, one arm trying to wipe the blood from the gash on the side of his head. Riker shook his head once more, letting everything regain its familiar focus.

"You came looking to ply your trade but instead, fell back on instinct. Whatever will the Council think," Riker teased.

"Not exactly . . ."

"Very exactly," Riker said, using his own sleeve to wipe at his bloody nose. "You've been stalking the command center, too."

"Yes," Worf admitted.

"It's this way," Riker said, gesturing toward the adjoining corridor. "They have strong internal sensors which have been tracking us. Have you noticed anything unusual about these people?"

"No."

"Then you haven't been looking close enough. I just fought my way through Klingons, humans, Romulans, and Ferengi, but all with yellow skin."

"A masquerade?"

"I think we just need to ask. If you'd please?"

Worf bent down and picked up Riker's phaser and tricorder, which had been knocked around during the battle. Riker accepted them, checked their functionality, and slipped them into his pockets. With each passing moment he was more and more alert, which also meant he felt each ache and pain with greater clarity. Trying to ignore them, Riker led Worf toward the corridor and they made their way to the Iconian bridge.

No one challenged the pair, which probably annoyed Worf but gave Riker a chance to catch his second wind. There was no question he would need Crusher's attention but he didn't dare contact her and possibly give away his position or compromise Crusher's. He gestured for Worf to stand on the opposite side of the door and then they raised their weapons in readiness. With his right hand, he banged on the door, knocking rather than activating the automation. The action was greeted with silence so Riker banged once more.

Finally, the door snapped open and an Iconian, one looking more like the first ones he saw, stepped into the entrance and spotted Worf. He let out a small sound before Worf clapped a large, dark hand across his mouth. He yanked the man out of the doorway, clearing space for Riker to step through.

Well, he was mussed, bloody, and less than at his best, but Riker was ready for that all-important first face-to-face contact with an alien leader.

The command center was not designed for comfort, or even efficiency, the *Enterprise* officer thought. Darker than even the passageways, the room was oblong with two large screens, showing fore and aft images. People sat in low-slung chairs, control panels to both sides. There appeared to be six such stations in a ring, three facing each screen. All six looked at Riker in horror but none dared move.

"Hi," Riker said. Worf stepped in behind him, letting

the door finally close. "Does one of you happen to be the captain?"

The Iconians proved to be less than a challenge to Grekor and his landing party, which infuriated him. These yellow-skinned weaklings might have possessed great firepower as witnessed by the crippling of the *Glory,* but they could not fight like Klingons. Trying to win a battle through sheer numbers proved nothing and was beneath his contempt.

Once the Iconians had been incapacitated or killed, he had his people fan out in the room, trying to decipher its purpose. This much technology, he concluded, meant it was a necessary location. Kliv, one of his better warriors, seemed able to learn the control panels and got it responding to his touch. This impressed Grekor, since he had never before considered Kliv as anything more than a career soldier. But one who could fight and make a computer sing was a valuable asset.

"Report," he barked at that asset.

"My best estimate is that this room is an engineering control station, my lord," Kliv said.

"Where are the engines?"

Kliv turned back to the console, knowingly risking Grekor's anger, but coaxed it into making a portion of the side wall roll back. It turned out to be an accessway to a platform overlooking a vast engine room. Now, this was something Grekor understood: a room throbbing with power. These engines could easily handle the highest warp for longer than those of either the Federation or the Klingon Empire. So, he would wrest its secrets and bring it back to Martok, insuring some victory, some advantage for his own House.

Grekor gestured for Kliv to join him on the platform. He gestured out toward the engines, idling, but still turning out terawatts of energy for the starship. "I want this ship's secrets," he whispered to Kliv. "How do these engines work? Find me that and we shall all benefit."

"My lord," Kliv began in obeisance, which pleased Grekor. Too few Klingons seemed to know their place anymore, but Kliv was well trained. Then the junior warrior turned his attention away from Grekor and down below. The captain craned his neck and watched nearly a dozen forms take shape near the engine core.

"Gorn," Grekor snarled.

"What shall we do, my lord?" Kliv asked. "They are allied with us in this."

"But they defy Picard's order," Grekor said. "He is not a man to cross."

The commander stared at the dozen grotesque forms swarming with sensors, trying to obtain the same information. He wanted to unsheathe a blade and strike a blow for Picard's honor but had to stop himself, second-guessing his gut. It galled him, but for the moment, he would look after the overall interests of his people—but he would not soon forget this transgression. Should Kahless wish it, his time would come.

"We will both have this technology, then, but they bear watching," he said in slow measured tones.

Kliv returned his attention to the control room and proceeded to coax the alien code into revealing itself.

"Captain, there has been an unauthorized transport," Data calmly announced.

Picard looked up with a look of alarm. The last thing he needed was the uneasy alliance to crumble because the Romulans or the Ferengi or the Gorn could not wait to plunder the Iconian ships.

"It came from the Gorn ships," the second officer continued.

Picard sighed. Given that they were the first to take lives despite his orders, this wasn't so unexpected.

"Picard to Captain Ralwisssh. I demand to know why your people are on the Iconian ship."

"To the victor go the spoils . . . is that not one of your phrases?"

"We are not victorious," Picard said, fighting to contain his anger. "We've merely gotten the upper hand for the moment. The gateways remain active and therefore the threat remains."

"I see it differently, but will send over no more crew," Ralwisssh said. Picard wished he could read a tone, an attitude or emotion from the voice.

Instead, Picard stood and approached Data, staring at the viewscreen, and wondered what was transpiring on the command vessel. What did these people know of the Iconians and how was his crew faring in person? Still, his primary thoughts had to remain with the fleet.

"Data, let's move our ships in an effort to corral the Iconian ships. We'll nudge them into a tighter group, making it more difficult for them to maneuver and fight or even flee. While they may outnumber us, we do seem to be in control for the moment. I don't want to waste the advantage."

The android agreed and began working out courses for the other ships, sending out signals in place of Commander Riker. In the meantime, with nothing else to do, Picard retired to his ready room, allowing himself a brief respite.

From his private sanctum, the captain ordered his favorite tea, and a small scone. Sitting on his couch, he held up a padd that contained current readings on the damaged ships. Desan and her crew seemed to have restored more power to the *Glory,* so it remained spaceworthy. He appreciated their efforts and dedication. On the other hand, the *Mercury* was having a tougher time. They remained on auxiliary power and were working nonstop to restore vital systems. Brisbayne's last report indicated his doubts as to restoring warp power and they were all too far away from the Federation to expect much backup help. Without saying so, the captain was ready to send his crew off-ship, a step before total abandonment. It no doubt hurt the career officer, and Picard had much sympathy for his plight. It was all he could spare right now; there were not enough resources all around to allow Picard to send La Forge over to lend a hand.

He gazed out the viewport and saw the three Iconian ships floating in the ether. They fascinated and infuriated him. Like a good chess master, he had surrounded the opponent, but it irritated him to not know exactly what it was he had surrounded.

What secrets could possibly be locked away on those ships and were they smart enough to discover them?

Chapter Nine

RIKER CONTINUED TO STAND impassively, waiting for someone to speak. The heavy breathing behind him would normally elicit a comment, but for now, he was just comforted to have Worf watching his back. It had been a full thirty seconds since they breached the control room, but the passive figures before him seemed more mannequin than life-form.

"Do I scare you? You'll forgive the appearance, but it was difficult finding your address. I shouldn't be scary, I'm really a nice guy. The man behind me, though, you don't want to wear out his patience. There isn't a lot to begin with." He flashed them a winning grin, not daring to steal a glance at his companion.

Finally, a man at a station toward the room's rear looked up and spoke. The voice was authoritative, although the body seemed ill formed, somewhat broad at the shoulders, and the human face certainly lacked definition. He idly thought that they sort of resembled the Changelings but with less control over their mimicry.

"I'm sorry, Commander," the man said, breaking into a smile. "This has been quite a reversal for us, as you can imagine. We're not used to that."

The first officer was surprised by the casual tone in the words, expecting something far stuffier. But he could adapt.

"Are you the leader?"

The man smiled benignly, briefly flashing flat, dull teeth. He had a fringe of dark hair from ear to ear, not dissimilar to Picard, but the unlined face offset the appearance of age. In fact, Riker wouldn't hazard a guess.

"Maybe not for the entire Iconian people," he began with a slight laugh. "But for the Alpha Quadrant, yes, I do speak for my people. I am Doral."

Riker grinned back at the unassuming figure but refused to lower the phaser. He did, though, step into the room, letting Worf further within. The bridge felt much fuller, almost annoyingly so, but he was not going to give up the advantage.

"I'd like you to order a cease-fire, and begin discussions with Captain Picard, whom you so rudely ignored."

"Oh, I wouldn't say ignored, just listened intently without much to say," Doral replied. "Still, you have me at a disadvantage so I will send out the signal."

Now Riker was getting annoyed. This leader was being too affable, showing almost no emotion. With caution, he watched Doral give brief hand signals to the officers nearest him and each hunched over the controls, tapping away. He waited, practicing patience, trying not to give away a thing. Instead, he absorbed the controls, how they were being accessed, and added it to his growing knowledge. If he had to fight his way off the ship, he would be damned if he would be caught ill prepared. No doubt, Worf was doing the same.

Doral, a little taller than Riker, but not as solidly built, turned and smiled once more. "There. I've also put out the same message throughout this ship so your people, and Ambassador Worf's, and the Gorn will no longer be at risk."

Mention of the Gorn surprised Riker, but he kept his poker face intact. Something told him, though, that Doral saw his surprise anyhow. This man seemed placid, but Riker could tell he was being measured up in much the same way. He was used to it by now, but still, these were unknown opponents and he had to think of them as such, much as he wished these were the mighty people Picard somewhat idolized.

"Thank you," Riker replied. "Now, are you ready to meet with Captain Picard and get this matter settled?"

"Actually, no," Doral said. "There are a few things I'd like explained, such as what you did to disrupt our technology. We came to your people, offering this boon, and here you are trying to sabotage it. That's not dealing with us fairly, now, is it?"

"I find it interesting how you've gone to great lengths to resemble the quadrant's key races," Riker said. "Haven't spotted any Breen, Kreel, Orions, or Cardassians around here, but I'm sure it's just a matter of looking a little harder."

Doral just looked at Riker and said nothing. The look in his eyes was not a happy one.

"I would imagine it was done for a purpose," Riker

said, hoping he could bluff through the exchange. "You have, though, ignored our pleas to turn off the devices while we and the other governments negotiate in good faith."

Doral smiled, looking deep into Riker's eyes, and the first officer started to feel more than a little uncomfortable. If he could read some tic, some movement that tipped off the bluff—he had nothing left but force and with a ship full of Klingons and Gorn, he was not going to be the aggressor.

"Of course, Commander, and perhaps we should have. But we could take this as a sign of aggression and retaliate against the Federation while continuing to negotiate with the dozen other governments in this quadrant."

"I would say, right about now, you don't have the ability to launch much of a fight," Riker said, surer of his ground. "If you've sent out the cease-fire, we'll be able to talk and settle this like enlightened beings."

Doral laughed at the word "enlightened" and waved an arm that gestured Worf and Riker further into the control room. The others remained at their stations and just watched, never taking their hands off the control panels. He and Worf looked around at everything with heavy suspicion but joined the Iconian at the far viewscreen. Doral nodded toward the closest officer and the viewscreen switched to a star map. Riker didn't immediately recognize the star patterns.

"That's the Beta Quadrant," Worf said, his deep voice startling more than one officer. "Is that where you hail from?"

"Me personally," Doral said, "no. I was born on a ship here in the Alpha Quadrant, but we've been making our way here from the Beta Quadrant, as you so quaintly put it, for quite some time. We flourished here once, and would like to do so again. For that, we will need resources and after studying the situation here, it seems the gateways were the greatest benefit we had to sell.

"You people, siding with one another and then turning on them. My people are long past that. We can't even recall our last war."

"Yet you were known as the 'demons of air and darkness,' " Worf said.

Doral paused a moment, seemingly thinking. Was he offended by the sobriquet, or was there something else? He watched the facial expression and with fewer lines to define the face, he had trouble telling. "That's a name I have not heard in a long time," he finally said. "I'm sure we seemed like demons to some of the worlds we visited but in the literal sense, no."

"It seems like you want to talk, so please, let's arrange a meeting with Captain Picard. Ambassador Worf and I should not be the ones to debate this with you."

"Perhaps, Commander, but I do enjoy the opportunity," Doral said. "But for now, I think I shall remain here."

"I do not think you should refuse Commander Riker's suggestion," Worf said in a menacing tone. Doral actually flinched at the sound, which secretly pleased Riker, but he did not want to settle this through intimidation.

Doral's eyes darted to an officer, who nodded in return. Just as Riker waved his phaser to cover the man, a transporter beam griped the Iconian and took him from the bridge. Worf's phaser fired first and the officer slumped over the console. Riker turned his weapon on the next nearest officer and inquired where the leader had gone. He was met with silence and Riker could tell it would remain that way.

"Riker to Picard," he said, stabbing at his chest emblem.

"Go ahead, Number One."

"We've found their leader, a man named Doral. However, Doral seems disinclined to meet with you and had himself beamed off the bridge. We're not sure where he went, but we do have control of the ship."

"Understood. The others have ceased the attack and we have positioned our fleet defensively. I'm sending Data and La Forge over to begin studying their technology."

"Agreed," Riker replied. "Worf and I will stay aboard to keep an eye on things."

"Very well; you'll stay in charge."

"Captain, what are the Gorn doing aboard?"

"They are there without permission but apparently have not acted violently."

"Just another wrinkle in the plan," Riker commented. "We've got it under control, so Data and Geordi can come aboard any time. I suggest they start in engineering."

"Done. Picard out."

Maybe some hot cocoa, Troi thought to herself, or better yet, a sundae. Instead, she gulped down the last of a cool cup of *raktajino* as she reviewed the latest in a steady stream of padds. The cascading effects of the fight meant one system after another had shown strain. Her damage-control teams had locked down the worst of the problem and the ship's power was almost back to normal. But it meant everyone was working without letup, in case the fighting started again. While the *Marco Polo* was a lean machine, its smaller crew meant there was little in the way of relief.

On the bridge, Hol had healed enough that he was back at his station, although his left arm was in a sling and he moved slowly. Davison had whispered to him a while ago and he actually cracked a smile so she knew he would be fine.

The turbolift doors opened and Mia Chan returned to the bridge after a checkup. While she hadn't been seriously hurt, Troi insisted the entire crew get a medical once-over just in case. She lingered at tactical for a moment, slipping her left arm through the space between Rosario's right arm and chest. Their fingers brushed one another's for a moment and she leaned into him, which resulted in a wince. Quickly, she disengaged herself and took her station.

"Dr. Buonfiglio pronounce you fit?" Troi asked mildly.

Chan turned and gave her a big smile, nodded, and returned to her readouts. She seemed very intent on looking forward, concentrating on nothing in particular. There was very little for the conn officer to do while everyone in the fleet maintained position.

The captain eased herself out of the center seat and moved forward, coming alongside Chan. "He'll be fine."

"Oh I know, Captain, but I don't like seeing him hurt."

"Only him?" she asked mischievously.

She blushed and shook her head, making the hair fly about. "Not at all! Well, okay, maybe those that fired on us, but you know I have feelings for him."

"As he seems to have for you. But I need you focused on the mission. If you can't do that, I'll have to summon relief."

"I'll be okay, Captain," Chan said, sounding all business. "No need to worry about me."

"As you have no need to worry about him," Troi finished.

Within five minutes, La Forge and Data were in the engine room, which now had more members of the alliance than Iconians. Kliv took most of the ship's complement and locked them in a nearby room, posting a guard. Klingon, Gorn, and Starfleet officers waved sensing devices over the equipment and Grekor stared with smoldering hatred toward the aliens.

La Forge thought Data was acting fine, betraying no sense of apprehension, but he suspected it remained with his friend. Despite having used the emotion chip for several years now, Data was still coming to grips with the powerful changes it effected on his perceptions of the world around him. Something like this was sure to rattle him, considering what happened the first time.

Turning his attention to the main engines, Geordi allowed his optical implants to go to work. Similar to the tricorder, his implants allowed him to scan things at almost the molecular level. He could determine the metallurgical composition of the hull plating, the kinds of monofilaments used to wire the control panels, and the number of strands in the weave of the fabric on the control chairs. La Forge never ceased to be awed by how his sight far exceeded his fellow humans.' Still, he not too long ago was also able to see the pure colors of a sunrise without artificial enhancements. He remained wistful over losing his natural sight once again but was at least aided by trusted technology.

Kliv, taller and far broader than the chief engineer,

nearly tripped over him. The Klingon swore an oath loudly but unintelligibly and Geordi took it in stride. Seeing the access panel, the Klingon also bent down, and the two men stared in through the panel.

"I see no dilithium in use," the Klingon muttered.

"Me either," Geordi said, hoping to share knowledge, which was more likely from a Klingon than a Gorn. "Their antimatter flow seems regulated through pulsed magnetic fields, which doesn't make a whole lot of sense to me."

"There is an imbalance in the warp field this engine generates as well," the Klingon said, trying to sound more like he was talking to himself than to a fellow engineer.

"I see that. The pulse seems to cause it, which also seems to form a tighter warp bubble, which I believe gives them some greater maneuverability than either of our ships."

The Klingon spat but nodded in reluctant agreement. "But I also see three types of alloy used for the housing, which also makes little sense."

"We think these ships are old enough that they have been patched with salvage. We've seen that sort of thing before," La Forge said.

The two went on exchanging technical small talk for a little while, and in so doing, seemed comfortable with their surroundings. Still, even as they moved around the engineering deck, no Gorn came near them. On the one hand, Geordi was just as pleased, but on the other, he wanted to know what they knew. He spotted one lingering near them, no doubt eavesdropping and doing a rather poor job of masking the task.

La Forge looked across the room and saw that Crusher was idly studying readouts that probably made as little sense to her as they did to him. He then looked to the left and saw that Data had literally climbed atop a control station and had removed the top paneling. Nothing seemed to stop his friend from researching the machinery and he was tempted to get his hands a little dirtier as well but decided to let his colleague start.

Data was waist-deep inside the paneling for several minutes and La Forge paused to look over the tricorder results. There was a great deal of information, some of which made sense, a lot of which seemed contradictory. His captain might have seemed somewhat in awe of these people, but they seemed awfully sloppy starship pilots after hundreds of centuries. Maybe they relied too much on the gateways and fell out of practice. He wasn't sure, but he would find it hard to take any pride in captaining ships like this one.

Suddenly, La Forge heard a somewhat muffled cry of "Eureka!"

Data scrambled out from the computer's innards and smiled at his friend and La Forge knew Data's child-like wonderment and positronic brain met up and reached a vital conclusion.

"Geordi, these people may have control of the gateways, but they are not the Iconians."

Deanna Troi could see the allure of command. It was something that fascinated her when she served with Picard on the *Enterprise*. Everyone had their own style and she had seen where Will Riker got his: a combination of not-his-father and Picard. Edward Jellico, who captained the vessel for a brief time, was bluster and hardheadedness, not to her liking at all. Even her close friend Beverly Crusher had a differing style, empathy covering a steel will that no one dared question. As a ship's counselor, Deanna found it all very fascinating, but as a ship's commander, she realized all made choices because it was how they wanted the crew to react. She had yet to really make those choices before now, and she was instinctually following her training. It meant a good rapport with this crew and she hoped it would prove correct should a crisis occur.

But right now, she was restless.

No longer aboard the flagship, she was commanding a vessel that was assigned guard duty and she missed the bustle of activity aboard the *Enterprise.* Things were quiet, the Iconian ships were at station-keeping, her crew had a chance to eat at their stations, and she sat in the command chair and felt . . . what was it Will called it once? *Ants in her pants.* She fully agreed with the description.

"Any chatter?"

Rosario looked up from tactical, amazed at the question that made her inwardly sigh. "No, ma'am. You expressly asked me to inform you and I have not been derelict in my duties."

"Thank you."

"If you're looking for something to fight the boredom," began Hol, "come look at this."

Troi rose, pacing herself, and casually approached the science station. She crossed the distance in seconds, momentarily forgetting that the *Marco Polo* was a much smaller vessel. The Tiburonian shifted in his chair and gestured at his largest panel. Displayed on it was a series of energy matrices, making very pretty, colorful patterns.

"These are from the Iconian ships?"

"Yes, the sixty-three vessels break down to these energy patterns."

"Interesting."

There was a long pause as she carefully read the breakdown of ships to power sources, wishing more than anything that Geordi were beside her to offer an explanation rather than force her to ask.

"Good work," she offered.

"And you're not sure what you're looking at," he replied, his tone serious, betraying no warmth.

"Actually, no," she admitted with a small smile.

"Counselors don't get a lot of engineering courses at the Academy, I bet," he said.

"Just the basics—and that was a long time ago," she said, letting her own warm smile show.

"We have five dozen ships emitting seven different energy signatures. For a scientifically advanced people, these Iconians seem to be using a lot of current engine types. And why not a uniform method of propulsion?"

"Very good questions, Mr. Hol. Speculation?"

Now it was his turn to pause and she liked making him think about the answer. People rose to command any number of ways, but she was fairly certain she was the only current ship's commander to come from the medical branch of Starfleet. She liked the notion but equally disliked not being able to keep up with the staggering amount of technical information most commanders seemed to have at their fingertips. Her respect for Picard was once again reinforced.

"They are not what they appear to be" was his response.

She nodded thoughtfully, picking up his pride in the analysis. "Captain Picard agrees. There's much more to this than the Iconians simply showing up to offer up the gateways for money. These may be a very diluted form of Iconian. . . ."

". . . Or not Iconians at all," Chan said.

Troi turned to see that her conn officer had been listening intently. She was grinning and seemed rather satisfied with herself. "Could be, but why such a big smile?"

"I bet a round of drinks on that answer," she said.

"There's betting on this?"

"Well, Captain Picard did not like it on the bridge," Chan said. "Sikluna had the pool going, in the galley, as soon as we got within scanner range. I lucked out and got that option. Poor Kranepool, he's my bunk-mate, got stuck with them being Changelings."

"Kid's barely more than a plebe," Hol said with a sniff. "He deserves to learn how it's done."

"Oh? And which option did you obtain?"

"Too many unknowns, so I didn't enter the pool."

Chan laughed. "He's just a chicken."

"My people tend to bet wisely with thorough analysis," Hol said in his characteristically somber tone.

"Your people haven't prospered much have they?" Davison said from her seat.

"Wait a moment," Troi said, her tone shutting down the conversation. Everyone turned to her expectantly. "We entered scanning range while I was in command, so why wasn't I invited to join the pool?"

There was a long silence as the crew exchanged surprised glances and tried to come up with answers—she could feel their anxiety. Clearly, they expected their captain to be just like Picard. She, though, was determined to lead in her own style. Chan, most of all, seemed most upset by the question, which she meant in good fun, but they took her seriously—a problem with any command.

"I can tell you why," she said, breaking the uncomfortable silence. "Because next to Ferengi, Betazoids are the quadrant's most feared gamblers. It wouldn't make a good impression if the temporary commander of a temporary crew fleeced you all. Perfectly understandable." With that she took her seat, basking in the surprise she felt from Hol, Chan, and Rosario. Davison, a more experienced officer, seemed content.

"Well, that may be true," Chan said, brightening. "But Hol just showed us these can't be the real deal so I'm going to win and the chicken here gave me the prize."

Picard was restless on the bridge. With Troi on the *Marco Polo,* Riker, Crusher, La Forge, Data, and even Worf on Doral's ship, he was suddenly without his closest allies. The captain relied on their skills as well as their counsel. A part of him was tempted to summon Dr. Crusher back to the starship just so he had someone to talk to, but he shrugged it off as foolishness.

He admitted to himself how desperately he wanted to be on the ship, be the one to study close-up these Iconians and find the answers himself. In some ways he felt cheated by his rank and allowed the frustration to eat at him, which caused him to mentally berate himself. What he wouldn't give for a distraction.

"Captain, signal from Taleen," said the relief tactical officer, a Benzite named Golik.

Well, be careful what you wish for, he chided himself. "On screen," he commanded.

Taleen's pleasant features filled the screen and he reminded himself all over again that he wanted to make time to be more welcoming to the lost Nyrians. They had proved themselves to him as they came to the fleet's defense hours earlier, so had gained a measure of trust.

"Captain, as I understand it, the Iconians' leader ran away."

Picard smiled at the image, but shook his head slightly. "Not exactly ran, Taleen, but did beam off their bridge."

"Are you looking for him?"

"We suspect he's hiding somewhere on the ship, but our people have not seen him. Why?"

"I wanted to see if you would like our help in locating him." She smiled at him, proud to be of service, and Picard warmed toward the woman.

"You know where he is?"

"Not yet, but it shouldn't take long if you want our assistance."

"Of course, Taleen, commence a search with your equipment. If you find him, let me know."

Taleen nodded off-screen and told Picard, *"It won't be a minute."*

This made Picard's eyebrows rise in question and she laughed, with a nice tone. She tried to look more serious despite her youth and explained, *"We specialize in translocators—what you call transporters. Our equipment sends out a continuous scan of the area our ship is in, ready to execute a transport at a moment's notice. The range of our equipment is much superior to yours if our experience with* Voyager *is an indication."*

"Really," Picard said, with genuine curiosity. He suspected he let his sympathy for a lost ship cloud his judgment over its capabilities.

"We can run our scans through the computer and

trace any other transport signature and . . . here we go," she said. For a moment she glanced below the camera and smiled broadly. *"Interesting. They seem to have a synchronized escape route. He went from his ship and bounced off eight other vessels before settling on a ninth ship, about ten thousand meters from the Glory."*

Picard glanced over to Golik, who punched up a tight tactical map showing the two ships. The captain nodded in appreciation and turned back to his new friend. "I thank you, Taleen. Trust me when I tell you we will help you find your way home."

"You've protected us so well, Captain, I'm trying to repay the debt. Good fortune." She ended the signal before he could reply.

"Mr. Golik, get me Desan on the *Glory*."

"What do you mean, Data?"

"Geordi, the large amount of equipment used to construct this, the flagship vessel, date at most ten to fifteen years. We have already observed that many of the defending ships seem to be patched with differing hull composites and systems technology. Everything points to this fleet of ships being scavengers from the Alpha and Beta Quadrants. Furthermore, none of the language on this ship resembles the iconology we witnessed on Iconia nor does it match the known roots of the Icco-bar, Dewan, and Dinasian languages which we already know to be formed from Iconia."

"Which explains the fifteen different energy signatures," La Forge added, feeling heightened emotions. He was genuinely getting excited at finding the truth, although a part of him knew this would crush Picard.

"Exactly. Based upon the data gleaned from the three gateways encountered prior to this current situation, there was a uniformity to the technology. That is not at all exhibited here."

"So who are they?"

"That, my dear Watson," the android said with a smirk, "remains a mystery."

La Forge inwardly groaned, not feeling like playing the able assistant to fiction's greatest detective personified by Data. It was fine for the holodeck adventures they shared, but on a mission it could prove distracting.

"We'd better inform Captain Picard," the engineer said slowly. He tapped his combadge, gave his report, and could hear Picard's all-business tone. He tried to sense the real feelings but his captain had spent a career masking them when necessary and for now, he would keep those personal feelings bottled up. As he made the report, the Klingons drifted over and listened, some nodding in agreement with Data's revelations.

"Commander, I think it's time Dr. Crusher examine one of these people and see if we can trace where they're really from."

"Fine," La Forge said, appreciating the extra familiar hands. "We'll find a volunteer."

"Please bring Mr. Riker up to speed, I'll start making my report to Admiral Ross. Picard out."

That's one disappointed man, La Forge thought. He tried to imagine what it must have been like to study a race as legendary as the Iconians, get your hopes up about meeting them, and then have them dashed to find out these were frauds. Not especially good ones at that.

He would want to smack the leader, but suspected that wasn't in Picard's character.

"You have a volunteer for me, Geordi?" Crusher asked, getting right to work and not even bothering to look around. She was in full doctor mode.

"Allow me, Doctor," Grekor said. With a hand gesture, two of his largest men strode out of the engine room.

As they waited, La Forge walked over to Data, laid a hand on his shoulder and said, "There was nothing to worry about after all."

"True," his friend replied. "Still, these may not be the Iconians but the gateways most certainly are. When we encounter them, my concerns will remain valid."

La Forge shook his head, unable to convince his friend to avoid fear. It was one of the toughest lessons any sentient being had to learn and Data was proving no different.

The doors snapped loudly open and the Klingons returned with a very frightened Iconian woman between them. They marched her directly before Crusher and with hands on the woman's shoulders, forced her to her knees.

"Don't worry, she won't vivisect you," Grekor said, trying to sound cheerful.

"We value our privacy quite highly," the woman said in a voice that was almost a squeak.

"I think you gave that up when the first shot was fired," Crusher said, sounding displeased.

Geordi, Data, and the Klingons stood back and watched as Crusher ran her Feinberger over the woman's body once, then twice. The doctor was constantly checking her medical tricorder and made little sounds to herself. This went on for several minutes and she did her best to ignore the impatient shuffling of the warriors' boots nearby. She reached into her bag and pulled out a hypo.

"Madame," she said to the frightened subject, "I'm going to take a small sample of your blood for a more complete analysis. I promise, this won't hurt."

"Please don't," she said, the first words since the exam began. The Iconian began squirming, twisting her shoulders to keep her arms away from the doctor, who did not seem amused.

Grekor, who had been watching from a distance, walked to the small grouping and stopped directly before the Iconian. His towering form loomed over the group and clearly, this woman had never seen a Klingon before. The eyes riveted the woman stock-still although her legs seemed to quiver just a bit. La Forge stifled a chuckle.

"lo'laHbe'," he muttered as Crusher extracted a small amount of copper-colored blood. When she was done, Kliv strolled casually back to his group of engineers.

"What did he say?" the woman asked La Forge.

"Sorry, I don't speak Klingon, but it didn't sound good, did it?"

Crusher connected the device containing the blood to her tricorder and set both down on a countertop. She fed in some information and then stepped back, waiting for the analysis to be completed. Both the doctor and chief engineer remained aware and concerned that as long as the gateways remained operational untold disasters could occur.

Nagging in the back of his mind, though, was the notion that these sixty-three ships might not be the entire fleet of Iconians . . . or whatever they turned out to be. If there were more out there, this small group of ships could never hold them off.

* * *

Picard was seated in his ready room, his ignored tea cooling rapidly, as he completed the report to Ross. He regretted revealing the aliens' duplicity, fighting off the sense of disappointment, and continued with a dry recitation of the known facts. Before completing the message, he added an additional note about the Nyrians, making it clear they were helpful allies and were to be accorded all due assistance from Starfleet when the time allowed.

A part of him yearned to bring his Ressikan flute up from his quarters and play the melancholy tune he learned years earlier. He found it brought him great comfort and relieved some of the tensions of command. Still, he pushed the notion away, since he still was holding together a coalition of species, outnumbered by potentially hostile ships with its leader refusing to deal with him. There was no time for personal needs—or so he convinced himself.

He sent off the report in a subspace squirt, estimating Ross would receive it within three hours. Deftly, his fingers played on the controls and called up the tactical display. All remained as it should be, which gave him some measure of relief. The captain thought he should consider himself lucky that they had lost but one ship. True, the Gorn displayed more of an independent streak than he would have liked, but they were mostly behaving themselves. All along, his instincts told him to be wary of the Romulans, but Desan remained an exemplary officer. When he reached her earlier, asking that the crippled *Glory* move closer to the ship harboring Doral as a safety precaution, she agreed without question. There was little doubt that everything seen and heard was being recorded for later analysis. That report would concern not just these aliens but how well the Federation ships and Picard in particular handled the situation. The Romulans were an arrogant bunch, he knew, but they still studied their opponents carefully.

"Crusher to Picard."

He was pleased she was getting in touch, afraid he would let things get even more maudlin if he remained on his own much longer. How he missed having his familiar crew with him. "Go ahead, Doctor."

"My conclusion supports Data's: these are not Iconians."

He let the words sink in, their finality feeling enormously heavy. "I see," he said, expecting the news. "Any chance of a biological link?"

"None I can see on first analysis," she replied.

"A match to any race we recognize?"

"No, Jean-Luc," she said.

"Data, given this information, can we conjecture who they are?"

"Our analysis indicates they come from outside the Alpha Quadrant but have made significant upgrades to their ships with familiar material," Data said.

"My thinking is," La Forge added, *"they're a long way from home so this is a first-contact situation."*

"I concur," Picard said, feeling like they were finally starting to get a handle on the situation. "But how did they manage to control the gateways?"

"I'm not sure," Geordi said. *"I do think they are responsible and have some highly sophisticated systems I can't pierce as yet."*

"Captain," Crusher added, *"although these so-called Iconians appear human, with standard color variations and markings, I also see old evidence of cel-*

lular tampering. Everything is organic, but not necessarily material they were born with. I believe this is elaborate makeup."

The conversation lasted another few minutes as they shared notes on the ship, its largely docile crew, and what the next step needed to be. As far as Picard was concerned, there was still the matter of Doral's escape that made him concerned. None of this, though, brought them closer to the gateway problem itself.

They were interrupted by a large noise and Picard overheard distinctly Klingon tones coming through the comlink. A few moments later, Captain Grekor came within range and bellowed, *"There is a gateway on this very ship! It's active, but we don't recognize the locations. With this, we can seize control."*

"Every other gateway was located on a planet, moon, or asteroid," Data observed. *"They must have transplanted one here."*

"Excellent work, Captain," Picard interrupted. "Mr. La Forge, check the power consumption rates on the ship and Mr. Data, begin an examination of the control mechanism. I'll take this time to track down Doral."

There was another commotion, so his crew's comments got garbled, but something unexpected happened. As usual, Picard yearned to be present but was left in command. Gripping the now cool mug in his left hand, he squeezed it tight.

"This is Ulisssshk of the Gorn Hegemony," the slow, rasping voice said over the link. *"Iconians or whatever you call yourselves know this: we will be given control of the gateway technology or this ship and those around it will cease to exist in two minutes."*

"I order you to cease this threat," Picard practically

yelled. With deft fingers, he called up sensor readings on the ship directly before the *Enterprise*. He punched in commands to look for energy signatures from engineering as the Gorn replied.

"We see no true bargaining going on and my lord commands me to take the lead," Ulisssshk growled.

"You are here at the Federation's invitation, after we helped your people during a time of crisis," Picard reminded him, hoping to find the cause of the threat and neutralize it from the *Enterprise*. Nothing was apparent other than an ominous energy buildup near the engines themselves.

"You acted foolishly," Picard continued urgently. "These people will surrender nothing with their leader, Doral, off the ship. He's as likely to sacrifice them as your are to sacrifice my crew. Data, Grekor—clear engineering."

With just over a minute left, Picard weighed options, unwilling to sacrifice any of his crew.

"Transporter room, prepare to use the cargo transporters to start evacuating that ship," Picard said.

Chapter Ten

THE SUN WAS NAMED RAO, after an ancient god of a religion long since abandoned by the people. It had shaded to red since recorded history first noted its size, shape, color, and illumination. Science rapidly replaced religion on this world, which saw one golden age after another.

But the inhabitants knew it would have to end one day. A red sun meant it was cooling, and someday, millennia hence, it would no longer be able to support life.

With a keen sense of self-preservation, the people had colonized other solar systems, and their culture was assured survival. Those who still lived on the mother planet enjoyed a high place in the social strata and with continuity now guaranteed, Sir Leop la mir Werstin, current lord of the planet, declared a new Golden Epoch had begun.

That was a month earlier. Now, Sir Leop sat in an empty palace chamber, head in his hands. Short, stubby fingers played idly with the twelve long braids denoting his supremacy. Courtiers who normally attended his every need had fled for their families. His own wife and three children were en route to the winter castle on Glavir, the coolest continent.

With tears in his eyes, he gazed once more up at the sun, the giver of life. It burned a deep red and filled nearly half the sky. Global temperatures were up, small lakes and ponds were losing water, and the air was filled with a cloying humidity. There had been widespread panic as they noted the sun grew in size by the day and now by the hour. Pockets of the lowest-educated people resurrected the old religious beliefs, praying to Rao for deliverance.

Master Oli ma fen Cordiek, Sir Leop's chief scientist, could only provide details on the phenomenon, not its cause. Their beloved sun was going nova so far ahead of schedule that no one could fathom it. The morning's projections showed that at best, the planet's population had weeks or days left to them. Werstin had sighed heavily at the news, aware there was no chance to send even a tenth of the people to one of their colony worlds. Master Oli's report was his people's death sentence.

"Why?"

"Because of the doorway."

The lord of the people looked up, not at all expecting a response to his rhetorical question. Entering the chamber was one of the lesser scientists, one not even at the master level in training or experience. Werstin struggled to summon forth a name but failed.

"The doorway that appeared on the island of Feld,"

the scientist continued unbidden. "As soon as it began to operate, it drew energy from the solar batteries. The longer it remained in operation, for whatever reason, the demands of energy increased exponentially. Something happened and it began sucking the life from Rao."

"Then we shall destroy the doorway," Sir Leop proclaimed, in his usual royal voice, but it echoed around the empty room.

"My friends on Feld tried, Your Majesty. They tried and failed. Our weapons cannot seem to breach its defense."

"Devils! What is this doorway? Where did it come from?"

"It had always been there, I'm told; found some hundreds of years ago and thought to be from the Second Golden Age."

Sir Leop thought about that, not up on his history. Nothing occurred to him of the Second Golden Age.

"Others theorize it was left by the Demons."

New insight appeared in Sir Leop's tired eyes. "The Demons of Air and Darkness! This is their doing? But they are myth!"

"The doorway says otherwise," the scientist said, dropping all pretense regarding titles and ranks. Had Sir Leop been focused, he would have been insulted.

Instead, he sat silent, brooding over the revelations brought to him that day. After all, it wasn't every monarch who got to oversee the ending of life as he knew it.

From ship ES135659, Doral was also seated and given over to great thought. Plans that should have gone flawlessly had backfired. He, the pod leader in control of the mission, had to escape from his own command ship, separate himself from his pod. Desperately, he needed time to think and regroup.

Ili, his eldest podmate, was now running the flagship and she had called to alert him to the Gorn threat. Although they had grown from the birth pod together, Doral was still uncertain if Ili could command with authority. It was not her strength. With less than two minutes to act, he was faced with utter destruction and failure for overplaying his hand. Could he reason with Picard, not someone he was mastered for, but certainly of the same breed? Maybe, but it would be moot if someone did not stop the Gorn. Perhaps he would have to bluff his way through a negotiation with the Gorn, find a way to stop the explosive, and then escape. They were so alien to him, he wasn't certain he knew how to act. All his training was for humans. A different podmate had studied the reptilian race and was unavailable.

Quickly, he signaled ES135659's captain, and relayed a terse instruction. Then, he tried to raise the Gorn ship, hoping everyone measured time in the same way.

In the command center, Worf quickly surmised the situation belowdecks. Without waiting for Riker to notice him, he tapped his communicator and ordered the *Chargh* to send him from the bridge to engineering.

"What do you think you're doing, Ambassador?"

"Saving your neck," Worf said. Before Riker could object further, Worf, gripping his *d'k tahg,* dematerialized.

All his training from children's games on Gault to his Academy training and experiences in Starfleet would come in to play as he had to vanquish his opponent in time to stop the explosive. Knowing Picard, he presumed the captain would beam his people from the ship, taking as many of these faux-Iconians as possible. Grekor would also retreat, he suspected, knowing the captain would rather fight from strength than blunder blindly in the name of honor.

Free of the transporter beam, glancing just once around engineering, he spotted three Gorn keeping watch over a console. Holding the personal blade in his right hand, Worf snarled a challenge at the reptilian beings. They moved slowly, turning their bodies toward him, their faces unreadable.

"This ship blows in a minute if these aliens don't give in to the demands," one of the Gorn warned Worf.

"You will be dead long before if you do not disable the device," Worf retorted.

That was all one of the Gorn needed to hear and he raised his left arm, pistol mounted at the wrist. He fired off one shot but Worf was nowhere near his original position. Instead, he had ducked, rolled, and lunged forward, his floor-length ambassadorial vest making him appear larger than he was. His momentum carried him forward, and he barreled into the trio. One grabbed at his sleeve, while another lost balance and fell. Worf's blade found the third, sticking him in the abdomen.

His left fist found a snout and his leg kicked out, striking the already downed Gorn. It felt good to strain his muscles, fight for a worthwhile cause. It was like shaking off the cobwebs and coming to life once more.

The downed attacker stayed that way and the one he sliced open made an odd, mewling noise, quite unlike anything Worf expected. All that remained was the one clutching at him, his talons biting through the layers of fabric and actually ripping open his skin. He knew enough to avoid the sharp teeth and continued to use his greater flexibility as an asset. He wriggled around, maneuvering his body so he could clasp a crushing bear hug on the Gorn. Planting his feet firmly on the deck plating, Worf hefted the Gorn into the air and smashed him to the ground.

With the *d'k tahg* at the Gorn's throat, Worf asked, "Will you disable the device?"

"So you see, Ralwisssh, we had no idea you were this interested in the technology to this degree. I have some of the technical schematics here to offer you as a sign of good faith. In turn, you can disable the explosive."

Doral felt the sweat begin to itch his chin, a flaw in the duraplast process which his people had never managed to correct. He ignored it, gazing at the viewscreen with as much sincere intent as he could muster. While he was used to reconstruction to deal with potential clients, he did muse for a moment that he was glad they didn't initially target the Gorn. Better his podmate endure the lengthy reconstruction.

His opponent seemed to consider the offer longer than expected, and Doral mentally counted down. They were at thirty seconds, maybe less, and time was against him.

"I agree to the terms. Once we receive these schematics, we will turn off the device."

Anticipating the move, Doral was prepared and stabbed a control as the words were still being heard.

"Done."

Ralwisssh was taken aback by the speed of the action, but also flicked a control that might have been the signal to his people aboard Doral's own vessel.

"Received. We thank you."

Doral faced the screen, but glanced with his eyes on the readouts from ES135659 and he saw the energy spike start to recede. There had to have been scant seconds left. He disliked doing what he just completed, but it was a necessary part of the overall program. Survival was all.

The Gorn had completed dismantling the complex wiring that forced the overload when his communicator beeped deep within his tunic. He started to reach for it, but Worf made a sound that conveyed his disapproval. As the beep continued, Worf checked his mental calculations and determined that the time had past—the ship should have been rendered into scattered atoms but nothing happened.

From behind, a door swished open and the ambassador heard the cries of victory from his fellow Klingons. Several got to him and they were smacking him on the shoulders. It felt good, but less than genuine, and he felt resentment start to build up. Before he could wave them away, they fell a step back, clearing a space for Grekor.

The older officer strode toward Worf, a look of consternation on his face. He kicked aside the wounded Gorn, ignored the other subdued saboteurs, and faced the ambassador.

"Has this one finished?"

"He has, Captain," Worf replied.

"Then why is he not dead?"

"He may have intelligence we can use," he said.

"Wise answer. *Qapla'!* You did well, Ambassador. Now, we have this ship and within it a gateway. We shall be victorious this day and your role will not be forgotten."

With a gesture, two Klingons flanked the Gorn, and Grekor headed back to the gateway, his crew following. Worf fell into line, having done enough in engineering. There was little need for him on the bridge and with his blood now racing, he chose to remain at the locus of activity.

As they walked, Grekor fell into step with the ambassador and grinned at him. Worf inwardly sighed, unable to extricate himself from the man's gaze.

"The House of Krad is a small one, I know," Grekor began. "But I've checked, and my *be'nI'*, Rorka, remains unattached. A man like you could benefit from a woman's companionship. Shall I arrange an introduction when we return to Qo'noS?"

Stuck, Worf was uncertain of the proper answer. He, of course, had no interest in meeting this man's sister, but he had less wish to insult the captain. Were he anything but an ambassador, Worf could hurl out an insult and be done with it. Instead, he represented not the homeworld, but the Federation.

"I shall . . . consider it."

"The Gorn ships are powering up," Perim said.

Picard bit back a curse. For all his good intentions, the alliance was proving shakier than he had hoped after all.

"Have we checked out the transmissions fully?" he asked Golik.

"There was definitely information exchanged between an Iconian ship and the Gorn."

"And of course, we still haven't cracked their communications code," Picard said quietly. "Put the Gorn on screen."

The Gorn ships hung against the stars looking innocent. Within, he knew, were people operating under their own agenda. In silent alarm, Picard saw them break formation, turning about. He didn't have to ask where they were going; the only place for them was their home. What, he wondered, did they take from the Iconians? It was not likely the gateway technology, so what could it be to make them break apart the alliance?

"Shall we pursue?" Perim asked.

"No, Ensign," Picard said sadly. "We won't fragment the fleet further. Alert Mr. Riker of the news."

He strode toward his ready room, his mind racing with new configurations of the alliance ships. Without the Gorn, there was little chance he could expect the Iconian ships to stay in line. With Doral also running free, it was clear something would happen— and soon.

Without sitting down, Picard punched some information into his desktop display and looked at the readings. He then tapped his badge and put his next gambit into motion.

"Picard to Taleen."

"How can I help, Captain?"

"Just how good are your translocators?"

She laughed and it lightened his spirits for a moment. *"Better than your transporters I would think."*

"Could you then help me move some of my people around? I think it's time I meet with Doral face-to-face, and he does not seem interested in doing so."

Once more she laughed and agreed to help. He outlined his plan and asked her to execute it within the next fifteen minutes.

"Picard to quartermaster," he next commanded. "Prepare a room for an Iconian guest. Also, have the conference room on Deck Four ready in the next ten minutes, please."

Okay, maybe this wasn't the best place to be, Riker mused.

He stood in the Iconian command center and had somehow managed to lose their leader, Doral, then miss out on helping stop the Gorn's treachery. It had actually gotten downright boring just walking around the command center, looming over the frightened Iconians. He did note that all of them seemed to be in their natural appearance, not at all needed for the fantasy of universal unity.

After Worf beamed below, Riker had plenty of time to consider exactly why the Iconians would need to imitate the various races. In fact, he had some theories and had sounded out the Iconians who remained at their station, usually avoiding his glance. Since they wouldn't chat, he needed to try them out on someone so he ordered a link established with the *Marco Polo*. With relief, he saw that Troi seemed fit and even happy in her temporary role.

"Bored, too?" she began the conversation. He was impressed she could tell from such a distance but after all, they had known each other so well, for so long.

"A little," Riker admitted. "How goes your crew?"

"Fine. A little beaten up but they're young and have learned from the experience," she replied.

"I have a theory and want to run it by you," Riker said. He briefly outlined his discovery of the Iconians' detailed makeups and the races represented. "I think these people are scam artists on a rather large scale. The makeups are intended to imply some form of genetic link to a common ancestor. Lull the governments into working with the Iconians rather than study them."

"That's an interesting conclusion," she said. *"My crew was wagering on them being anything from a rogue offshoot of the true Iconians to the legendary long-lost fleet from Acaramenia."*

"But does it make sense?"

She looked directly at the camera and Riker felt her gaze, taking strength and comfort from it. He was never happier to have rekindled their romance. *"It does, Will, and it's an excellent deduction. Captain Picard will agree, I think."*

"Thanks, Captain Troi, I look forward to seeing you when this is over."

"As do I, there's much to thank you for," she said, and Riker saw an expression cross her face he wasn't entirely certain he liked.

He disliked being stuck on this smaller ship, with its high-backed seating and oily smell. It had been picked up when it was apparent the pod would grow long before they could get another ship from home. Doral was not fond of adding alien technology without an overall plan; it disturbed his sense of order. The ship was also in constant need of maintenance with precious little time available for such matters.

Doral preselected escape to this ship for the very reason that it was weak and likely to be overlooked by the various sensors, which had ceaselessly been probing his fleet. Of course, he had done the same with each ship encountered since entering the Alpha Quadrant a year earlier. From their records, none of his ancestors had been to this section of space for something like eighty years. It made Doral wonder what would have directed his people away from such a quadrant, teeming with intelligent races, but it was not for him to ask that aloud. The people's leadership would be the ones to question, probe into their past and chart their future.

He did know the pod that did find the first gateway did so at great cost. Lives were lost and the first gateway might not have been worth the effort. As he learned from his teachers, the gateway that arrived on his homeworld took many lifetimes to master and even then, the one they field-tested elsewhere in the quadrant flickered inexplicably on and off. The greatest engineering minds tried to master the alien technology, he was taught, and they had come only so far. It had been decided to send the pods back to the quadrant, trying to find the aliens who originally built the wondrous devices or someone who knew how it worked.

Times had gotten tougher for his people, Doral was told when given his ship. Their drive to explore the farthest reaches of the galaxy, and set up colonies, meant they were spread exceptionally thin—too much so, as they had lost contact with one colony after another. No doubt the colonies established themselves and then went farther out among the stars. It meant his people controlled vast portions of space, but it also meant they lacked cohesion and as an empire teetered on the edge of collapse.

Doral's team was to acquire more technology, maybe even the keys to the gateways, to once more reestablish contact with the far-flung people.

At first, their studies showed no one using the devices, going so far as to ignore them entirely. It then became apparent no one knew what they were. Their builders, he came to learn from tapping into computers from derelict starships left over from the just-concluded war, had gone from fact to legend. No race seemed to possess a similar enough technology to allow Doral to make a substitution, and he was left in need of ships for their growing pod family and supplies for the next leg of their never-ending journey. All contact with home had ended before they even reached the quadrant, and Doral was left to his own devices.

Such thoughts occupied him as he sipped at his bowl of tepid soup. The ship's cook had thrust it upon him, a woman he had never met before. There was something comforting about her natural appearance, while he retained his human masquerade. He would have to deal with Picard, but how could he gain some advantage, any advantage over the human? How could he acquire what he needed to go forward since back was not an option?

The door to the galley seemed to sizzle, waver, and then melt in a matter of seconds, letting people gasp and little else. For a mere moment, the pod leader thought the oily air itself might burst into flame. Doral began to rise and as he did, three Federation people burst into the room, equipped in protective armor, phaser rifles swinging back and forth like a pendulum. The one in the center pointed directly at him and the other two surged forward, flanking the confused leader as he completed rising.

They gripped him firmly, maybe even a little roughly. As soon as they had him in their grasp, the remaining one tapped a control on the armor and suddenly Doral was caught in a transporter beam. His last thought before the beam fully caught him was how tasty the soup had been.

The putative leader of the Iconian people appeared in a transporter bay, on a ship he presumed to be the *Enterprise*. More security officers awaited him, and he didn't bother speaking to them, since his chances to play off their petty interests and effect an escape seemed poor. It seemed, also, that if they could punch through his transporter defenses once, they could repeat it before he could improve the screens. Affecting a docile manner, he quietly followed the security detachment through the corridors and he took in the sights. What he caught first was the harmonious blend of color that suffused the ship. Clearly, this was designed to comfort the crew and visitors. Black paneling split the walls in two, and from its polished sheen, he imagined these were computer interfaces with touch-sensitive surfaces.

The people who passed him by gave him a glance but continued on their way, but Doral soaked in their variety. A mixed crew, male and female, human and other assorted races. Truly, everything the Federation had boasted about their harmonious ways was true, which probably meant everything else they told him was mostly true. Not every race was so forthcoming, Doral knew. His own history was spotted with despots hoping to take advantage, swindlers, cheats, and outright thieves. There were, of course, other races he had cheated out of technology or resources. To him it was all part of a galactic game of repositioning resources, with his sole objective being that of helping his people.

The walk stopped before wooden doors that slid open soundlessly. Inside the room was a long table with chairs. Decorating the walls were images of other starships, starscapes, and one captivating image of a molten pit spewing forth lava like a geyser. But Captain Picard, standing at the table's head, riveted his attention. He gestured for the security detail to leave and then it was just the two of them in the room. Picard was not especially tall, or physically imposing. For a human, his lack of hair or muscle should have made him something less than a commander. This puzzled him until the man spoke; then he understood.

"Welcome to the *Enterprise*," Picard said.

"A pleasure I truly wanted to enjoy, but at a time of my own choosing." He had little in the way of options, but practice and habit forced him to stretch out the conversation.

"You left me little choice," Picard told him. The voice had a charm to it, a cultured quality lacking in many of the humans he had dealt with. Certainly none of the ones from Starfleet itself. He then gestured to the chairs as he sat down himself. Doral took one close enough for a civil conversation. He had to continue projecting the same sense of confidence that had gotten him this far even though he had no clear-cut idea how to excise himself and his people from this problem.

"I have a great deal of respect for history," the captain continued. "This part of the universe can trace intelligent life back for hundreds of thousands of years. Some races we know of by legend, others by the little bits and pieces that have survived. The one that I've studied the longest has been the Iconians."

He let that hang and Doral was faced with two

choices: further deception or the truth. Picard had dealt fairly to date, but giving up their plan was rarely done and it galled him.

"I must disappoint you," Doral said, letting the scene play out, hoping to chart its course before too much longer.

"Oh you do," Picard replied coolly. "Very much. Technology to have survived intact and still function after two hundred thousand years is remarkable enough but for the technology to transport instantaneously, that's the stuff of legend."

"We weren't called the demons of air and darkness by every planet we visited," Doral said. "Just the less sophisticated ones."

"Legends have a funny way of growing over time so the original picture can get distorted. In my days at the Academy we swapped tall tales of officers who preceded us. Ones who single-handedly stopped war or bedded an admiral's son during exams and still graduated. We even told stories that couldn't possibly have happened but were there in the records. Garth, Pike, Rabin, Garrett . . . the giants among legends.

"Every so often, you actually get to meet one of these legends in person. You get to gauge for yourself if the man matches the myth. I had such an opportunity when I met Captain James T. Kirk and he was even larger than the legends. That impressed me."

Picard seemed very contemplative, not at all angry or upset with Doral, which confused him. These names meant nothing to him and his training had no instances of great exploits drilled into them. As they approached each new sector of space, current events filled his data screens. What had been acquired, how it had helped reshape his people, where they were growing next. All this talk of his, frankly, baffled him.

"A very few get to meet legends. I consider myself fortunate, because in my career, I've met far more than my share. I should have been satisfied, but in the back of my mind I held out the tiniest shred of hope that I would figure out what happened to the Iconian people. You can imagine, then, what it was like to be told we'd deal with one another."

Finally, an opportunity and Doral sprang for it. He grinned and said, "Your career has turned you into a bit of a legend, hasn't it?"

Picard seemed thoughtful, almost embarrassed by the concept. "I suppose, in the natural course of things, students today can look at my record with the same feelings I had when I studied Decker or Harriman."

"The admiralty spoke very highly of you, actually, so I suppose the legend can run both up and down the scale. While I may disappoint you, you certainly live up to the reputation." Doral admonished himself to be wary of using too much flattery.

"Disappoint is perhaps the mildest word I can think of," Picard said. His brow turned inward for a moment. "The one word I keep returning to, though, is fraud."

He stopped talking and let it hang in the silent conference room. No doubt the captain had figured out they were not the Iconians, so prolonging the conversation seemed pointless. Truth or silence?

Was there any doubt, he asked himself.

"We're a dying race, Captain," he finally said. And this time, he let the silence hang over the two of them. Picard's expression changed quickly, from anger to

confusion to concern and then passively back to inquis-
itiveness.

"Who are you?"

Doral took two deep breaths and then began: "We're
the Petraw. For a quarter as long as the Iconians have
been gone, my people have explored the galaxy. We're
bred this way, to explore and acquire, building out our
empire. One continent, long ago, led to a planet, to a
solar system, then two, then more. Whatever we managed to acquire through trade or guile was always sent
home for study and application to the race.

"Imagine, Captain, over fifty centuries of growth and
expansion, always being driven further among the stars.
Our birthing planet became a legend, some unvisited
place you sent your belongings to. My pod was born in
space, far from home, but the drive remained. To survive, pods began to pair up, keeping what we needed to
get further in our quest, and sending the rest back by
drone. There was never acknowledgment of receipt or
news from home. We're too far apart and can't return."

As Doral paused to calm himself, he looked over at
Picard, who now seemed thoughtful, his real chin resting on top of his knuckles. Whatever anger was in this
room previously had dissipated and all that remained
now was the confession.

"Why this deception?"

"My people found this technology years ago, on our
last visit to this section of space. You draw your maps
into quadrants and sectors, but from our frame of reference, it's all nonsense. We know no territorial boundaries and can't imagine fighting over imaginary lines in
space. It took us years to figure out what it did and how
to make it work.

"Not long ago, we lost contact with the other pods. Our thinking is we've drifted too far apart and now we're isolated, alone in space. You might turn around and go home; we can't. We're driven to go forward. Whatever is left of our empire is a matter of speculation and we rarely indulge even in that.

"We're running out of space, running out of time and resources. To acquire what we needed required a major infusion of something—raw materials or currency—to buy better ships and equipment so we could continue our lineage. We thought of the gateway device, offering such a wonder for the most money."

"You just found it," Picard repeated in a neutral tone.

"Years ago, in what was once the edge of the Federation. It was brought to my homeworld and studied."

"You've never even met an Iconian, yet you plunder their legacy," the captain said, this time with some heat. It made Doral feel small despite his greater physique.

"Before recently, we've never even heard of them."

"Turn them off and leave."

This was unexpected. Doral thought at the very least that the vaunted Federation would offer some assistance. He was just beginning to count on it, thinking it would be the best he could expect given the way this operation had fared. Certainly the Federation would offer something and leave them alone, unlike, say, the Klingons, who would merely use them for target practice.

"No."

Picard eyed him carefully and Doral could sense the penetrating stare. This was no longer a history lecture or a listing of disappointments. It wasn't even diplomacy anymore. For Picard, this was personal and that was unexpected.

"No?"

Doral considered and felt he had revealed this much truth, what did it matter if the rest came out?

"We can't."

"You can't what?" There was steel in the voice and he knew he was bested.

"We can't turn off the gateways, but we can leave."

Picard's brow knit once more, clearly absorbing and calculating the information just received. Doral recognized the feeling, one he had to employ time and again. "You dared to turn on something with such far-reaching implications with no way to disable the system?"

"No, not really, well, yes." He began to feel stupid, which eroded whatever was left of his bargaining position. "This wasn't a careful ploy, this was desperation." Doral's statement came out flatly and he merely nodded, no longer feeling like bantering. Or saying much of anything.

"Is there anything else you've done that was as stupid?"

"Not that I can think of."

At that moment, Picard's communicator came to life with a call from the bridge. *"Perim to Captain Picard. Sir, the Gorn ships just blew up."*

Chapter Eleven

"WHAT?" PICARD STOOD, staring angrily at Doral, who merely wanted to hold what little ground he had left. Right now, though, it was beginning to feel more like water than dirt.

"As they were exceeding warp four, there seemed to be some sort of chain reaction and they all had warp-core breaches."

"Full sensor scans, alert the other captains. Picard out."

He stared at the Petraw leader.

"I had to save my ship. I promised Ralwisssh and Ulisssshk the gateway schematics but sent them a bit of software we bartered from the Relisa. It overwrote their engineering systems and forced the breaches."

Picard stared, took a breath, and said in a low tone, "My God, have you no conscience?"

Doral hung his head and said, "I am desperate to save my people."

Picard was left speechless. Everything he expected when he left Earth had failed to materialize and now he found himself with a new race in desperate straits. Worse, they unleashed a threat to the galaxy that had no obvious resolution. He felt equal parts pity, compassion, and fury for Doral and his Petraw.

"I'm sending teams from my ships to oversee your fleet. Clearly, your word means nothing and I can't trust a desperate man."

"You'll do what you have to, like I did" was all Doral would say as he continued to stare blankly.

The captain summoned a security detachment to escort him to guest quarters. The brig would serve no useful purpose and treating him well might make a difference later. Right after they removed Doral, Picard was collecting his thoughts, shaking off the emotions and assuming a dispassionate countenance when his communicator signaled again.

"La Forge to Picard."

"Go ahead Geordi, what have you learned?"

"Nothing good. We've looked inside the control console and have noticed an exponential increase in its consumption ratios. From what Data can determine, it exhausted its fuel cells some time back and has been draining power from the engines. We've calculated the consumption and this ship will overload and explode in the next twelve hours. We can extrapolate that the larger gateways can suck a planet dry in less than a week."

Alarmed, Picard put his hands on the tabletop and

asked, "Best guess, how long before a planet might be endangered?"

"Any planet using pure ecology for their power production has maybe four days before the damage is too severe to repair. Anyone drawing solar energy just might fry themselves in a week."

"Merde," Picard muttered. "Geordi, pick an engineer to watch over the device. You and Data come back to the ship."

"Aye, sir, La Forge out."

"Picard to Riker."

In brief terms, the captain outlined the latest developments and revelations to the first officer. He tried to keep his voice neutral but he knew the strain was creeping in. There was not enough time to rest, not enough time to save countless planets, not enough time to absorb the things he had learned. But if he didn't take the time, there might be costly mistakes.

Riker shared his own theories behind the false faces of the Iconians and, like Troi, thought the assessment sound. But right now, it mattered only as an intellectual exercise. They needed to focus on the gateways and how to turn them off.

"Will, if Ambassador Worf does not mind, leave him in control of Doral's ship and come back to the *Enterprise*. I think I'm going to need my best team at the ready. You've also been on duty too long."

"And you haven't? I'll come back, but only if it means you can rest, too. Riker out."

Before he could even think of resting, Picard went to his ready room, prepared a new report for Admiral Ross, complete with information sent by Data. It would become clear that the gateways would either have to be destroyed—if that was even possible—or as many people as possible evacuated. He couldn't even imagine what it would entail. If Ross grew gray during the Dominion War, he'd be snow white by the time this was over.

"Picard to Data," he said wearily.

"Data here."

"As soon as you are situated, please begin coordinating with our fleet. I want teams to board every Petraw ship. I want all helm controls slaved to our ships and the teams are to stay in constant contact. Once the first teams have boarded, please work out rotation schedules so everyone on duty is already rested."

"Understood, Captain."

Picard was ready to close the signal when he came to a small realization, one he chided himself for not having thought of sooner. "Data, ask Commander Desan if she would be willing to have her crews mix with the others on the ships. The warbirds have much larger crew complements and she can easily spare them."

"Of course, sir."

"It goes without saying, the Romulans and Klingons should not mix."

"True, but you just did say it."

Picard definitely needed some rest. He sat on his couch and allowed his mind to sift through the day's revelations.

Troi remained restless and she could only imagine how her crew was feeling. They had been out of action for some time, merely keeping observation of the Iconian ships. Petraw, actually—she had learned that from Picard's report to Admiral Ross. There was a sense of the tragic in Doral's story, but she couldn't muster that much sympathy given the scale of the problems caused by the gateways operating. The reports from Starfleet indicated skirmishes and devastating losses to ships and lives. The Carreon and Deltan conflict was a shoving match compared to some of the battles starting to break out. Intelligence also indicated the problems were definitely being felt across the quadrant, although no official word had been received from the Romulans.

After discussing the boarding plans with Data, she and Davison looked over the duty rosters to determine the size and qualifications of those being sent over in the first wave. Most of the crew had some experience, but not as many had been in combat-ready situations such as this. She didn't need to be an empath to register the eagerness Davison had for visiting a Petraw ship and she could spare the capable woman.

Shift change was completing as the first watch settled into their positions, running diagnostics and checking for notes from their predecessors. She surveyed them with a measuring eye and made some judgments.

"Hol, Rosario, a moment of your time."

The two whipped around, with curiosity on both their handsome faces. She stood and they approached the command chairs with quick steps. The others on the small bridge looked over with some curiosity, especially Chan.

"We're sending over a boarding party to two of the Petraw vessels."

"I thought they were Iconians," Rosario asked, perplexed.

"We have learned their true nature and that is their name," Davison answered.

"Poor Picard," Hol said quietly. "He seemed very eager to meet them."

Troi nodded in sympathetic agreement but pushed onward. "Davison will lead the first party. Mr. Rosario, I'll ask you to lead the second, if you're feeling up to it. Mr. Hol, go with Mr. Rosario and learn what you can of their technology. We're sending over security and engineers with both parties. You leave in fifteen minutes."

"Aye, aye," Rosario said, filled with enthusiasm. He then glanced over his shoulder at Chan, who seemed disappointed. He stepped over toward her, and put a comforting hand on her left shoulder. She used her right hand to cover his and they shared a silent moment.

In the office of the Federation President, Admiral Ross and several other members of Starfleet filled the room. They had been going over reports from the various ships, including the mapping efforts of the *T'Kumbra*. Their work had been prodigious but still presented an incomplete chart and the various lines, indicating the two, three, or four destinations of the gateways, was giving him eyestrain. Even more maddening was the growing number of deaths directly attributed to these infernal devices.

"We've increased the frequency of the warnings," his communications and media officer reported. "All member planets with identified gateways have posted guards and barricades."

The president sighed heavily. "But the people on the other side don't always come from the Federation."

"We've asked the Klingon forces to enact similar safeguards but Martok is hard-pressed to cover them all," Ross added.

"Bill, were we wrong to send the Iconian representative away until we could convene the Council? Could this have been stemmed?"

Ross shook his head, remaining stiffly at attention. "No. They turned those on as they made simultaneous approaches across the quadrant. They caught us by surprise and I'm certain it was done on purpose to force us to negotiate quickly."

The men and women discussed security procedures and precautionary moves to protect planets under attack. A surprisingly large number of saboteurs and fanatics were stepping through the portals, thinking they were able to strike a note for their cause. Of course, there were a large number of causes that tended to blunt each screed. The damage, however, was painfully obvious.

Ross was interrupted by the arrival of an aide with a data padd. He took it, crossed to the quietest corner of the room, and read Picard's latest report. As usual, it was succinct and exact in its presentation. He had to credit the captain with never once showing how much pressure he was under. In person was one thing, but for the record, he was exemplary. Upon the second reading, he fully grasped the import of the Petraw's revelation and how it just might serve as an epitaph for long-term peace in the galaxy.

"Madame President," he said, "we have news from the fleet."

"We have it timed—on the eighth micron you jump through, then every fifteen microns thereafter."

"We understand."

"Once you're all through, it's sixteen mics to the target. Make it quick. In, out, and back."

"You said it was guarded. We might have to kill more than one."

"A price worth paying to regain our sovereignty.

These portals came at exactly the time we needed them. We can move the revolution timetable forward and be free people once more."

"It shall be my knife that drinks the blood of the dictator."

"As it should be. After all, you lost your entire family, I only lost a wife."

"We can all begin life anew when this is done."

"Have you prayed yet?"

"Yes, the minister came by and administered rites to us all after breakfast. We're as ready as we're going to be."

"Then go forth and begin the revolution. When you get back, this colony world shall be free of the Praetor's influence once and for all."

The ship wandered aimlessly through the region of space called the Briar Patch. Its sensors were rendered useless and even their communications failed them.

To the Breen privateer, this was madness. Her small scout ship was on its way back to the Black Cluster, its hold full of dilithium and trilium. The pickings had been good, once she detected the battle near Rimbor. It was child's play to selectively target and beam plunder from the dead ships. She couldn't have cared less about why the two races engaged in battle, and hadn't even shown any curiosity why one ship was totally unfamiliar to her. The trading at Sherman's Planet was pitiful, so this more than made up for a trip that was originally written off as a failure. Once the cargo was moved, the profits would allow her to upgrade the ship and take six months off.

She had been idly thinking of ways to spend the free time when she was caught up in the vortex created by a gateway. Thrusters couldn't stop the scout and it jetted right through the aperture and she found herself here. Almost immediately, she noticed her manifolds were overheating and she slowed her ship to a crawl as she tried to flush them clean.

It became apparent that the area was full of cosmic clutter and not safe for stardrives. Her mapping programs showed the region to be near Federation territory and nowhere near home. How this had happened baffled her until she visually spotted the gateway, hanging open near an asteroid belt. Whatever it was she would reverse course and slowly, very slowly, approach it and return to her original course. She would make a note of the phenomenon in her computer logs and tag the sector to be avoided in the future.

Half an hour later, she managed to turn her ship around, make certain her engines were clean, and head back for the gateway. She was eager to be back on course; there was a growing demand for trilium as a building ornament on some of the colony worlds near her homeworld. That made it more valuable than the dilithium.

She approached the gateway, maintaining one-third impulse, and was merely a hundred meters away when she began to notice the gateway was actually fluctuating, with differing readings coming across her barely functioning sensors. She spotted her original path, but was also reading high measures of helium, and then something the ship could not register. Her hands flew to the controls, trying to pull the scout off the course, but there was too much momentum and she would go through.

She screamed briefly but then the ship emerged on

the other side and was in a region without stars. It was totally black. Just the scout and the gateway on her sensors. This was worse than the other side, she immediately decided. With no stars, there was nothing to navigate by and she would be trapped with dwindling power supplies.

There was little choice but to go through the gateway one more time.

She tried and failed to find her way back. So, once more she entered the gateway.

And once more she entered the gateway.

And once more she entered the gateway.

The brief nap actually took five hours but left Picard somewhat refreshed. He stretched and got himself a fresh cup of tea from the replicator. At his desk, he took a sip and called up ship's status and everything seemed fine. A quick look at the communications log showed only a terse acknowledgment of his report from Ross so he presumed things were quiet for a change.

It wouldn't last, he knew, given the deadly situation he found himself in. While he had hoped to find the Iconians for real, he hadn't. Their influence was felt, however, as their gateways continued to cause strife across the Milky Way galaxy. For a brief moment he wondered if it extended beyond that but quickly dismissed the notion. Things were complicated enough without adding in other galaxies.

He stared at an image of the gateway he found on Iconia and thought about the influence these people left behind. He couldn't begin to imagine what people would think of the Federation two hundred millennia from now; it was just too vast a period of time. Sol would still be burning yellow, although beginning to enter middle age.

Influence.

He quickly reviewed his frustrating conversation with Doral. They had been to Federation space before, found the gateway on an abandoned world at what was once the edge of the Federation. Now, where would that be?

"Picard to Data. Meet me in stellar cartography."

Chapter Twelve

STELLAR CARTOGRAPHY never ceased to impress Picard. It was huge, round, and able to project star charts with startling clarity. He often worked out their problems in this room and it was one of the starship additions he most approved of. Right now, he and Data stood on a rounded platform extending into the room's center. Lieutenant Daniel Paisner stood at the console and executed the commands.

"What exactly are we seeking, sir?" Data asked.

"Doral referred to the edge of the Federation, approximately a century ago. I want to see if we can find the world where his people found their gateway."

A star chart filled the space, engulfing the duo. It was large enough to allow individual solar systems and key planets to be named. At first, they began one hundred twenty years earlier, scanning for anything obvious based on what they currently knew. Allowing for Data's more rapid visual receptors, Picard flashed around the edge of Federation space, marveling at how much they had grown in such a relatively short span of time. There had been their skirmishes and wars, repelling invaders of all sorts, but they held together and prospered. Could they ever reach a point like the Petraw, a point where they were too far apart? He certainly hoped not, but he was also reminded of how Starfleet Command had grown to the point where they weren't communicating as effectively.

Once finished, Data admitted to seeing nothing obvious. With a shrug, Picard ordered the view forwarded by a year and again by a year. Paisner kept his fingers moving over the board, his wavy hair shaking with each movement.

"It might help if we had more context to work from," Data admitted after five circuits.

"I agree, but it was not discovered by Doral, but his ancestor. I gather the records are scant," Picard replied, hitting a control to forward the image another year.

Finally, at 2269, Data saw a smudge to the top right of the dome. Paisner enlarged the sector until it filled the area and then Data looked once more.

"What is it?"

"Although we are seeing the star charts as they existed around stardate 5700, the computer is also providing us with updated geological data. This faded area, for example."

"Something is missing?" Picard felt the tug of something on his memory but dismissed it to concentrate on Data.

"Yes, sir, a planetoid was here and is not now."

"It vanished?" Picard's mind reeled at the possibility of a planet-sized gateway.

"I do not believe so. One moment." He manipulated several more controls and then a stream of information was projected next to the faded space.

"An artificial world existed here, but exploded at approximately stardate 5750. Detonated by Commander Spock . . . of the *Enterprise*," Picard read aloud.

"Interesting," Data said.

"Wait a minute," Picard suddenly interrupted, his brow furrowing. "What was it Scotty told me? They were thrown one thousand light-years away. . . ."

"Actually 990.7 light years," Data corrected, reading from a report on the console.

"The Kalandan people were never explained, were they?"

"No, sir," Data replied.

Things were starting to fall into place for Picard and he felt his blood beginning to rush, his lethargy replaced with renewed vigor. Taking over the console from a bemused Paisner, he fed in several planetary names. Within seconds, a brand-new map appeared before them. Several planets were highlighted, forming a crude line, almost bisecting the Alpha Quadrant.

"We know the Iconian civilization left its mark on Iccobar, Dewan, and Dinasia, but look if we link them to the Kalandan outpost and Iconia itself."

"A clear path is formed," Data observed.

"From Iconia, in the Romulan Neutral Zone, right across the Alpha Quadrant toward the Gamma Quadrant border. When their enemies bombarded Iconia, the people seemed to move across the galaxy. Maybe they stopped on each world to regroup or build new gateways."

"It is certainly a possibility," Data said. "Since we do not know how many Iconians could have survived, it is unclear what their needs were."

"Or if they were followed. We only found the one operating system on the homeworld. And Kirk found one at the Kalandan outpost." Picard briefly thought how his life and Kirk's seemed to endlessly intersect, a link from one *Enterprise* captain to another.

"I do note that the remainder of that mission seems to be missing from the official Starfleet records."

Picard nodded in agreement, a tight smile across his face. "I wonder at times if the classified records are larger than the public records."

"I could perform an analysis, calculating the time allowed for all official log entries of active captains during Starfleet's existence against the public record and come up with a total number of missing days. It might take some time, however."

"Never mind," Picard replied with a sigh.

The captain once again programmed in a series of commands and the screen shifted with a new projection, this one seemingly brighter than the ones seen previously. "When the universe was two hundred thousand years younger," Picard said admiringly.

"Donald Varley found Iconia by adjusting for the galactic shift. If I do that for the worlds we know had Iconian influence, we get a brand-new direction." He gestured at the new path that led straight across the Alpha Quadrant, avoiding the Gamma Quadrant entirely.

"Computer, adjust map to accommodate the highlighted planet's position during the first known evidence of Iconian activity." It beeped compliantly and the planets shifted ever so slightly on the dome, once more changing the line's direction.

"The Kalandan outpost was the last known visit, just ten thousand years ago. Perhaps an offshoot or the last remaining people. Now, Data, look at the distances from planet to planet," he observed, having the computer add measurements to the screen. It became apparent, there was a mathematical progression from point to point.

"Excellent detective work, Captain," Data said.

Picard gave him a genuine smile, his first in a while. "You have your Holmes, I have my Dixon Hill, and neither liked to be stumped. These were not capricious people, Data. Everything the Iconians left behind spoke of high intelligence and precision. These markers reinforce that belief."

"Do you believe they still exist?"

"We need them to exist since they hold the key to the gateways. Unless you've managed to decipher their language."

"I have not been successful," Data admitted.

"Then we have to find them or their records, don't we?"

Data turned and studied the captain's determined face. "You have a plan, sir, do you not?"

"When don't I, Data?"

Riker was waiting for them on the bridge. Like the captain, he was a little better rested but still felt the strain of the mission. And he missed Deanna. Now that they were together once again he found himself reluctant to let her be apart. Still, there was a time for love and a time for duty.

He wished he were beside Picard, finding out more about these Petraw, but someone had to remain on the bridge, coordinating information from the fleet. It seemed as if everything had progressed smoothly once Doral confessed. The Petraw acted like a beaten people, which made them seem more than a little pathetic. It irritated him, but there was nothing he could offer them other than a stern lecture, and that was something Picard was far better at.

Vale had returned from the Petraw ship, changed into a clean uniform, and was once again on alert behind him. She never seemed to sleep and was always at the top of her game, which impressed and surprised him. How did she manage to do all that?

When the turbolift doors snapped open, Riker turned and was pleased to see Picard and Data stride onto the bridge. Picard seemed refreshed, so something had gone right down below. In fact, the captain seemed positively eager, not something he imagined would have happened. Picard nodded in acknowledgment of his first officer and tilted his head toward the ready room. Gesturing to La Forge, who had been bent over the engineering post, the two went into Picard's sanctum.

"I believe I know where the Iconians are or last were," he said.

This took Riker aback. He didn't think Picard or Data had enough to go on but clearly something had changed. He was pleased by this but began to suspect there was more to it and was trying to think ahead of his captain.

"Can we get there?"

"Not all of us, Number One," Picard replied. Riker was now definitely getting a sense of why Picard was getting to be so eager.

"So you're going into the gateway," he said.

Now it was Picard's turn to look surprised. He and Riker looked at one another, as a silent discussion—one they had had many times before—played out. Data and La Forge kept silent, waiting for someone to speak next.

"Can I send Vale with you?"

Picard smiled slightly, Riker noting he had the better argument—who else knew the Iconians well enough to deal with them should they still be there? Who better to eloquently state the urgency of the problem? Of course Picard was going to risk this, not Riker. Circumstances pointed to Picard this time, when on so many occasions, Riker won the day.

"If I'm wrong, I will not risk another's life."

"Even a volunteer's?" This from La Forge, who displayed as much curiosity about things as Picard did.

"Even yours, Geordi."

"When?"

"We can't wait long, Number One," Picard replied thoughtfully. "I want to talk to the other captains and send a quick report to Admiral Ross. If this fails, I want Starfleet to know it was entirely my doing."

Riker nodded and waited for the dismissal. After a moment, the men were released back to the bridge and they slowly walked out. There was nothing left to argue, but they didn't necessarily want to leave the captain either. After all, if there was a danger, he'd be lost to them.

Once back in the command chair, Riker didn't feel comfortable, but had to make peace with the situation. He also had to start thinking like the officer in charge, because once Picard made the attempt, everything would fall to him. Grekor would object and Desan might even try a play on her own, so he had to plan accordingly. He was like a chess master preparing to play multiple opponents, some of whom he had never met before.

Turning the watch over to Data, Riker excused himself to the observation lounge, where he began reviewing reports, statistics, and tactical readings. If he was going to be in command, he needed every shred of information to be familiar so he could react accordingly. Those plans, though, were interrupted by Vale, who told him a signal was coming in from Troi on the *Marco Polo*.

The wall screen shimmered and the smiling face of his lover greeted him.

"How can I help you, Captain Troi?" he said, giving her a broad grin. She seemed concerned, though.

"You're troubled, Will. What's wrong?"

Riker was surprised by this long-range diagnosis. "Now how did you know that?"

"Imzadi, *I can read you even when surrounded by thousands of life-forms. Especially when you're agitated.*"

"Strong emotions again?" Riker filled her in and he saw her expression grow concerned. She fully understood; how could she not after spending most of her adult life with Riker, as well as Picard.

"You know this is something he has to do for himself as well as Starfleet," she said.

"Of course. He'd never forgive himself if one of us strolled through and made a faux pas in front of a real Iconian."

"Do you think he'll be successful?"

"He got us this far, Deanna. Outnumbered, we held off the Petraw and got the truth with minimal loss. Even the Romulans are behaving around him."

"Are you ready to take over?"

"Now that's an entirely different question," he admitted. "I've never had to coordinate this much before. He can do it his way, but I need to be myself."

"And so you will be. You've gotten Klingon respect before. If there's anyone to worry about it's the Carreon. We know so little about them. They've behaved so far, but who knows what will happen with them next? Desan will play along while there remains information to be learned. Even repaired, she won't leave the area until we know what happens to Captain Picard. And it behooves her to help out, just in case she needs help herself."

Riker shook his head in amazement. "Are you sure you shouldn't be doing this job?"

"Oh, I'm quite content sitting here with my own little crew. I'm growing quite fond of them actually."

"Good enough. Wish me luck."

"You won't need it when you have Klingons and Romulans at your back," she said, and ended the message.

Grimly, Riker mused, wondering if those people were supporting him, or plotting against him.

Picard nodded to the security guard posted outside Doral's cabin. The officer turned and unlocked the door, allowing the captain to enter.

Doral was seated at the small desk, the computer screen showing an image of his ships. Picard appreciated the concern a leader was showing for his people.

"Is there anything, in any of your records, that will tell us how to read their language?"

Doral slowly shook his head and gestured for Picard to sit. The captain took the chair opposite the Petraw pod leader and they sat in silence for several moments.

Picard saw that the bed was untouched, the replicator empty. He suspected Doral had been at the desk the whole time, wondering how he got into this mess. Still unsure of how he felt about the Petraw, Picard kept his own counsel for the moment.

"With no other choice, I am going to use the gateway on your ship and try to find the Iconians. We need to turn off the network and do it before more lives are lost. Those deaths will have to weigh on your conscience. If I don't try, they will be on mine, too."

"If you find the mechanism, will you keep it to yourself?"

"I will do what needs be done to turn them all off, and then if it means sharing it with those we normally consider our adversaries, then yes. Whatever our differences, we will not allow the innocent to die."

Doral looked deep into Picard's eyes, and the captain met the stare with equanimity. He held it for a moment, then two, and finally blinked. "Such a strong will," the Petraw softly said.

"The mark of a captain," Picard said. "And the burden of one."

"When you return, and the gateways are turned off, what of my people?"

Picard sat thoughtful, not really having spent much time on the issue. He admitted as much and then added, "What you did was criminal. I don't know if there's a way to charge you for such reckless endangerment, but you certainly cannot be allowed to go unpunished. Your current plight has to take a place behind the more immediate danger."

Doral nodded in understanding. Picard stood and

walked out, not saying another word, letting the guilt hang in the air.

La Forge and Kliv were bent over the gateway console when Picard arrived on the Petraw ship. They were passing equipment back and forth, having opened up a panel on the Iconian console, spare parts littering the floor by their boots.

"If we can place the microfusion initiators here . . ." La Forge muttered.

"Then the EPS power stabilizer can fit below it," Kliv finished. They continued working and muttering, totally ignoring Picard's presence. He smiled toward them but walked over to Grekor and Worf, who seemed irritable, just watching.

"Regardless of race, engineers always speak in their own tongue," Grekor said.

"They are a breed apart," Worf said.

Picard came aboard equipped with field medical kit, tricorder, hand phaser, and rations. There was little knowing what awaited him on the other side, but Picard knew enough to be prepared. Crusher had berated him for going alone but then had stoically talked him through how to use some of the latest diagnostic devices, how to store readings in case the Iconians allowed themselves to be studied, and how to counteract the dozen most common poisons.

She seemed to go into lengthy detail, forcing him to spend more time in sickbay. He knew she wouldn't like the solo nature of the mission, but he refused to argue the point. With great patience, he had allowed her to discuss the kit's contents, noting how often her hands found his. There never seemed to be enough time for these feelings, but in case he wasn't coming back soon, he stored the emotions.

As he had begun to leave sickbay, Crusher had called to him one more time and he found himself in a tight embrace. She had said it was for luck but he knew better and said nothing.

Riker had been waiting for him in the transporter room, padd in hand. He had tried to convince Picard there were some orders needing his thumbprint but the captain knew his friend better than that.

"I'll be fine, Will," he had said confidently.

"I hope so, sir," Riker had said, the twinkle appearing in his eye. "I want my own command, but not like this."

"Careful of the fleet," Picard had said. "It's fragile and will need a gentle hand. Bractor will try and gain any advantage while Mel Rosa may continue his battle with Oliv when this is finished."

"At least the Gorn are out of the picture," Riker had said, a grim smile on his face. No one wished their deaths, Picard knew, but not having them around would certainly make Riker's job simpler.

"Look after my ship, I'll be back for it."

"As always," Riker had said with a laugh.

They had looked at one another for a moment and then Picard had taken his place and simply said, "Energize."

Now he was aboard the Petraw ship and felt how alien it was to him. Every race had their own sense of design and functionality but again, there was not time to study the hodgepodge vessel. He hoped there would be when he returned.

"From what we saw on Iconia, my best guess is that the coordinates are input here," La Forge said, gesturing to a hooded portion of the board. It contained three triangular areas with brightly colored buttons.

"I want all portals to have the same coordinates so as it rotates, all doors lead to the same place. It seems safest."

La Forge shrugged, "Guess we can try it. I'll need another photonic amplifier or two. . . ."

"We have determined each color represents a set of binary data combinations and tapping them begins the sequencing," the Klingon engineer added.

"We're taking an awful lot on faith," La Forge added.

"Sometimes, Mr. La Forge, faith is all we have." Picard handed his friend a tricorder with the coordinates on it. "Based on the mathematical progression of each planetary jump, and then factoring the shift over the millennia, I believe I'm going here."

Grekor and Worf had drawn closer, looking at the information. It seemed to Picard that Grekor was more interested than he had let on, but he would not remark on it. Worf, however, turned to Picard with some alarm on his face.

"Sir, that's uncharted space. You have no idea what sort of planet that might be. You should not go alone. Or first."

"Fortune favors the foolish, Ambassador," Picard said. He smiled at his friend. "I will allow no one else to take the risk."

"You are a warrior after all," Grekor said.

"He has the heart of a Klingon," Worf said with pride.

"Actually, I have a heart of steel thanks to Dr. Van Doren." He chuckled at the confused expression on Grekor's face.

La Forge had ignored the exchange, concentrating on the coordinates. He tapped a few, looked at the tricorder and tapped again, muttering to himself, "amber, amber, blue, red, amber, blue . . . no, amber."

The equipment suddenly chirped and La Forge scrambled backward. Lights blinked on and off and as Picard looked; the space within the gateway's arch began to shimmer. Within a few seconds, it cleared to depict a starfield.

Then it began to rotate, and the starfield became a solar system . . .

. . . then a green planet . . .

. . . then a brown continent . . .

. . . then a golden field . . .

. . . then a lush rain forest . . .

. . . then a high domed building, glistening damply in the sunlight . . .

. . . then a high domed building, glistening damply in the sunlight . . .

. . . then a high domed building, glistening damply in the sunlight . . .

"I think that's my port of call," Picard said, more to himself than anyone.

"Good luck," La Forge said.

"Qapla'!" Grekor and Worf said simultaneously, their voices resounding off the walls.

Without turning his back, Picard took two steps and entered the gateway without knowing what lay beyond.

To Be Continued In . . .

STAR TREK: GATEWAYS, BOOK 7 WHAT LAY BEYOND

Acknowledgments

No book writes itself, especially when it is a part of a seven-book series.

First, thanks to John Ordover, who helped me shape a vague idea into something strong enough to sustain this crossover. People wonder what an editor does and to some people it means a wordsmith, someone to polish the author's prose. John is the big-picture kind of editor, spitballing ideas and drumming up enthusiasm from his authors. It was John, for example, who hit upon the Kalandan connection which allowed us to tie in The Original Series. The fun of it was, most of the event took shape through Instant Messages, and then e-mail, showing just how far technology has come. An appreciative nod goes to my cowriters, Susan Wright, Diane Carey, Keith R. A. DeCandido, Peter David, and

Christie Golden for joining me on the journey. All credit to Susan for taking the name Petraw and bringing them to life.

If you liked this, then a large portion of the credit goes to editor Keith, who stepped in to edit the manuscript late in the process. However, having been there from the beginning, and helping make this richer by sending me IMs that started, "Could you work in . . .," he is now here to make sure this stands tall. We go back way too long to cover here, and it's neat to work together like this. Others at Pocket who provided help, encouragement, or just a smile include Marco Palmieri, Jessica McGivney, John Perrella, and Margaret Clark.

Thanks also to my old pal Paula Block, at Paramount Licensing, who makes sure these books are as good as possible. Additional Paramount people to thank include Mike and Denise Okuda for their exhaustive and incredibly useful reference tools, including the *Star Trek Encyclopedia*.

Coming from the world of comics, I find it appropriate that the Iconians were co-created by fellow comics denizen Steve Gerber. Along with Beth Woods, they added a layer to the galactic history that has allowed us to explore and have some fun along the way. We worked together a few years before he wrote the "Contagion" episode and it's nice to sort of be working with him again. I may even forgive him for the Dry Cleaners incident.

I was encouraged along the way by friends, colleagues, and coworkers, including Mike Friedman, Mike Buonfiglio, the usual Shore Leave contingent, and the gang at PsiPhi.org. Of course, I wouldn't have gotten this far without the support from my family, including Mom, Neil, and Judy.

As always, my patient wife, Deb, and children, Katie and Robbie, understood the need to lock myself away in the basement nights and weekends, making sure I could hit this deadline. Robbie's enthusiasm for the space battle kept me going while Katie signed off on the crew of the *Marco Polo*'s dialogue. Every author should be as lucky to be surrounded by such a support group.

About the Author

Bob Greenberger has either watched, read, edited, or written something about *Star Trek* since he was a mere lad. Along the way he has found ways to make a living never straying far from the universe Gene Roddenberry created.

After graduating from the State University of New York at Binghamton, Bob started his professional career at Starlog Press, where he worked on *Starlog* and *Fangoria,* creating *Comics Scene* along the way.

In 1984, Bob began a sixteen-year career at DC Comics, first as an Editor and then later as Manager of Editorial Operations. As an editor, he discovered some of today's top talents and handled some of DC's best-known characters in addition to media tie-ins, including an eight-year run on *Star Trek.* He's especially proud of the numerous awards won by *Star Trek: Debt of Honor,* the first hardcover graphic novel to feature Gene Roddenberry's characters.

Taking a break from comics, Bob joined Gist Communications, a leading provider of Interactive Television Programming Guides, where he was a producer, mastering the challenging world of the Internet.

Marvel lured him back to comics in early 2001, and he currently serves there as Director of Publishing Operations. The words "excelsior" and " 'nuff said" have crept into his conversation with increasing frequency.

Along the way, he has done some freelance writing, including historical articles on comics, and most recently fiction. He has collaborated on several *Star Trek* books with Peter David and Mike Friedman, some of which are still in print, and has written the *Next Generation* novel *The Romulan Stratagem.* Bob also conceived the acclaimed *Enterprise Logs* anthology and will be contributing to Pocket's program in the future. Beyond *Trek,* Bob has written several short stories, mostly original works, the next being a contribution to DAW's *Oceans of Space* collection.

In his spare time he is an avid baseball fan and, along with Mike Friedman and Keith DeCandido, a member of a fantasy league. His team? The Final Frontiersmen, of course.

He makes his home in Connecticut with his wife, Deb, and children, Katie and Robbie.

Look for STAR TREK fiction from Pocket Books

Star Trek®: The Original Series

Star Trek: The Next Generation®

Star Trek: Voyager®

Star Trek®: New Frontier

Star Trek®: Starfleet Corps of Engineers (eBooks)

#1 • *The Belly of the Beast* • Dean Wesley Smith
#2 • *Fatal Error* • Keith R.A. DeCandido
#3 • *Hard Crash* • Christie Golden
#4 • *Interphase, Book One* • Dayton Ward & Kevin Dilmore
#5 • *Interphase, Book Two* • Dayton Ward & Kevin Dilmore
#6 • *Cold Fusion* • Keith R.A. Decandido
#7 • *Invincible, Book One* • David Mack & Keith R.A. Decandido
#8 • *Invincible, Book Two* • David Mack & Keith R.A. Decandido

Star Trek®: Invasion!

#1 • *First Strike* • Diane Carey
#2 • *The Soldiers of Fear* • Dean Wesley Smith & Kristine Kathryn Rusch
#3 • *Time's Enemy* • L.A. Graf
#4 • *The Final Fury* • Dafydd ab Hugh
Invasion! Omnibus • various

Star Trek®: Day of Honor

#1 • *Ancient Blood* • Diane Carey
#2 • *Armageddon Sky* • L.A. Graf
#3 • *Her Klingon Soul* • Michael Jan Friedman
#4 • *Treaty's Law* • Dean Wesley Smith & Kristine Kathryn Rusch
The Television Episode • Michael Jan Friedman
Day of Honor Omnibus • various

Star Trek®: The Captain's Table

#1 • *War Dragons* • L.A. Graf
#2 • *Dujonian's Hoard* • Michael Jan Friedman
#3 • *The Mist* • Dean Wesley Smith & Kristine Kathryn Rusch
#4 • *Fire Ship* • Diane Carey
#5 • *Once Burned* • Peter David
#6 • *Where Sea Meets Sky* • Jerry Oltion
The Captain's Table Omnibus • various

Star Trek®: The Dominion War

#1 • *Behind Enemy Lines* • John Vornholt
#2 • *Call to Arms...* • Diane Carey
#3 • *Tunnel Through the Stars* • John Vornholt
#4 • *...Sacrifice of Angels* • Diane Carey

Star Trek®: Section 31

Rogue • Andy Mangels & Michael A. Martin
Shadow • Dean Wesley Smith & Kristine Kathryn Rusch
Cloak • S. D. Perry
Abyss • David Weddle & Jeffrey Lang

Star Trek®: Gateways

#1 • *One Small Step* • Susan Wright
#2 • *Chainmail* • Diane Carey
#3 • *Doors Into Chaos* • Robert Greenberger
#4 • *Demons of Air and Darkness* • Keith R.A. DeCandido

Star Trek®: The Badlands

#1 • Susan Wright
#2 • Susan Wright

Star Trek®: Dark Passions

#1 • Susan Wright
#2 • Susan Wright

Star Trek® Omnibus Editions

Invasion! Omnibus • various
Day of Honor Omnibus • various
The Captain's Table Omnibus • various
Star Trek: Odyssey • William Shatner with Judith and Garfield Reeves-Stevens

Other Star Trek® Fiction

Legends of the Ferengi • Ira Steven Behr & Robert Hewitt Wolfe
Strange New Worlds, vols. I, II, III, and IV • Dean Wesley Smith, ed.
Adventures in Time and Space • Mary P. Taylor
Captain Proton: Defender of the Earth • D.W. "Prof" Smith
New Worlds, New Civilizations • Michael Jan Friedman
The Lives of Dax • Marco Palmieri, ed.
The Klingon Hamlet • Wil'yam Shex'pir
Enterprise Logs • Carol Greenburg, ed.